MYSTERY OF A WOMAN

MYSTERY OF A WOMAN

RECHA G. PEAY

URBAN SOUL
URBAN BOOKS
www.urbanbooks.net

URBAN SOUL is published by

Urban Books
10 Brennan Pl.
Deer Park, NY 11729

Copyright © 2006 by Recha G. Peay

All rights reserved. No part of this book may be reproduced
in any form or by any means without the prior written con-
sent of the Publisher, excepting brief quotes used in reviews.

ISBN 1-59983-004-3

First Printing: September 2006
10 9 8 7 6 5 4 3

Printed in the United States of America

This is a work of fiction. Any references or similarities to ac-
tual events, real people, living or dead, or to real locales are
intended to give the novel a sense of reality. Any similarity
in other names, characters, places, and incidents is entirely
coincidental.

PROLOGUE

The mystery of a woman has yet to unfold.
The mystery of a woman has not been told.

"In here, on the bathroom floor!" Rowan Miller emphatically shouted as though the life he was attempting to save was his own. His voice bounced off the walls of the small bathroom and vibrated down the narrow hallway. In his several years of responding to emergency calls as a paramedic, he had never witnessed anything as intentionally brutal as what he saw before him. An intruder fled a violent crime scene, leaving the victim for dead. The uneven and broken seams of the barely glued linoleum floor provided a trough for the blood that seeped without form from her body. Using his hands to support himself, Rowan knelt to evaluate her wounds and feel for a pulse.

She was propped against the tub where she'd seemingly collapsed. Her legs were drawn into her chest and a blood-soaked towel was draped over the lower half of her body. Bloody fingerprints covered the telephone handset that lay on the floor beside her. Her ripped blouse hung loosely from her body. It looked as if she attempted to nurse her right arm, which appeared to be severely out of place. A sudden rush of adrenaline made Rowan dizzy; he stood slowly to clear his head. *My God, it will be a miracle if she survives*, he thought to himself. Speaking aloud, his more experienced partner immediately began to make a thorough assessment.

"She has taken several hard blows to the head, primarily the left side." Parker moved slowly and cautiously around the small bathroom. "Her right arm is swollen, possibly broken, with excessive bruising on the legs."

The victim heard voices, yet she couldn't move. She mustered just enough strength to barely open her eyes, seeing a blurry vision of Rowan. As their eyes met, he saw straight into her soul and was immediately affected by the pain, violation, and shame he saw in her. His heart was filled with compassion for her. Though his partner occupied most of the available space, he moved closer, attempting to offer her comfort through their brief connection.

"You're going to be just fine, miss," Rowan said calmly and assuredly as he'd been trained to do, although he himself wasn't quite convinced.

She could feel slight movement as Rowan carefully stepped over her limp body, and though she tried to focus, she was unsuccessful at preventing her eyes from closing. They began to roll to the back of her head.

"She's going into shock, don't move her. If we don't get her stabilized within two to three minutes we may lose her. She needs oxygen immediately!" Parker sternly stated.

We may lose her? Did she hear him correctly? She wouldn't die. She *refused* to die. Her spirit began to disconnect itself from her earthbound physical being to help her endure the pain.

God, if you are there, please listen to me, she prayed. She felt she was a small voice among the faithful, but she was still young and had her entire life ahead of her. *Whatever I did to deserve this, please forgive me. I want another chance.* Even in her state of near-unconsciousness she knew she wasn't ready or willing to die, but it seemed to her as though she had no alternative. Suddenly everything was completely dark.

Rowan responded quickly, darting to the ambulance to get both the oxygen she needed and a stretcher to transport her. Hurriedly, he grabbed the equipment and returned. Two more paramedics arrived at the scene, followed by a team of investigators, and wasted no time getting inside to assist. Although he wanted to be near her, the limited space of the bathroom would no longer allow Rowan entrance. From the hallway where he stood, his eyes instinctively searched the area. He took note of the décor of her modest home and made several assumptions. In the bathroom, scented candles and bath oils were neatly placed around the small space. The living room walls were painted a deep gold and accented with burgundy swag tie-back curtains and matching rugs. A beige couch and matching love seat were asymmetrically arranged, while the tables were askew. A picture of a mixed floral arrangement within a green frame hung above the couch. Her kitchen, highlighted in yellow, had a happy tone. A brass and glass-top table with coordinating pastel striped chairs was in a corner designated for eating. A vase holding fresh tulips was placed in its center. The refrigerator displayed an assortment of fruit magnets, and ceramic fruit wall hangings were positioned above the oak-colored cabinets. She attempted to have her décor appear to be expensive even though it didn't necessarily materialize. He concluded that this young lady was modest and virtuous.

As he looked again over the disarray in the living room he guessed she was attacked shortly after entering her front door, signified by the contents of her purse strewn about the doorway. Her lipstick was nearly beneath the couch. Her makeup compact had been separated and the halves lay on both sides of the room. Three textbooks and a few notepads had been knocked off the coffee table, and loose sheets of papers bearing school notes were everywhere. A laptop, turned on its side, was tilted against the arm of an easy chair. Rowan watched the investigators tape off the scene and begin their work, first tracking the trail of blood between the bedroom and the bathroom where she was found. He imagined finding the culprit would be a nightmare for any forensics investigator. There was nothing left behind that Rowan could see that would provide them with clues of a potential suspect. *If she can't identify her attacker, the police will have a difficult case to solve. It could have been anyone*, he thought.

Among the remnants of broken glass he spotted a small card on the floor. Straining to look at it, he realized that it was her faded Louisiana State driver's license identifying her as Maria A'Twanette McCory. The woman fighting for her life in the bathroom wasn't the picture-perfect woman captured in the license photo. Her strong facial features and pointed nose revealed her rich ethnic background. Her shoulder-length, wavy black hair was parted on the right side and locks hung tenderly over her left eye. Her smile was radiant and flawless. Her prominent neckline was given proper attention by the soft pink V-neck blouse she wore. As Rowan documented her personal information, he again felt compassion for her. She was such a beautiful woman whose privacy had been violated.

"She's stable. Let's get her on the stretcher." The announcement of her stability propelled him outdoors toward the ambulance. Rowan was somewhat relieved, but knew she still had a fight ahead of her.

"Let's get her out of here, we don't want to lose her," his

colleagues said while working together, giving the care necessary to ensure her life for a few more minutes, at least long enough to get her to the hospital. Rowan, ready to take the driver's seat, watched as the others cautiously stepped over shattered glass, moved down the hall, through the living room, and onto the gray slab that functioned as a front porch, transporting the victim to the ambulance.

"Ready? On three. One . . . two . . . three." They hoisted her into the vehicle while Rowan got behind the wheel.

"We have a black female, late twenties, 125 pounds, several blows to the head, possible broken right arm," Rowan said sharply into the radio, advising the nurses at the hospital to prepare for her arrival. As he waited for them to signal that she was secure, he made a quick assessment of the neighborhood.

It wasn't the poorest Rowan had ever seen, but wealth wasn't the common denominator either. Renovated duplexes and triplexes lined both sides of the street. There was a mixture of expensive, midpriced, and more economical vehicles parked along the side of the street, indicating various incomes. Some homes featured neatly manicured lawns adorned with blooming flowers, while for some yards it seemed that the grass refused to grow.

Having heard the sharp whistle from his partners, he flipped on the siren, demanding respect from both the inquisitive adults and the undisciplined children who had gathered nearby. Collectively they moved back, heeding the siren's command. There was no time to waste; if he didn't get her to the ER soon, they would lose her, and he wasn't willing to let that happen. Rowan pulled out of the driveway and hurled the flashing vehicle into the street, burning a path to Tulane University Hospital.

* * *

The last thing Maria remembered was the sound of the siren, loud, desolate, and lonely. In her mind, the flashes of bright red light symbolized the blood trickling, not only from her body, but also from her wounded heart.

The emergency room's double doors were nearly dismantled as the paramedics rushed through them at a startling speed. The black rubber wheels of the stretcher barely touched the floor. Rowan's heart pounded inside his chest as her vitals and condition were again communicated to no one in particular while she was quickly maneuvered down the crowded corridor. As they approached the nurses' station, his frustration peaked. The lack of concern on the faces of the nurses annoyed him. Saving her life was a priority to Rowan, even if no one else felt the same.

"Get the doctor. Now!" he barked, startling the team of nurses, who seemed to be chatting casually. His actions made it extremely clear that he wouldn't allow her to be ignored. As if by magic, a doctor swiftly appeared, assumed a steady pace beside the stretcher, and began giving directives. Two nurses, ready to immediately carry out his verbal orders, followed suit and pursued his steady pace.

"Okay, listen up, this is a delicate one! Blood pressure now sixty over forty, heart rate steady with substantial blood loss. Jackie, I need a type and cross for two units of blood, comprehensive profile, and serum pregnancy drawn STAT. Follow rape kit protocol before she's prepped for surgery." The nurse beside him repeated each detail as she recorded the information on the chart. Rowan grabbed both corners of the starched white sheet above Maria's head while Parker secured the corners at her feet. In unison they lifted her body and moved her onto the awaiting gurney. Immediately she was wheeled into the operating room. The doors shut and the work began.

Standing on the outside of the room, Rowan realized his assistance was no longer required; he felt helpless. He backed out of the triage area and whispered a silent prayer. Unfortunately, his extensive training in emergency room procedures and protocols didn't go beyond the double doors of the operating room. He made his way back to the ambulance, his mind flooded with thoughts of Maria. *She has to pull through*, he thought, as he held her picture-perfect image in his memory.

CHAPTER 1

It has haunted the minds of men since the beginning of time; until the end of earth men will never find . . .

My day at the station was stressful as hell . . . four fender benders, a teenage suicide attempt, and a false domestic violence call were the main contributors. The rest I owed to Parker for calling in sick. Lieutenant left me with no option but to swap duties with his cover. He was a new driver and jerked me around in the back of that damn ambulance for all of twelve hours. I drove home with double vision and a pounding headache. I swore, switched my bag to the other shoulder, and pulled my keys out of my pants pocket. I could smell dinner before I opened the door. Hmm . . . steak, sautéed onions, and oriental vegetables. On a normal day, it was my favorite meal, but my headache had taken my appetite.

"Hey, honey." Vickie looked up and smiled as she diced two cucumbers into small cubes. With the back of her hand she moved her bangs away from her face. "How was your day?" She paused for a few seconds before speaking again. "Anything interesting?"

"No, not really," I said between sighs, not mentioning my headache.

"My days are so routine and sedentary. You may not believe it but your reenactments are the highlight of my day." She paused for a minute, then continued. "Do you think I would be good in the medical field?"

"Sure," I responded nonchalantly. My mind was too cluttered at the time to assist her with entertaining the idea of a new career path.

"Your blood-and-guts encounters are so cool. By the way, I thought you would want something light to go with your meal today, so I'm tossing a salad for you. Dinner will be ready in a few."

I tossed my bag with my extra uniform in the closet and put my keys on the table. I couldn't wait to take off the dark blues I'd been wearing for the past twelve-plus hours. I undressed right there in the middle of the living room. Seconds later, I was standing in front of her in just my white T-shirt and boxers. Not feeling like talking, I kissed her on the forehead, then retreated to the bedroom to take a hot shower and unwind.

Before stepping into the shower, I turned to the mirror to study the dumb-ass look on my face. I had mixed emotions about our relationship. Something was missing. Vickie satisfied me mentally and for damn sure sexually. Honestly, most times she overdid it. Yet, I wasn't satisfied. I tried to shake the feeling but I didn't know what it was. I knew what I wanted . . . a soul mate connection. For whatever reason, I didn't feel this with her. Yeah, I loved her, but I wasn't in love with her. *If a woman is my soul mate, will I have to grow to love her or will the love already be there?* My mind wandered off again.

I'd met Vickie at an Italian restaurant on Decatur Street about three years ago. The atmosphere was casual with a flare for romance. Knowing it was a popular hangout for singles, I left the house dressed to impress. It was the middle of August so I wore a pair of off-white linen pants and a loose-fitting shirt that emphasized my broad shoulders. I looked damn good, I said so myself. I spotted her when I walked through the front door, sitting at the bar sipping on a margarita, her lips making passionate love to the straw with each sip. She was wearing a seductive red halter dress, nothing too revealing, just sexy. Her long locks of red hair were pulled up and held in place with two chopsticks. It was difficult for me to play it smooth, seeing how attractive she was, but I managed to do a pretty good job. I walked around pretending to look for someone, but really I wanted to find out if she was alone and if she was approachable. I slowly and confidently walked to the bar, sat down beside her, and ordered a Heineken; then I turned toward her only enough to make eye contact. I didn't speak right away, not wanting to appear anxious and lose my cool points. I wanted to make her feel comfortable without invading her space. After a few minutes more, our eyes caught again and I made my move.

"Excuse me, did they tell you how long the wait was?" I cleared my throat because I already knew the answer; I counted on it being a while before either of us was seated.

"I think it is about forty-five minutes to an hour. I've been waiting about twenty minutes already."

"Thanks."

"You're welcome," she said, slowly sipping the last of her drink.

"Would you like another one while you wait?" I asked, motioning toward her now empty glass.

"Sure, why not?"

Lucky for me, if she had a date, he hadn't shown up. While we waited to be seated, we kept each other entertained with light conversation. Vickie told me she worked as a legal assistant for a prestigious law firm downtown, where her best friend, Lisa, was an attorney. It was through Lisa's encouragement that Vickie decided to major in prelaw. Soon, one topic led to another and we agreed to have dinner together. Thirty minutes later we were seated in a cozy, dimly lit corner. Talking to her was easy. We discussed our likes, rather than our dislikes. The things we had in common, instead of our differences. I had such a good time that our predetermined racial differences never entered my mind.

The odds were already set in motion against us. Although interracial couples weren't uncommon among most communities, there were still a select few that preferred to keep their bloodlines pure and sacred. Mixing with "unclean" blood was sinful, or so they thought. I myself sincerely believed that the "pure" would cease to exist within the next twenty years. While today, my doubts regarding our relationship weren't specifically hinged on those challenges, there were yet barriers for me to identify and resolve.

I stepped out of the shower, dried off, and threw on a pair of sweats and a clean T-shirt that Vickie laid out for me. As I shuffled toward the kitchen, the void in our relationship was still heavy on my mind. How did Vickie feel about us? Did she sense the same emptiness that I felt?

"Are you okay? You seem to be a little distant." Vickie took a sip of wine as she served dinner.

"Yeah, baby, just a hectic day at work. You know those calls can be overwhelming at times," I said before taking two Extra-Strength Tylenols and sitting down at the table.

"Let me know if you want to talk about it, dear." Her concern was genuine.

"I'm fine, just a little worn out." I was starving and all I wanted to do was get some food in my system. To discourage questions, I reached for the television remote and searched for a good game. Before I could finish my evening meal the phone rang.

"I'll get it baby, it's by me," I said, reaching to answer it.

"Hey, man, what's up?" It was Josh Stephenson on the other end. The reception from his cell phone was terrible, but right away I detected tension.

"What's on your agenda for tonight? My anxiety level is at an all-time high."

"I know what you mean. What do you have in mind?"

"Hell, I don't know, I need a drink or something. Isn't tonight open mic at Enchanted Notes?" Josh asked.

"Yeah, every Wednesday and Friday." The quaint jazz and reggae club downtown was a familiar spot for music lovers to kick back and relax during the week. "I can be ready in about an hour. I'll meet you at the bar."

"Thanks, man." Josh sounded relieved.

Josh and I had become acquainted during my junior year of college. Being shy and intimidated by large crowds, he'd limited his circle of friends. He had the heart of a saint and the physique of a Roman god, standing six feet four inches with dark blond hair and blue eyes. Once Josh and I became friends, girls used me as a passport to enter and survey his territory. With X-ray vision, they beamed his muscle definition straight through starched khaki pants and polo shirts. The fellas and I could only imagine the opportunities he had with the ladies, which he never took advantage of. In college . . . fine girls, shit; what was he thinking? Josh majored in computer engineering. Talking his computer lingo blew his opportunities and turned off the average female. They found nothing romantic about that storage space and RAM bull he talked all of the time. He was incredibly serious and focused. I admired that about him. Ironically, by my senior year Josh was married and had a child on the way. Free time became a rare gift for him. All of his energy was devoted to his pregnant wife and finishing school.

Though our majors led us down separate career paths, we kept in close contact after our college days were well spent. Josh was still just as committed to his wife and Josh Jr. as he'd been back then. As a matter of fact, he would turn down a night with the fellas without a second thought, preferring to read a book to his son, or paint his wife's toenails.

Now I wondered what could have been going on to have him so set on trying to get out of the house. I had never heard him sound so exasperated.

Although I was tired, I used this opportunity to escape my thoughts about myself and Vickie. Lisa usually came over on Friday nights for their regularly scheduled gossip forum. I wasn't trying to be home for that anyway. I would just end up in the bedroom watching pretty much nothing on TV while they babbled and gossiped. I explained to Vickie that Josh was really depressed and he needed me to be there for him. I saw a glimpse of disappointment in her eyes, but she leaned across the table and pecked me on the lips.

"I was hoping we could cuddle tonight a little bit, but go ahead. Have a good time, sweetie."

I returned her display of affection and went into the bedroom to change into something more appropriate for the ambiance of Enchanted Notes.

I arrived first. The club catered to a crowd twenty-five and above, and on Friday nights the music was usually a smooth mix of jazz and rhythm and blues. Couples seated at tall, round tables were on both sides of the entrance. These tables, sized only for two, made intruders the least of their worries. Up a few steps and to the left were several larger tables and a section of booths covered with shiny red vinyl along the back wall. A five-piece band sat to the right of the front door. The band was well respected and known for their original jazz compositions. In front of their setup was a dance floor. I smiled and shook my head as I looked at the couples out there doing their thing.

I took a seat at the bar and ordered a Crown and Coke. It wasn't my usual choice, but this was no usual night. Before my drink was served, Josh walked up beside me.

"Hey, man, what's happening?" he huffed. He seemed weary as he plopped down next to me dressed in a pair of wrinkled faded jeans and a dingy cotton T-shirt.

"Man, what the hell?" My expression showed my disapproval of his appearance. He looked like shit. "Did you just finish cutting the grass or something? I'm surprised they let your ass in here. What's up, man?"

"I don't know. Jana is just stressing me out lately." He stared at me, then looked over his left shoulder as though Jana had followed him there. "She's been having some sort of mood swings, I guess. I'm doing everything I can to be patient and understanding. Man, I just don't know how much more I can take. She's really been on my ass. I needed a break tonight, you know?"

"Then the drinks are on me tonight." I gave him a reassuring pat on the shoulder.

"Jana's at home all day and I can't imagine what could be so difficult about that. She's going through something, man, and I don't quite understand her insecurity. One minute she's all over me, the next I'm not wanted and being accused of having an affair. What's going on?"

I had never really cared for Jana much from the get-go. She made a bad first impression, which I'd never let go of. She struck me as a user with no limits. I could never figure out how Jana got his attention or how she kept it. She wasn't attractive at all. She was about five feet six inches tall with a medium build. She kept her thin dyed blond hair in a shoulder-length bob. In my opinion, nothing about her face or body warranted a second look. Once Jana realized that Josh was soft-spoken and easily influenced, she held back nothing to get what she wanted. Even if it meant using a pregnancy to manipulate a man with a promising future. She knew that by carrying his child she had his heart, his time, and all of his money. She was nothing but a damned parasite.

"Is she pregnant, man? Or maybe it's just her time of the month. You know a female will lose her mind and flip on a brother quick when her 'auntie' shows up."

"Naw, man. Not unless she got a thirty-day cycle! Cheating on her is the last thing on my mind. All I know is that she ain't giving me none and I'm about to explode, you know what I mean?" He chuckled slightly, in an attempt to make light of what he'd said, but we both knew he was serious.

"Yeah, Josh. I feel you, man," I answered, trying to offer a little comfort, but honestly, I had no idea how he felt. Vickie was always on me. Every night and every day. Two or three times a day when I was off work, like the Energizer Bunny. Hell, sometimes I had to push the woman off me, which would generally lead to an argument, and I'd end up having to satisfy her anyway. So, in all actuality, no, I couldn't relate at all.

"I don't even go out like I used to, just so that she can feel secure, but when I do go out, she has to have the number to where I'll be, the address, and a list of everyone there."

I couldn't help but laugh. "When did you start going out?" Josh almost never left the house unless he was on his way to work. Josh, showing authority at home. Yeah . . . right. I wasn't drunk yet.

"Man, shut up and listen." He motioned his hand as if he was going to back-slap me.

"All right, all right. I'm listening."

"Rowan, I'm tired and I'm frustrated." Josh sighed heavily, folded his arms, and looked down at the floor. He leaned back in his chair and took a deep, raspy breath. I had no idea his home life had been falling apart. He looked so confused. His facial expressions alone convinced me that my situation with Vickie was insignificant and petty. He actually had issues.

The band started to fade as the lights were dimmed and a

spotlight focused on the stage. It was time for the poets to take the microphone. A tall, dark, brown-skinned man wearing ethnic attire was the first to take the stage.

"Good evening, everyone, and welcome to open mic night at Enchanted Notes. As you all know, I am not a stranger to free form. I would like to share a bit of knowledge with you in the form of the spoken word. Is there a man out there tonight who knows you've got a real woman?" There was applause from every man who sat with a woman, whether it was sincere or not. "This is for you."

> *The woman I speak about is the epitome of every*
> > *woman.*
> *She possesses strength, inner and outer beauty, grace,*
> > *poise, and attitude.*
> *She has no race or color—she is a woman.*
> *When she sits, all men stand.*
> *As she turns, the room is quiet; no one knows where*
> > *she'll glance.*
> *When she talks she has everyone's attention . . . they*
> > *know they had better listen—she is a woman.*
> *Her height surpasses the highest mountain.*
> *Her value cannot be measured in gold.*
> *Her demeanor is unlike any other ever told.*
> *When she walks, the earth trembles and winds cease to*
> > *blow—she is a woman.*

I was getting a light buzz from the Crown and Coke and was now totally relaxed.

I closed my eyes and actually felt the words of the poet. At the same time, I was suddenly reminded of the woman whose life I'd helped to save earlier today, Maria. For some reason, I wondered how she was.

Applause interrupted my thoughts of Maria; as I opened

my eyes I noticed that a poet was now taking his bow and exiting the stage.

"Next to the microphone we have a newcomer. She calls herself Ebony. Let's give her a hearty Enchanted Notes welcome, shall we?"

There was more applause as Ebony took the stage. She was a little "big-boned" for my tastes, but she was an attractive lady. She wore her hair short and natural and was dressed in a colorful dashiki. I prejudged her, expecting her strong and confident presence to be an indication that she would recite a male-bashing piece. Much to my surprise, the words that spilled from her soft brown lips weren't those of an angry woman, but a woman who seemed to know the trials and tribulations of love.

Love surrenders, it is not a sacrifice.
When you fall in love it is not a struggle to remain faithful in your day-to-day life.
Everybody thinks the grass is greener on the other side.
Once you cross over you realize it was just a field of over growing weeds needing to be destroyed by herbicide.
You stand there puzzled not knowing what to do.
You've destroyed a blessed relationship because you thought it was better to have two.
When the light came on inside of your mind . . . it was too late. Then you had wasted all of your time.
Romancing and dancing seemed cool for a while . . . but while you were playing you lost your wife and your child.
The drummer beat and the piano player played, I hope you now realize what was thrown away.
Love surrenders, it is not a sacrifice.
No hard feelings, forget about the damage that was

> *done; I asked for God's forgiveness so the battle has*
> *been won.*

The bartender slid two beers across to me. My eyes remained glued to Ebony. For a second we made eye contact and I detected pain in her eyes. She spoke out of personal experience. She made me think of Vickie and I shook my head a little, jilting the thought. My third drink had me tripping. I looked down at the glass, feeling a little guilty, I suppose, then glanced back to the stage. Ebony had ended her poem and left the stage just as quickly as she had come, receiving a standing ovation. That was atypical for this crowd, but the words she spoke were truth personified.

"Rowan, man, thanks for listening. I hate to sound like someone stole my first red tricycle, but the past couple of months have been rough. In the beginning it was so much easier. I only had my needs to consider."

His pat on my shoulder made me turn to look him in the eye. I leaned forward and rested my elbows on the edge of the bar. I couldn't help but stare as his facial expression changed from dazed to worried.

"More than anything, I have to think about my son's future. I'm not willing to walk out on him over something as trivial as this. Rowan, man, I can't stand the thought of another man raising my son. So, whatever is going on, I *have* to figure it out." The wrinkles in his forehead disappeared as he finished his beer.

"Yeah, man, I feel you, but I can only imagine." As a friend, I was very concerned, but didn't know what to say to boost his spirits so I ordered us another round of drinks.

The sweet sounds of jazz continued to flow through the atmosphere as more poets worked the stage. I looked over at Josh and noticed that he had unwound a lot. Mission accomplished.

"I'm out, man." Josh got up, stood still to compose himself, shook my hand, then headed toward the door.

"Do you want me to follow your drunk ass home?" I didn't think Josh realized how much liquor he'd consumed. His slurred speech was a warning that his intellectual capacity and judgment were impaired.

"No, I got it." He generally held his liquor well, so I didn't attempt to stop him. After listening to him I needed more time to unwind my damn self. I stayed a little while longer and listened to more music before calling it a night and heading back home.

When I turned into our complex I noticed that the bedroom light was on. Vickie never slept with the lights on in the bedroom. *Why?* I asked myself. *Why tonight, of all nights, is Vickie waiting up for me?* I knew what she wanted. I had a lot of things on my mind and wasn't in the mood to make love to her. I unlocked the door, eased it open, then put my keys on the counter, quietly. When I entered the bedroom, there she stood with one foot propped up on a chair, dressed in what she knew to be my favorite, a see-through, black lace teddy, fishnet hose, and high-heel shoes. She wasn't going to take no for an answer.

"Come over here and sit down." She patted the chair to confirm her instructions. "I know you had a rough day at work. Let me give you a massage and a little something to help you let go and relax."

With firm circular motions she started at my shoulders and worked her way into my lower back, soothing every nerve with her fingertips. Her movements seemed effortless and within minutes I felt like a puppet on a string. Her hands moved around to my chest and down toward the part of my body that was betraying me. Mentally, I wasn't prepared, but physically I wasn't in control. She skillfully used her gift of persuasion as a woman to get exactly what she wanted. As much as my mind fought against it, she was doing a hell of a job, as always. She rubbed slowly but aggressively while kissing me on my neck, then moved down my back. Gradually she moved in front of me.

My physical impulses took over and with a firm grip on her waist, I pulled her toward me. I kept my eyes closed; I didn't want her to see into my soul. She climbed on top and took full responsibility for the experience. As I entered her, my nature expanded and grew even more inside her wet walls. The rush of pleasure caused my head to roll backward, but Vickie pulled my head toward her and forced me to stare into her eyes.

"I love you, Rowan," she whispered. I felt bad, but there was no stopping this train. She held firmly on to my shoulders and began to moan from the enjoyment of her journey. Vickie was holistically making love to me, with her mind, body, and soul, but I couldn't display the same level of passion. She gyrated up and down, causing me to soon explode in pleasure, and, no doubt, we were both totally satisfied.

When we finished, the routine was the same. She got up and took a shower while I crawled into bed where my pleasure abated.

CHAPTER 2

*. . . the source of our strength . . . the origin of our beauty;
the field where our sweet smells grow . . .*

I passed my damn exit even after a long night's rest. It
wasn't like me to miss details, so I chalked it up as a typical
boring Monday morning ride to the station. I got off on the
next exit and drove fifteen minutes out of the way to get to
work. As I pulled into the driveway on the south side of the
station, I made a personal confession. I was thinking about
Maria. I had never allowed myself to get emotionally attached
to anyone I saw on the job. Subconsciously, I was saying a
silent prayer for her recovery. Feeling guilty, I stopped midsentence, shook my thoughts, then willed her out of my mind.
She had no business there in the first place.

"The brew is strong and hot this morning," the lieutenant
said as he passed by me.

"Thanks, I definitely need an eye opener." I patted him on
the shoulder, grabbed a copy of the morning newspaper, and
fixed my usual cup of black coffee. The guys were sitting
around the old kitchen table with the one weak leg and eight
mix-and-match chairs watching TV and telling their usual

weekend lies. I worked with some real characters. Thomas and Jordan were the most comical of the crew.

Thomas was an excellent cook. We called him "the flaming chef." No matter what was going wrong in the world, his first priority for the day was always the dinner menu. Jordan served as our in-house Reverend T.D. Fakes. He preached hellfire and brimstone twenty-four-seven, constantly reminding us that we were all going to hell if we didn't get our lives together. He owned and carried every version and interpretation of the Holy Bible. He was praise God for this . . . praise God for that, but let us play a video game where he'd lose . . . he'd call you a cheatin' son of a bitch in a minute. And as if that weren't enough, he told the most sexually explicit stories at the station. He knew more women than he did Bible verses. Go figure that shit out. He was twenty-five or so; guess he hadn't realized he was thinking with the wrong head.

Their conversation moved from rehashing the weekend to views about being involved in a relationship with an older woman. As usual, Fakes took his place as the facilitator. His hands flew through the air as he made his points.

"Man, I would never date a woman ten years older than me. I have one mother, I ain't lookin' for another one. The Bible says the man is the head of the household. Y'all hear that? Not woman. A man! I guarantee if you date a woman that's older than you, she'll want to be the boss. Have you doing the laundry, cooking, vacuuming, and changing the baby's diapers. I'm not feelin' that. Y'all can walk around here whipped if you want to, but not me, man."

Chef piped in next.

"I would. Personally, I don't see nothing wrong with dating someone older than me. If you're secure within yourself, her age won't matter. An older woman is mature, stable, and ain't about no games. You'll still be the man of the house and she'll respect that. I'm thirty-one years old. Have you seen the way forty looks now?" He paused long enough for us to stare into the air and visualize forty. Our uh-huhs echoed across the room. "And a forty-year-old woman has a hell of a sex drive. Those younger women can't keep up with me, man. Besides, you're just intimidated by a real woman. You need one of them young chicken heads that would do any- and everything you say!"

Chef had successfully made it a debate.

"What kinda bull is that, man! I ain't intimidated by no woman, I just know where their place is . . . in the kitchen, or on their knees!" The whole station shook with laughter. I couldn't help but laugh myself. Where was his Bible now? Fakes was gonna bust hell wide open if you asked me!

"Like I said, you want some little weak woman that will bow down to you and do everything you say. I'm just sayin', I have no problem dating an older woman."

"Well, of course you wouldn't have a problem with it. You would date—"

"Head-on two-car collision. West-bound Interstate Ten. Driver of vehicle number one reported to be unconscious. Vehicle two . . ." the voice blared out over the static-filled loudspeaker. Before the dispatcher finished the call, Parker and I had left the station. We could get the rest of the call in-side the vehicle.

We dashed in and out of rush-hour traffic and soon ar-rived at the scene of the accident. From what we could see, a 1996 black Pontiac Bonneville had hit a green Toyota Corolla head-on after the driver lost control of his car. The driver was in his early twenties and undeniably intoxicated. The woman who drove the Corolla was rendered uncon-scious from the impact and had to be airlifted to Tulane. The Corolla also had two small children inside; fortunately, they had been properly restrained and sustained only minor in-juries. This situation could have been much worse. We trans-ported the children to the same hospital as the mother for evaluation.

When we arrived, we found out that the mother wasn't responding to treatment and the children were too young to identify a next of kin. Things weren't looking good at all. The two children would have to be taken into custody by a social worker. Situations like these always saddened me. I chose this career to save lives, not to watch the innocent suffer because of someone's poor judgment. Man, I was doing it again. I was thinking about Maria and the traumatic state we found her in.

Since I was there, I made a quick decision to take the opportunity to meet her. I convinced myself that I just wanted to make sure that she was all right. I'd seen many physically injured people in my day, but Maria really touched my heart. It was hard to imagine how a man could treat such a beautiful woman, or any woman for that matter, with so little respect. Finding her to express my concern before I left the hospital became a priority. I told Parker that I was going to grab a sandwich from the cafeteria and I'd meet him back at the ambulance in fifteen minutes. As soon as he turned his back, I headed straight for the nurses' station.

Miranda, the head day-shift nurse in the emergency room, had always had a big crush on me. From the end of the hallway I could see her grinning and nudging the nurse beside her. She pulled a compact out of her coat pocket and began to primp a little. I turned my head to keep from laughing.

"Miranda, good to see you. How is everything going?" She flashed all thirty-two, no, twenty-nine of her teeth. "Girl, are you working out? It looks like you've lost a few pounds since I last saw you," I said, trying to ease into a conversation with her.

"Well, I guess I don't have to watch my figure, since you're going to watch it for me." She batted her thin lashes, and puckered her lips in a mock kiss. I looked at her penciled-on eyebrows and shook my head.

"You're too much, girl." I chuckled to stroke her ego.

"Listen, I know this is a bit much but I need your help. We brought in a young lady, McCory, I think the name was . . . she came in about a week ago with severe head trauma, deep facial wounds, and a possible broken arm. Does this sound familiar to you at all? It might not, it was opposite your shift."

"Hmmm . . . I thought you wanted to know how I was doing." She saw right through my game.

I crossed my fingers behind my back for luck, hoping she would still give me the information I wanted.

"Well, those come in a dime a dozen. I vaguely remember this one girl, though. Everyone felt very sorry for her. I heard she won't really have a home to go to once we release her. She was messed up pretty badly when she came in, a pretty girl too."

"Is she still here? What room is she in?" I slowed my pace; I couldn't sound anxious.

"Give me a second and let me see what I can find out for you." She disappeared into the back for a few minutes. When she returned, she had a sheet of notepaper in her hand. To tease me she pulled it into her chest.

"What is it worth to you? Are you going to take me out like you promised?" she asked with a goofy grin. Miranda was definitely not my type. I returned the grin and winked while thinking, *hell no!* Maria's room number was definitely not worth a date with Miranda. I had other resources, like picking up the telephone and calling patient information.

"You know I'm in a relationship. But as soon as I'm through . . ." I winked again.

"Yeah, whatever! You're gonna stop playing with my emotions, Rowan Miller!" She rolled her eyes, then slapped the notepaper down on the desk. "Maria A'Twanette McCory, 704 North."

Whew, she had a-t-t-i-t-u-d-e, but I didn't give a damn. I thanked her, then walked away before she got any more ridiculous ideas.

Before heading to 704, I really did go to the cafeteria, but instead of getting a sandwich, I talked one of the workers into putting together a small fruit basket. It would only be right to have something to offer. As I walked toward the elevator, I second-guessed myself. I didn't want Maria to have any misconceptions about my visit to her room. I only wanted to see her and make certain that she was okay. I felt the need to reach out as a potential friend; this was harmless.

One by one the floor numbers lit up and the elevator came to an easy stop as I reached floor seven. It was time for me to get off. *You moron*, I thought to myself as I strolled down the hall; *how the hell is she going to know you? She was nearly unconscious when you found her.* I took a deep breath and thought about how I'd introduce myself. *Hello, my name is Rowan. I responded to the 911 call the day you almost died.* I rethought my actions, but managed to tap softly on the door.

MARIA

I'd awakened that morning feeling disoriented and nauseated from the pain medication that had been administered to me earlier. My physical injuries held me captive within the confines of a minuscule hospital room. The solid walls of gray concrete seemed to close in on me. From imprisonment, my thoughts were overwhelming. My life as I formerly knew it resided in another plane of existence. Though I was horrified by the fact that I'd awakened in a hospital, I was eternally grateful to God for answering my prayer. I had a very close call with death, yet I was still alive. Through all the pain and suffering, God had given me one more chance. I lifted my head and stared at the wooden cross beneath the wall-mounted television. I wanted to pray a prayer of thanks; the only problem was that I only remembered one simple prayer from Mass. I whispered something less formal than the prayer from my childhood, believing that God knew the sincerity of my heart and would both hear and help me.

I gazed blankly out the window of my room rehashing the entire event, wondering what I could have done to prevent it. Was it my fault? Why didn't I make sure the door was closed securely before I turned my back to him? I knew not to be too trusting of anyone, yet I managed to allow someone to take advantage of me. Why didn't I see through him? Why hadn't I been a better judge of character? I was angry with him and all he represented. He had brutally beaten and humiliated me, then left me for dead.

An unpleasant thought suddenly immobilized me—pregnancy? I lowered my head, closed my eyes, and covered my face with both hands. Explaining to a child they were conceived during a rape was unthinkable to me. I shivered as a cold chill ran down my spine. Did I even have a reason to worry? I asked myself. I'd been taking birth control pills since high school to regulate my monthly periods.

I had finished a stressful day at the bank and wanted to relax a few hours before class. I was exhausted and had to complete a biology research paper, not to mention the fact that I had encountered more irate customers disputing checking fees in the last two hours than I had during my entire day. Nevertheless, I was still in a good mood. It was Friday, the summer sun was still shining, it was about ninety degrees outside, and I was off for the weekend. As I listened to the mellowing sounds of Alicia Keys on the way home, I smiled and bobbed my head to the music while entertaining the thought of a Saturday afternoon matinee. One study-free weekend was long overdue. I had unwound and was pleased to finally see my street sign.

I rented a one-bedroom, one-bathroom duplex. Basically, on my salary and with a very small savings, it was all I could afford working at the bank as a teller and attending college at night. The neighborhood didn't seem too bad. It consisted of mostly single mothers with two or three children. I spent very few daytime hours at home, so the laughter and playfulness of the children never really bothered me.

A FOR SALE sign had been in the yard of the duplex two doors away for at least six months. Four days prior, I had noticed two men viewing the property. They walked around, had a brief conversation, then got into a car parked in front of the house. One was an average-looking white man, medium build, muscular, conservatively dressed in navy blue khakis, an oxford shirt, and a pair of worn leather loafers. The other was a very handsome black man, tall with a slender build, bald, and wore dress slacks, with a starched shirt and tie. Their behavior didn't seem to be out of the ordinary; I assumed they were either inspectors or looking to purchase the property. The following day only one of them returned. He'd been there before, so to see him again triggered no red flags.

Two days later he returned again. When I drove by his parked car, he looked up and gestured hello with his head. As I got out of my car and walked toward the house, he seemed busy taking notes. I could see the legal pad against his steering wheel. I adjusted my books and turned my head to look in the other direction. I opened my front door, set my books and purse down on the table, then took off my shoes. My cushioned pumps didn't provide the needed support for my long shift. All I wanted was to take a few minutes to stretch out on the couch and relax before class. About five minutes later there was a knock at the door. I got up and looked through the peephole. Since I recognized his face, I opened the door to see what he wanted. He stepped forward and stood close enough for me to see his bloodshot eyes and striped oxford shirt.

"I'm . . . ahh . . . looking at the property a few doors down from you." He pointed toward the duplex for sale. "The battery on my cell phone seems to be dead or something." He placed his hands inside his pants pockets and took a step back. "I need to call the real estate agent. May I borrow your phone? I will make it brief." He looked around as he rustled the loose change inside his pant pocket.

"Yes, sure." I left him standing on the porch as I went to get the phone, not thinking to close the door while he waited. Apparently he crept in behind me. I didn't realize it until I turned to bring him the telephone from the kitchen and ran right into him. With a tight and restricting hold, he grabbed me.

"What's going on? Please let me go!" I squirmed to get loose. The more I struggled, the tighter his grasp became. "If you want my money you can have everything in my wallet. Take anything you want but please don't hurt me!" I panicked as I begged him to let me go.

"It's not the money that I want. Everything I want is right here."

I looked over my shoulder and saw a brass candleholder on the table. I squirmed out of his arms, picked it up, and pulled my arm back with every intention to hit him and render him unconscious. Before I could hit him, he snatched my wrist midair and knocked the candleholder to the floor. Hearing it land with a thud made me feel more vulnerable. My attempt to protect myself upset him.

"Why are you resisting me? You know you want it just as bad as I do."

He twisted my right arm tightly behind my back, forced me into the living room, then shoved me down on the couch. During the struggle, my blouse inched far above my waistline and the look in his eyes pierced me like a sword as he pinned me down with his body. I closed my eyes and my life flashed before me.

"Hmmm . . . you are so fine. I bet you didn't realize I was watching you . . . now, did you? You made me work really hard to see you but I managed." My breathing became shallow as I listened to him and feared his threats. "My, you're such a beautiful little black thing." He roughly fondled my breasts. "Is all of this for me?"

I leaned into the couch as he spat his words into my face. I didn't know what to say. If he had been watching me, then he already knew that I was single. But if he was lying, maybe I could use that to scare him off.

"My boyfriend is at work. He'll be here . . ." I stuttered as a curt slap landed on my face. I gripped each thigh with my hands to tolerate the pain as physical reflexes caused my body to tremble.

"How can such plump luscious lips form themselves to tell such a huge lie? I've never seen a man at your place. I see everything you do."

So, he had been watching! His observation let me know that I needed to get out of the house that very second! I quickly looked away to survey the room. The front door was to my right and the back door behind me.

"That's what I thought."

I felt a shift in his weight and took advantage of the small space by rolling onto my stomach and sliding off the couch on to the floor.

"Oh no, did you think it would be that easy?" Before I could stand and run toward the door, he pulled me up by my hair and pushed me against the wall. With his hands on both sides of my face he pressed my head tightly against the wall. "I'm not letting you get away."

The liquor on his breath was offensive. Small beads of his sweat burned my eyes as he flicked his wide and obtrusive fingertips in my face. I could see each layer of dry skin underneath his bitten and uneven nails. The pressure from his hands left my face tender to the touch as he vocalized his verbal threats in my ear. "All about me . . . the pleasures will all be mine."

Suddenly I had another thought. Maybe if I reversed the roles and pretended to seduce him he would consider letting me go. The goal was to make him calm enough to believe I'd submit, then make a mad dash toward the front door.

"Hey, if you found me interesting you should have introduced yourself." As I spoke, my words were broken and shaky. He loosened the grip on my face and took a step back. My back never left the wall as I turned my head and looked into his eyes. My act needed to be sensual, not too fast and not too slow. I spread my legs apart as wide as I could, moved my right leg sideways, and rubbed my inner thighs. To him it would be interpreted as a sensual gesture, but for me it would be another step toward the front door. Looking confused he let my face go but maintained his stance in front of me.

"We don't have to go through this drama. All you have to do is sit down and talk to me. Tell me what you want. I promise I will make it worth your while." Maintaining eye contact was becoming impossible. While I spoke, I slid my fingers along the wall and estimated how many steps there were to the front door. If I could divert his attention for two seconds I knew I could make it.

"Shut the hell up! I'm not that damn drunk. You're only trying to get the hell out of here. You can't fool me. You give me what I want and then I will leave you alone."

He saw through my every move. I panicked and bolted for the front door. I had to make it; I had to get out. He thrust his body forward and grabbed my arm. I tripped on the corner of my area rug and hit my head on the end table. Scared for my life, I began to scramble toward the door that held my freedom behind it. Despite my attempt, the door moved farther away. I didn't make it.

"It's not over till I say it's over."

From my peripheral vision I could see something flying

swiftly across the room. The maniac had ripped a sconce holder off the wall and thrown it at me. It struck me on the side of the head.

"Don't make this worse than it has to be! All I wanted was just to have a little fun. But, oh no! You're going to make me go there. The way I feel now, I want double the pleasure. You want a good time? Your fantasy man is going to give it to you. Yeaaah."

Kicking the pieces of broken sconce, he walked toward me, reached down, wrapped a handful of my hair around his hand, and dragged me into the bedroom. He rummaged through my dresser drawers, pulled out a pair of panties, and sniffed them. "Ummm, smells so good. I wonder what it tastes like. Cherries? Chocolate?" He unwound my hair from his hand, threw me on the bed, and grabbed my throat to hold me down. Every second of my life equaled an eternity.

With both hands, he lifted me off the bed by my neck and shoved me against the dresser. I bounced off the hard wooden dresser onto the floor. I was too weak and dizzy to fight back. He then picked me up and shoved me into the dresser again. The mirror on the dresser liquefied and transformed itself into several large pieces, and I immediately felt another sharp pain in my head. He picked up a piece of broken mirror and turned my head, forcing me to stare into it. My vision was blurred by my tears, blood, and hair. I could only imagine what I looked like.

"See this pretty little face? Take a good look at it. This is the last time you will ever see it," he snarled as he cut across my cheek, then stepped back to admire his artwork.

I could feel the warm blood form a stream with my tears before flowing down the side of my face and continuing below my chin. The kick he gave me to the stomach knocked the wind right out of me. I rolled over onto my side and held my stomach in pain. All I could hear was his laughter as he turned me on my back, twisted my skirt until it was above my waist, ripped off my panties, and forced my legs open. He plunged his offensive nature deep inside me over and over again. The pain was so bad that I could no longer scream for help. My barren lips continued to move even though void of sound. Again and again he thrust himself forward, while using his right hand to repeatedly slap me.

"Yeah . . . pretty girl, huh? Too cute to speak? Who will want your tainted black ass now?"

A knock on the door brought me out of my trance.

ROWAN

"Yes, Who is it?"

I cleared my throat and shifted the fruit basket to tuck in the back of my shirt.

"Rowan Miller." I stepped closer to the door. "One of the responding paramedics the day of your incident." I knew I was taking a chance by showing up unannounced. Because I didn't see a man the day of the incident didn't necessarily mean she wasn't in a relationship. He could have been at work, out of town . . . anywhere.

"Rowan? Come in."

I entered the room but kept a safe and respectable distance by standing just inside the doorway and leaving the door open. I was relieved to see that she was alone. She turned toward me and squinted her eyes. I knew she couldn't remember my face and didn't know what to say.

"Hello, I'm Rowan. I responded to the 911 call at your house a few days ago. I wanted to check on you to see how you were doing." I spoke calmly. Yes, this was definitely Maria. From out of nowhere, I felt the grip of a soul mate connection clutch my heart.

"Well, thank you for checking on me." She pressed the button on the side of her bed to elevate her head.

Her voice was sweet and tender. Even through her head bandages her warm smile made me speechless. I didn't know what more to say or how to say it. My nervousness caused me to unnecessarily clear my throat again and shift my weight from one leg to the other. I felt like a moron.

"I brought you some fruit." I placed the basket on the rolling tray at the foot of her bed.

"Thank you, Rowan. I appreciate your concern."

"I . . . was very concerned. I feel better now that I know you're recovering well." She was even more beautiful than I remembered. I wanted to reach out, touch her, and give her a consoling hug. I wanted to make all of her problems disappear and tell her that everything was going to be okay. "I, uh . . . I guess I'll be going now. You take care of yourself."

"Thank you very much for the fruit and for coming by."

I took another direct look into her eyes as I moved slightly toward the door to leave. "You're welcome. Take care now." I turned and walked out of her room, with that grip still tightly around my heart.

CHAPTER 3

Diamonds are made, not created;
they are carved and shaped by life's minor altercations.

As I waited to be discharged, I laced my tennis shoes, then braced myself on the edge of the bed to stand up. In the mirror I adjusted the oversized family reunion T-shirt and faded baggy blue jeans left in my room by Social Services. Misinterpreting the soft tap on the door for my nurse, I reached to open it. It wasn't my nurse but a stocky black female with a short Afro wearing black slacks and a white cotton shirt. Standing directly behind her was a very tall thin white man with salt-and-pepper hair wearing dark gray pants and white shirt with gray stripes.

"Ms. Maria McCory, my name is Detective Renee Madison and this is my partner Detective Peter Sturges." She removed the leather pouch containing her identification badge from her waistband and held it up so I could see it. Her partner did the same.

"Yes . . . ?" I took another look at their identification as they pardoned themselves and stepped inside the room.

"We were assigned to your case and followed the ambulance to the hospital. Due to your physical state before and after surgery it was impossible to proceed with questioning. Until this point we've investigated based on evidence found at the crime scene."

"We're very sorry if this isn't a good time. It seems as though you're preparing to leave," Detective Sturges said as he looked around the room.

"Yes, my discharge paperwork will be ready this afternoon."

"Before proceeding we want to let you know personally how sorry we were about your incident and we're pleased to see you're well enough to go home." Detective Madison's facial expression was sincere as she shook her head and placed her hand on her chest.

"Yeah . . . just wanted you to know how relieved we are to see you going home." Detective Sturges leaned forward slightly as he spoke.

"Thank you." I folded my arms and took a deep breath. I wasn't ready to deal with the reality of my situation just yet.

"We want to assure you it's our goal to process every piece of info—"

"And follow any leads to that no-good son of a bitch. Oh, excuse my French. I mean put whoever did this to you behind bars." Detective Sturges had stepped forward and blurted this out before Detective Madison could finish her sentence. Apparently embarrassed, he wiped his forehead and covered his mouth with his hand.

"I'll feel safer when I know he's in jail," I responded sternly as I sat down on the edge of the bed. Detective Madison walked to the side of the bed and placed her hand on my shoulder.

"Yes . . . we're very sorry it happened to you. With your help, maybe we can stop it from happening to someone else."

The other detective took a small notepad and ink pen out

of his pocket. "If you don't mind, I know it's been two weeks but we'd like to ask a few questions."

"Sure, I can't leave until I've signed my paperwork."

The gentleman stepped closer to me and leaned back against the small sink opposite the bed.

"First, can you give us a detailed description of the intruder?" Detective Madison said as she removed her hand from my shoulder, gently clasped them behind her back, and leaned her head to the side as Detective Sturges prepared to take notes.

"Well . . . he . . . was . . ." Wanting justice to be served but unable to verbalize my thoughts, I found a knot in the white bed linen and twisted it with my fingers.

"Maria . . . we understand. Please take your time."

"He was white, about . . . honestly I'm not good with height or weight descriptions. I'm sorry."

"Tell you what . . ." Before walking to the foot of the bed she rubbed her temples and placed her index finger on her chin. "Do you know how tall your father is or perhaps an uncle?"

"Yes, my father is about five feet eleven inches."

"Visualize him standing beside the intruder."

After a short pause and a deep breath I spoke again. "He was a few inches taller than my father, so I would guess maybe six feet two inches and very muscular. Most of all, I remember his eyes . . . they were blue."

"Did you know him? Had you seen him in the neighborhood before?" Anticipating my response Detective Sturges shifted his weight from one leg to the other.

"No, I didn't know him!" My back became stiff as I looked them both in the eye.

"Please, we don't mean to offend you. Many times women are victimized by men they know. Men from the neighborhood, even next-door neighbors."

"Oh, I'm sorry. It's just that . . . I've tried to forget and now I have to relive it again in my mind."

"We do this every day and believe me, we understand. We want to help you but we really need you to help us."

I released the tension in my back as she explained their purpose to me again.

"You're doing great." Detective Sturges looked up from his notepad and rested his ink pen against his chin.

"No, I didn't know him. I noticed him in the neighborhood four days prior to the incident."

"Four days prior . . . never before then?"

"No. He was looking at a duplex a few doors away from me."

"Anything else . . . like his car, anything peculiar that would lead us to him?"

"He was driving a black Volkswagen Jetta."

"Can you give us an idea about the year?"

"No, not exactly, I can only assume."

"Did the car look new, used? Were there any obvious dents or details?" He tapped his ink pen on his notepad.

"It didn't look very new to me. It was very clean . . . spotless to be exact."

He nodded his head, then made a circular gesture with his right hand for me to continue my thoughts. "It would help us if you could remember at least one detail about the car. Did anything stand out in your mind?"

I looked down, closed my eyes, and attempted to remember anything about that day. One detail did come to my memory.

"Hmmm . . . I do remember a large dent on his bumper."

"That might help us. Do you remember which side?"

"Yeah . . . it was on the left side." I closed my eyes tighter and dug my fingertips into the edge of the bed, searching my memory. "His car had Louisiana tags and I remember the letters DDB . . . but that's all."

The detective smiled and nodded his head. He made a combination of notes before closing his pad and putting it inside his jacket pocket.

"Thank you very much. The information you've given should help us get one step closer to the scum that did this to you." He leaned forward to shake my hand.

"Maria, we wish you a total recovery and you'll be hearing from us soon." Detective Madison shook my hand and patted me on the shoulder before leaving the room.

My legs suddenly felt like molds of cement as they turned to walk away. The thought of having to leave the hospital and face society with only the clothes on my back made me ill inside. My car and all of my personal property were still at my old place. Until I knew for certain that the criminal was behind bars, going back to my old neighborhood frightened me. The only other place I could go was to my aunt Bethany's. I didn't want to go back to Aunt Bethany like this, but I had no choice. My loss of pride left me with no inhibitions. Mentally unprepared to return to my duplex, I was willing to temporally abandon personal possessions for peace of mind. In time I would face those demons, go back, and retrieve my things.

The nurse knocked on the door before she opened it, making sure I was dressed. As if they were memorized, she reviewed the discharge paperwork, then prompted me to sign the release forms. She cleared her throat and handed me a brochure. Her details were few as she softly explained the contents, which consisted of free counseling for rape victims, and directed my attention to the 800 number on the back side. I looked at it, folded it in half, and placed it inside my back pocket. Self consciously, I touched the bandage that concealed the wound on my left cheek. With a smile she wished me luck. I knew she meant well by her expression of kindness.

My heart skipped beats as I picked up the telephone and

dialed Aunt Bethany's number. "Hello," the raspy voice said on the other end.

I took a deep breath. "Aunt Bethany, hi. I know I haven't talked to you in two weeks . . . but I . . . I've been in an accident and I need somewhere to stay. Is my old bedroom still available?" I tried to steady my voice.

"Oh my good Lord!" Aunt Bethany began to panic. "Baby, where are you? You okay?"

"I'm at Tulane University Hospital."

"I knew I shouldn't have listened to Clara. She told me you were probably busy with school and work. I knew better. She changed my mind each time I wanted to stop by. You call me every other day and it's not like you to ignore my messages. I just felt like something was wrong. Baby, Aunt Bethany is on the way."

"I'll be waiting for you in the main entryway." Hearing Aunt Bethany's voice humbled me and made me cry. I hadn't cried since the attack, and now all of my emotions rushed forward uncontrollably. After hanging up, I went inside the bathroom to pull myself together. I hadn't meant to have an emotional outburst like that, but then again, I was thankful that I could attempt to get all of my tears out before my aunt arrived. Even though I had every reason to cry, I felt obliged to show myself strong by hiding my expression of tears from her. Not only that but an overabundance of tears would surely bring about an overabundance of questions, questions that I wasn't ready to answer. My tears subsided as I took one final look around the room. Under no circumstances did I want to see this place again.

I left the room and proceeded to the front lobby; thirty minutes had passed when I saw her approach the front door. She hugged me, rocking me from side to side. Warm tears trickled down her face and onto my shoulder.

"Maria, why didn't you call me? How long have you been in this dreadful place?" Just as I expected, her questions went on and on. I embraced her tighter in exchange for the answers. I didn't want to give her the slightest indication of what had happened.

"Aunt Bethany, it's a very long story. Please don't make me talk about it right now. I don't have the strength. I promise I'll tell you later." I had no intentions of ever telling her the truth; I simply didn't have the heart. There was no need to burden her with it.

When I was a child, my life with Aunt Bethany was emotionally rewarding; I was blessed to receive from her the nurturing that I needed. No character or personality traits led anyone to assume I was the daughter of two socially misfit teenagers.

My father was an only child. At the age of fifteen, his parents were killed in a tragic automobile accident after attending a social function during the Christmas holidays. His father was slightly intoxicated, so his mother opted to drive back home. An unexpected rainstorm came from nowhere and the wet, slick pavement mimicked a sheet of ice on a bridge and provided no traction for their automobile tires. She lost control of the car; it spun madly and was stopped temporarily only by the embankment. Before long, the vehicle slid downward and Lake Ponchartrain opened her mouth and formed a liquid grave. With no biological parents to guide him, my father lost all interest in education by the age of sixteen and soon promoted himself to the school of hard knocks. Forced to live with only the bare necessities provided by his grandmother, he found a job to provide himself with the things he truly desired. Armed as he was with only a tenth-grade education, his first exposure to labor was a job he took working as a bagger at a small corner grocery store. There he was introduced to several moneymaking opportunities. While my father worked, men from the neighborhood would gamble in front of the store. His curiosity began to get the best of him and he soon took interest in their activities.

One evening after work he went over to watch the game of chance. He was not only good looking, but cunning as well. He was smart enough to observe a street game and master the rules. It all seemed pretty easy to him, so he asked if he could play.

"Got any money, youngblood?" an older man asked my father jokingly as he rattled the dice in his right hand.

"I wouldn't ask to play if I couldn't pay." He stepped back and reached into his pockets with an attitude. He started to play and win. That was the beginning of the end for him.

What started out as a little game of chance soon turned into more. Every Friday the fellows would get together for a game of "craps" and the fixings that went with it, beer, whiskey, and drugs. My father's youth gave him an advantage. The neighborhood guys showed more interest in his moneymaking potential. Before he knew it he was making more money on the streets gambling and hustling than he would ever make at his job, so he resorted to gambling and stealing for his income.

My mother was in junior high when she and my father met. Because she was three years younger than he was, there was hardly any effort required on his part in seducing her. He allured her quickly with his fast money and slightly used Buick LeSabre. Expensive gifts were the tools used to control her young mind. It was then, at fourteen, that she discovered her cat could do more than just meow. When it roared she ended up pregnant with me. She had two choices. Live with her grandmother in Mississippi or give birth to me in Louisiana and allow my father's aunt to obtain custodial rights. Her choice was the latter of the two. She carried me to term, had me, and graciously let Aunt Bethany do the rest. Aunt Bethany provided me with love, security, and most of all an awareness of God. I would describe her as a devout Catholic, and sincerely believed that there was a golden robe and a pair of slippers reserved in heaven for her.

We got into the car and she drove off. As we turned onto the highway, she kissed her fingertips, then rubbed my bandage.

"How is yo' daddy?" she asked. "You'd think he'd be gettin' old and tired by now. All of those women gonna kill him one of these days. I guarantee it!" She shook her head as she drove.

"I guess he's okay. I really don't talk to him much anymore. You know he has a better relationship with Jamilia."

Somewhere between the streets and home, my father had hustled up Jamilia. My "sister" was distinctly different from me; her mixture of black and white genes gave her long silky hair, and a pair of beautiful green eyes. These physical differences gave her royal status in his heart. He was very proud of his "other" daughter. Two years later a telephone call from her mother for milk and Pampers blindsided my mother. The news only forced a breakup of two weeks between my parents. To make amends my father showed up at her door with a rabbit fur jacket.

We rode the remainder of the way in silence, which gave me more time to think. How was I going to get back to living my life? Scheduled to return to work in three weeks, how would I look my coworkers in the eye? Again, I was overcome with emotion. Here I was, suddenly displaced, broken, and stripped of everything I once was. My confidence . . . gone, my self-esteem . . . that too had been stolen. My self-worth, at this point, I greatly questioned. I felt more tears beginning to burn behind my eyelids, but I didn't dare let a single one fall.

I'd already missed two weeks of school and I wasn't ready to go back right now. I was so ashamed of what had happened; I wasn't up to having to explain the situation to a professor or a dean, or anyone for that matter. In my contemplating, I had unintentionally started a list of reasons why I couldn't go back. My struggle with organic chemistry made the top of the list. It would be impossible for me to catch up on a full load of missed assignments.

As we got closer to the house, the familiarity of home began to embrace me. Aunt Bethany's elegant eighteenth-century home, which encased many of my favorite child-hood memories, greeted me with a smile. The front door creaked as she opened it. With every step the hardwood floors sang a welcoming melody. I stood in the doorway, looked around, then inhaled and exhaled slowly. Since I'd left, her furniture hadn't been moved. The antique Victorian couch was still stern against the back wall. Two wing-back chairs were on both sides of the window to the right of her room. Her marble-top coffee table held its place neatly in front of the couch. I played a few notes on her old piano as I passed by, then picked up a crystal whatnot from the curio in the corner. The antique grandfather clock constructed with mahogany wood stood with dignity at the end of the hallway. I followed the path of the woven hall runner into the kitchen as aromas of old and new competed for my attention.

Aunt Bethany pulled some fresh yeast rolls from the oven, while I instinctively poured two cups of honey-lemon tea. Just like old times. Together we sat at the table in the small breakfast nook and took advantage of the opportunity to reminisce. She shared with me fond memories of my up-bringing; I did the same. I knew everything was going to be just fine. I was back at home.

CHAPTER 4

Are we listening to the warnings?
Are we paying attention to the signs?

I'd been so busy at the fire station the last couple of weeks that I hadn't gotten a chance to visit Maria again until today. I promised myself that I would see her and actually hold a conversation longer than two minutes this time. With great anticipation I slowly eased the door open. Dang, I was so nervous I had forgotten to knock. As I peeped around the door I could see her small silhouette in the bed, her back turned toward me. This was the day. I was going to tell the woman of my dreams, possibly my one true love, my soul mate, how I really felt about her. I'd fallen in love.

"Did I disturb your nap?"

"Oh no. I was only resting." Her voice sounded weak and feeble, as if she wasn't recovering so well after all. She turned her head from the window to look at me. My eyebrows shot up toward the ceiling. This was definitely not what I had expected. This was somebody's grandmother.

"Ma'am, I'm so sorry. I have the wrong room. Sorry for the inconvenience." I backed out of the room, turned around, and walked away disappointed. I'd missed my opportunity.

It was exactly what I deserved. I wasn't being true to Vickie or myself. Never had I been so embarrassed in my life. I guess it wasn't meant to be.

Disappointed, not wanting to accept this outcome, I went back to the ambulance. Reaching for my cell, I decided to give Josh a call. Maybe he wouldn't mind going out to the range with me. I hadn't talked to him since the night he was nearly in pieces over that wife of his. He answered on the second ring.

"Let's go hit some balls this evening. I know you aren't doing anything," I started.

"What's up, Rowan?" He seemed to be in much better spirits than the last time we talked.

"Come on out and play for a while. Can you get a hall pass?" I joked, knowing how Jana kept him on lockdown.

"Whatever, man. That sounds good. I'm off today. What time are you talking?"

"As soon as I pull off these blues. I'll be around there in a few, I just need to get my truck."

Josh didn't live too far from the station, and I was in no rush to get home. We were at the range thirty minutes later, perfecting our swings.

"So, are you and Jana going to make it?"

"Oh yeah, oh yeah. We're fine, man. It took a couple of arguments, but we're working it out." He shielded his eyes from the evening sun as he watched his ball sail into the distance.

"So she put you back on the schedule?"

Knowing that I was referring to his sex life, he looked at me sideways. "Rowan, can I have a personal life? Do you have to know about everything?" He moved aside, allowing me to position myself for my next swing.

"Damn, man. Calm down! I'm just checking on you. You're the one who called me crying and sniffling like a little girl," I teased.

Josh knew I meant no harm. "Forget me! When are you gonna marry Vickie?" A wide smile broke out on his face. It was his turn to ride my case.

"Shut up, man." I really didn't feel like talking about her, especially as it related to marriage.

"I mean, you're living with the girl . . . you milking the cow, right? Sounds like it's about time to make a purchase." He doubled over with laughter, but I didn't see a damned thing funny.

"You can't rush love." I tried to dig my way out. He knew I was nowhere near ready for marriage.

"Oh, so you're in love now?" That was even funnier to him. "When did your big ass fall in love?" He crossed his arms over his chest with his eyebrows raised and awaited my response.

"You didn't hear me say I was in love. I said, you can't *rush* love." I paused momentarily. "I don't think things are going to work out with us, to be honest with you, man." I was baring a little of my soul and couldn't even look him in his face; I watched my ball instead.

"What? Man, you're gonna throw three years away?" His eyebrows now scrunched low, nearly touching his lashes. "All right, come clean. What's her name?" He pushed me aside and teed his ball.

"What are you talking about?" I tried to play it off.

"Rowan, how long have I been knowing you? You're not just gonna walk away from what you have and not have a contingency plan. That's not you. You've got something working somewhere."

"Ain't nobody got nothing working. I just don't want to continue to waste the woman's time. She ain't the one," I admitted. I wasn't ready to tell him that I thought I had met "the one," particularly after what had happened earlier this afternoon.

"And I guess you're just finding that out, huh?" he asked sarcastically.

"How did we get on me? I thought we were talking about you." We both chuckled and left well enough alone.

MARIA

Little by little, I was beginning to settle back into the routine of life. Aunt Bethany's home was as comfortable and nurturing as it had always been. Every evening, we would share a cup of tea and enjoy the simple pleasure of conversation. I came to notice that Aunt Bethany had lost a considerable amount of weight in the few short weeks that I'd been there. One evening as she stood in the kitchen preparing dinner, I casually mentioned it to her, thinking it was odd that she'd lost weight so rapidly. She thought nothing of it, but I did. She was already fairly small, and the weight loss made her look sick and malnourished.

"Aunt Bethany, have you seen a doctor lately?"

"A doctor? Maria, stop being silly! What do I need a doctor for? Now you know I don't believe in spending all of my hard-earned money on a doctor. They run tests that make you sick. I'm doing fine."

"Okay, Aunt Bethany. Calm down. You're losing a lot of weight. I'm only concerned."

"You just concern yourself with finishing my homemade biscuits. I don't cook like this for my health." Flour flew from her fingertips as she pointed them at me to make her point.

"Yes, ma'am."

At sixty-two, Aunt Bethany was yet a very active woman. Every morning she would walk for about forty minutes before doing yard work. Her yard was immaculate. She took pride in her award-winning rose and azalea bushes. To see a weed of any sort was sinful. She maintained the acre around the house, while her nephews managed the remaining forty.

After Uncle Brewster died she didn't want to sell their land to some young hotshot developer. She said they would mess up her good land with a bunch of good-for-nothing houses that wouldn't stand a good strong gust of wind. She also ran bingo nights at church every Wednesday. She refused to sit still, yet it became very obvious to me that her activity level was decreasing. Later she started to complain about her stomach. She said she was bloated frequently and always uncomfortable. My worry prompted me to take her to our family doctor for a routine physical. He was the first of several doctors she saw who wrote her symptoms off as old age.

"Oh, it's not a big deal. Everyone either loses or gains a few extra pounds with age," they responded halfheartedly. "She'll be fine. She needs to decrease her activity and get a little rest. She isn't twenty-five anymore."

Rest was their prescription for her recovery. No physician could convince me it was only old age, but I wasn't a physician and couldn't diagnose her problem. Having to rest would kill Aunt Bethany.

Her weight loss persisted and she was always tired. One of her friends suggested a specialist at the hospital. Fortunately, he had a cancellation and was able to see her within a week. Even though I'd returned to work only three weeks prior, my immediate supervisor understood when I scheduled a day off.

MARIA

"If you have completed the paperwork I need a copy of her insurance card for our records." I gave the clerk her paperwork and insurance card. "Thank you, ladies, the nurse will be with you soon."

It was at this moment the clock on the wall hid its face from the both of us. The waiting room was very quiet. The occupants either watched the Health Channel or read old magazines as they waited in their choice of hard tan chairs or a barely cushioned sofa.

"Bethany McCory. Bethany McCory," the nurse called. I held her hand as we walked through the door.

"How are you doing today? I need to get your weight. Step on the scale for me. Please take your time." She recorded Aunt Bethany's weight on her chart. "Now step down and have a seat. Next, I'm going to take your blood pressure, pulse, and temperature. This is routine to prepare you for the doctor." After getting a reading, she removed the black cuff from Aunt Bethany's arm and asked us to follow her down the hallway into an examination room. "Please have a seat. The doctor will be in to see you shortly."

We both whispered silent prayers as we waited on him.

The knock on the door startled us as he came in. "Good morning, Mrs. McCory. My name is Dr. Eastlan. I have reviewed your chart and I understand you are concerned about a dramatic weight loss?"

"Yes, Doctor, I am. To be honest with you I wouldn't be here if it wasn't for my niece over there. I think I have lost twenty pounds this month. I'm not on a diet, I eat three good meals every day. I'm too old for diets, you know."

"Any other problems?"

"Yes, I get so weak and tired. After a stool, my stomach never feels completely empty. It always feels so full."

"I will do a routine examination and blood work, then evaluate the situation based on the results."

To watch him examine her was interesting. He removed a black instrument from the wall and looked into her ears, eyes, and throat like a baby. With his fingertips he gently felt behind her ears, below her throat, and under her arms. His facial expression changed slightly. Then he asked her to lie back on the examination table. With both hands he kneaded her stomach like dough. He told her to stop him if it became too painful. Aunt Bethany withstood the exam, but told him a couple of places he touched were tender. He stopped to make notes on her chart. Next, he requested routine blood work and asked her several questions about her eating habits, lifestyle, and weight loss. What did a normal meal usually consist of? How many meals did she eat a day? How many times did she eliminate? How active was she? Any hereditary conditions? Her rapid weight loss was his main concern. Otherwise she appeared healthy.

Tension started to build as we sat in the office and waited impatiently for him to tell us something. It took him forever to come back. Finally, he appeared in the waiting room and asked us to follow him to his office. He shut the door and asked us to have a seat. We watched him thumb through her chart, make a note, then close it.

"I have your preliminary lab results." The discontentment on his face was obvious. "At this point I'm very concerned about your positive fecal occult blood test result. It isn't normal. Before I make any assumptions I want to perform additional tests." He wanted to admit her into the hospital for additional testing.

Displeased with the frown on Aunt Bethany's face, I asked him to elaborate. "Dr. Eastlan, could you explain your comments to us in everyday terms?"

"During a routine physical we perform a battery of tests for women over the age of fifty. The tests include a complete blood count, urinalysis, chemistries, and a fecal occult blood test. Well, your aunt's test results, specifically the fecal occult blood test, weren't normal. At her age this can't be taken lightly. Her age and certain predetermined genetic factors make her risk higher for certain diseases. I want to take every precaution to make sure that she is okay. If not, the necessary treatments need to begin immediately. I would like to admit her into the hospital for a colonoscopy, X-rays, and a CT scan."

"What exactly does the positive fecal occult result indicate?"

"I would rather not discuss that with you until the testing is complete. I don't want you to be alarmed if it isn't necessary. Please understand and trust my better judgment. I have been in this profession for twenty years. Believe me."

Aunt Bethany started to cry, then asked if she could spend the night at home and admit herself the next morning. The doctor wasn't too happy but he honored her request.

Aunt Bethany cried all the way home. She never said a word as she held her head and shook it in disappointment. I couldn't fully describe what I was feeling other than a void in my heart for her. After an uncomfortably quiet dinner, she prepared herself for bed, then called me into her room. She patted the bed beside her, motioning for me to sit. As she talked I listened intently, respecting her enough not to interrupt. In the next few minutes, she was sound asleep.

I sat there for nearly ten minutes longer, silently weeping, pondering on all that she said, and knowing that she'd fully prepared me for her departure. Emotionally drained, I finally rose from her side and retired to my own room. I tossed and turned in my bed until I finally fell asleep. It wasn't a very deep sleep. I woke up in a panic around three o'clock in the morning sensing something was wrong. I went into Aunt Bethany's bedroom where she was gasping for breath . . . each breath she took was short and hard.

"Aunt Bethany, Aunt Bethany! Please wake up! Oh, God, please don't let her die. She's all I have. Please not now, never!" I called 911.

When will I wake up? Am I reliving a nightmare? Once the ambulance arrived they asked for a brief medical history. I could only tell them we had been to the doctor's office earlier the day before. The paramedics were able to contact Dr. Eastlan, who then gave specific instructions regarding her transport and admission. After several private conversations the admitting physician disclosed that Dr. Eastlan suspected colon cancer. Aunt Bethany's treatment would totally depend on the metastasis and stage of the cancer.

I was allowed to see her once she was stabilized. My heart was broken as I watched her fight for her life. I hurt with every breath she took. Her eyes were weak and tired; the oxygen mask hid her face and IVs restricted her movements. I wasn't ready for our relationship to end. She was my guardian, my hope; how would I make it without her?

CHAPTER 5

She opened her heart to love; she provided a hand to heal; she willingly enacted God's will.

I'd been at the hospital for three weeks and was reluctant to leave Aunt Bethany in her room alone. For me, spending every second by her bedside was a must. I listened to her monitors and tried to interpret the beeps and red indicators as they flashed across the screen. I wanted to hear every breath she took and possibly wouldn't take.

There was a faint knock on the door just before Rhonda, the evening nurse, came in. Her smile was warm as she stepped inside the room. She checked the very same monitor I was trying so desperately to interpret, and then she made a note on her chart. Gently she pulled the bed linen back, initialized the instrument to check Aunt Bethany's blood pressure, then lifted her wrist to check her pulse. She responded with a slight "hmm" before making additional notes on her chart.

"Maria, have you had anything to eat today?"

I responded honestly and told her no. Basically, I had barely left Aunt Bethany's room since she'd been admitted into the hospital, except once to get a few toiletries and fresh

clothes from the house. She shook her finger and repri-
manded me for my self-negligence.

"Look, honey, you need to take care of yourself while
your aunt is here. That means eating right and getting some
rest yourself. Your immune system is very vulnerable."

I knew her concerns were right. She covered Aunt Bethany's
arms and checked the monitors one final time.

"If you're hungry, now would be a good time for you to
get something to eat. When you get back she may be ready
to wake up. I'll be back in a couple of hours to check on her,
but you can call me if you need anything."

Suddenly I longed for some fresh squash, corn, green
beans, and a piece of Aunt Bethany's mouthwatering corn
bread. My mouth started to salivate the more I thought about
it. I contemplated leaving her alone for only a few minutes
as she slept, to get a hot meal from the cafeteria. For the last
few days, candy bars and potato chips from the vending machine had become my only means of nutrition.

"Thanks." I looked at Aunt Bethany and even though she
was sleeping and sleeping well, I was still reluctant to leave
her alone. The nursing staff was great and they never gave
me any reason to doubt their care. I sat on the edge of my
chair before convincing myself it would be okay to leave her.
I stood up and rubbed Aunt Bethany's forehead before I left
the room. The nurse saw me walking down the hallway and
gave me directions to the cafeteria. She assured me again
Aunt Bethany would be okay until I returned. As I stepped
on the elevator, I repeated in my head the directions she gave
me.

"Elevator to the first floor, follow the hallway to the end,
left, end of the hallway, another left." When the elevator
stopped, my taste buds started to tingle as I could smell the
aroma from the hospital cafeteria. The lightly seasoned food
made my mouth water. I must have really been hungry.
When I walked through the double doors, I saw that my op-

tions were actually much better than I thought. To my right was an all-you-could-eat salad bar; to my left were choices of steaming hot meats and vegetables; and in the middle, sandwiches. I picked up a tray and made a decision to have hot vegetables instead of a salad. As I stood in the short line selecting my green beans someone tapped me on my shoulder.

"Maria, hi. How are you doing?"

"Hi." The greeting took me by surprise. "Rowan, right?"

"Yes, you remembered. I'm surprised to see you here. Are you visiting someone?"

Seeing him made me acutely aware of my scarring, but I resisted the sudden urge to hide my face.

"Actually I'm here with my aunt. She's been in the hospital almost three weeks now. I'm expecting her to be released any day."

"Is she okay?"

"Well, she was diagnosed with colon cancer." There was a few seconds of silence while he searched for the right words and moved his tray along the silver serving rail.

"Wow, Maria, I'm very sorry to hear that."

I smiled at his kindness. "Thank you very much. I'll have to say she's responding well to her treatments. She's been through a lot in the last few weeks."

"Again, I'm very sorry." He paused to receive his food from the server.

I didn't realize how tall Rowan was until he leaned across the steam table. He was at least six feet, if not taller, and very well built. I noticed the flex of his biceps through his short-sleeved uniform shirt.

"Are you going to eat in the cafeteria? You can join me if you'd like. I promise not to ask for any of your macaroni and cheese," he joked to lighten the mood.

"Well, I was going to get my food and take it back to the room. I want to be there when my aunt wakes up."

"I understand." He nodded. By this time we had made it to the end of the line. "I'll keep you and your aunt in my prayers. It was really good seeing you again."

"Likewise," I said as I paid for my lunch and thanked him for his prayers. Another prayer certainly wouldn't hurt. As I turned to walk away, I reflected on his sincerity when he visited me during my stay in the hospital. Then I thought he'd be good company for at least a few minutes. I could use someone to converse with. Deciding to accept his offer, I turned back.

"My aunt is asleep. I have at least thirty minutes to sit down and eat." He smiled, obviously pleased that I had reconsidered. After paying for his lunch I followed him to another counter for condiments, napkins, and utensils.

"Where would you like to sit?" he asked.

I wasn't familiar with the cafeteria so I wasn't particular. I shrugged. "It doesn't really matter to me."

He found a small table by a window and we both sat down.

"I still can't believe I bumped into you here today." He leaned his head to one side as he spoke.

"Why are you so shocked?" I responded jokingly. "This is a public facility. I'm sure you see familiar faces here all of the time."

"Tell you the truth, I never thought I would see you again. Especially after my second—"

I responded before he completed his thought. "Well, I'm glad to see you. I was so disoriented from the pain medication given to me in the hospital, I'm surprised I even remember."

"I know . . . you seem to have recovered very well from your injuries." Rowan looked down at his plate as though he had said something wrong or offensive.

He hadn't, but knowing the subject was awkward, I changed it. "Do you have any brothers or sisters?"

"Yes, I have three brothers."

"Wow . . . I can't imagine being the only female in the house with five other men, four boys and a husband." I assumed his parents were married and had jointly raised them.

Rowan chuckled as he placed his fork down on his plate and finished chewing his food. "My mother had no problems at all. She kept us boys in line . . . including my dad! What about yourself? Any sisters or brothers?"

"Well . . . I have a half sister. We didn't grow up together, though. Sometimes being alone bothered me, but Aunt Bethany did her best to take care of that. She kept me so busy with all kinds of activities."

"I'll be honest with you, there were a lot of times I wished I were an only child. But now that I think about it I wouldn't trade my experiences for anything in the world. Especially when one of my brothers got into trouble."

"Oh . . . so you found it entertaining?"

"Are you kidding? I remember one time, I caught my oldest brother kissing a girl on our back porch. Boy, you would have thought I was running from a vicious dog the way I sprinted into the house and reported it to my mother. The eyewitness news had nothing on me! I gave her every single detail and then some. When I finished she was on fire. She humiliated him so bad and I thought I would never stop laughing. But you know what happened, right?" He paused to laugh at his own story. "He kicked my butt later that night after my parents went to sleep! He made sure that I would think long and hard before I *ever* told anything else he did! I think I know a couple of things about him right now that I'm taking to my grave!"

I laughed so hard I spilled my tea. "Rowan, thank goodness I wasn't very thirsty." Realizing my spill embarrassed me, he passed me a napkin to place beneath my glass. I gasped slightly after looking at my watch and realizing I'd been away from the room for nearly forty minutes.

"I better get back upstairs. I need to be there when my aunt wakes up." He was understanding and said it was time for him to leave as well. Our conversation had gotten so involved he hadn't even eaten all of his lunch, while my plate was completely empty. I giggled in spite of myself.

"I haven't had a hot meal in several days," I explained as I began cleaning up the table.

"Don't worry about that, I'll get it on my way out," he offered, standing up and taking the tray from my hands.

"Oh," I said, semisurprised. Our eyes met for a few seconds, coupled with an endearing and mutual smile.

"Listen, thanks for a great lunch." He extended his hand for a friendly shake. I accepted. His grip was firm but gentle.

"No, thank you. I've enjoyed your company."

"Maybe the next time I see you, it won't have to be in the hospital."

"Maybe." I blushed, then turned quickly and made my exit, leaving him at the table. As I walked back to the elevator, I smiled at our interaction. I couldn't remember the last time I had laughed. He was great company and it did my heart good having someone to chat with. I didn't suspect that we would meet again, though I had to admit to myself, I imagined it would be nice. I quickly refocused my thinking as I rushed back to Aunt Bethany's room, dismissing the thought altogether.

MARIA

Aunt Bethany's final prognosis was good. The cancer and affected lymph nodes had been removed and tested for any other malignancies. Her initial chemotherapy and radiation treatments were done in the hospital, but ongoing treatments would be completed as outpatient procedures. Initially, hair loss was her only side affect, but eventually the treatments made her very nauseated and weak. And while she received the best care New Orleans had to offer, her soul was getting tired and I knew it. Within two months of the first diagnosis, her health took a dramatic turn for the worse. In spite of my concerns for her health she refused to see the doctor for further evaluation.

"Baby, those doctors will not touch any parts of me. I will not let them open me up again. They made me worse. I didn't get sick like this until they 'treated' me."

For the sake of her health I tried to reason with her. "Aunt Bethany, please consider continuing your treatments."

"Maria, I know you don't understand. You don't feel my pain. The final answer is no." Her will to fight was gone.

At this point I could only respect her wishes. She was satisfied with the life she'd lived and couldn't take any more pain. From that day on, she treated every day like her last.

Knowing that I wouldn't have her with me much longer, I was constantly by her side. Every morning, we made it a priority to have breakfast together in bed. Still, I wasn't ready when it happened. There were still so many things we had to talk about.

"Maria, look outside. Isn't it a beautiful day?" She talked to me as she sipped on her cup of green tea. As I looked out of the bedroom window I saw skies overcast with dull gray clouds threatening a downpour of rain any second.

"Yes, it is." When she looked out of the window she saw a beautiful day. Her illness completely opened her mind and allowed her to see each day clearly without clouds or rain. I had a newfound respect for her new outlook on life and envied her vision.

"You were very special to Uncle Brewster and me. Before he passed, he made me realize you were the child we never had. Your birth was no mistake. Your mother did have you at a very young age, but you were a gift from above to all of us. So don't let nobody make you feel like your life was a mistake." She raised her weary finger and pointed it toward me. "You listen to me now. I want you to get on living your life, you hear me?" I nodded solemnly as tears began to flow down my cheeks. "Now you haven't told me what happened to you, but this I do know, you can't let it hold you back." She gently ran her thumb across the scar left on my face. "You're still beautiful . . . you're still beautiful. Don't you let nobody strip you of who you are." I pressed her palm into my face, then kissed her hand. "Get yourself back in school. I know you needed a break, but don't let the break break you." She tapped her finger on my chest. "There's something inside you that's gonna cause you to overcome. You don't see it right now, and you might not feel it, but it's there. It's the mystery of a woman. It's gonna cause you to press forward and press on and be all that God intended for you to be." She smiled at me. "You're so precious." There was a long pause as a pained expression came across her face. "I love you but it's time for me to go to my heavenly home. Don't you worry about me none. I'm okay now. You hear me?"

"Yes, ma'am," I answered slightly above a whisper. She ended the conversation by giving me specific instructions of how to handle her passing. When she finished she pulled me toward her, gave me a kiss on the forehead, then smiled.

As if I were watching a movie in slow motion, I saw her gradually losing muscle control. Her head fell backward as her arms went limp. Tea spilled onto the bed as the cup she held shattered into small pieces on the floor. Within a matter of seconds she had taken her last breath.

Accepting that she had seen the best and last of her days, I inhaled slowly, lifted her arms, and crossed them gently on her chest. I gave her one final kiss on the forehead before rubbing my hands across her face to close her eyes. I straightened the blanket, pulled it over her body and above her head. I paused to whisper a silent prayer. First, for forgiveness, realizing my desire for her life was selfish. I had only thought about Maria. I never thought about the pain or discomfort she was feeling during her illness. Then I remembered to be thankful for her unconditional love. Aunt Bethany knew in her heart why I came back home. She saw it in my eyes. Not once did she judge me or treat me like an outcast. She mended my wounds with love.

MARIA

I called my mother and father, uncles, aunts, and cousins. They all expressed their condolences, which were appreciated, but the burden of the arrangements was on me. Aunt Bethany had shared with me her requests and I knew it was my responsibility to honor them. She wanted a homegoing celebration, nothing too long or sad. During her life she had demanded love and said tears were useless after she died.

It had been years since my family had been together. I couldn't remember the last wedding or funeral. I endured the general courtesies from the neighbors and church members. The usual fried chicken, gumbo, and pound cakes were delivered to my door constantly. Phone calls ended with "baby, if you need anything just call." I knew the comments were sincere, but I also knew that honestly, life would return to normal in a few days. We'd all cry, hug, and kiss before and after the funeral, and then I'd be left alone to deal with the onslaught of loneliness and depression.

ROWAN

It was the first Saturday off that I had had in almost three weeks. Vickie wasn't up yet. It was just me, my cup of coffee, and the morning paper. There was always an advantage to getting the paper before Vickie. The first advantage was being able to read it in its entirety before the "coupon queen" struck and left holes all over it. The second was being able to learn the news firsthand, rather than from Vickie. She had an annoying habit of rehashing each and every article like she was an anchorwoman out at the scene. Today, though, the *Daily Gazette* was mine, all mine! I propped my stockinged feet up on the coffee table and began my journey into the news.

There didn't seem to be anything new or interesting in today's articles. I had already learned all I could learn about the overseas warfare and the Michael Jackson scandal.

"They need to leave Mike alone, man," I mumbled as I set aside yet another section. Looking up, I saw Vickie entering the kitchen to pour some coffee for herself.

"Good morning."

"Good morning, Rowan," Vickie responded as she made her way to my side for a morning kiss. "I see you grabbed that paper up pretty quick."

"Yep, sure did. Sometimes it is nice to actually read it before you start making paper dolls out of it."

She gave me a playful punch on my shoulder as she picked up the sections I had already completed. "Did you read these already?"

"Yeah, baby, I'm on the Life section now."

"Why do you read that section? Nobody reads that part, there's never anything in there," she said, retrieving a small pair of scissors.

"I read the whole paper, baby. It's cover to cover or nothing at all, and besides, there are some very interesting things in this section." Today I was looking to see if there was an article detailing a fire from the morning before. I hadn't gotten all of the details before the end of my shift. I did know that a young man and a small child didn't make it out alive. Unfortunately, the neighborhood of the house that burned down was that of an old friend of mine. His name was Robert Gist, if memory served me right. I was praying to God that he wasn't the one victimized by the fire. We had known each other years ago; he was one of the guys that hung with Josh and me in college, but we had lost contact once I became a paramedic. I scanned each article, not finding anything, then quickly read over the obituary section, as morbid as it seemed. Although most names and faces I didn't recognize, one name in particular caught my immediate attention. Bethany McCory. That last name sounded so familiar. Where had I heard that before? I began to read her obituary.

She is survived by her niece Maria McCory.

My heart stopped.

MARIA

As we stood outside to enter the church our sorrow turned into appreciation. Side by side, in two lines, we entered the sanctuary. My parents stood behind me to provide their version of support. I knew after the funeral they too would leave me to grieve alone.

Aunt Bethany's facial expression could only be described as angelic. Her warm smile had been immortalized. I leaned forward and rubbed the lapel of her favorite coral linen suit. We were seated; the attendants lowered the lid of the casket, secured it, then placed the spray on top. I smiled within as her neighbors and friends spoke kind words about her. Clara's humor made us laugh.

"Giving thanks to God. To the bereaved family and friends. We're here to celebrate B's homegoing. Y'all know the life she lived. So I know she's looking down from heaven with a smile. But let me tell ya'll 'bout her and her yard. She was always in the yard! You know, she was the mold they used to make those little garden statues. My husband and I bought land across the road from the McCorys. It was wintertime when we moved, so everything was dead and nothing was growing. The large oak tree in B's backyard was the only evidence of life I could see. I knew she didn't plant it herself, so I was okay. Wasn't long before bulb-planting time came. By early spring her house came to life. I told Earl we had to get in gear. We worked days on end to catch up with her. One day she just came over to help. She was a sweetie and became the best neighbor and friend I ever had." Clara paused, blew a warm kiss toward the casket, then presented me with live roses from a bush Aunt B had given her two years ago. The moment was heartfelt, so I thanked her with a hug and kiss before she returned to her seat.

CHAPTER 6

The Mystery of a Woman ceases to amaze.
She performs little miracles every day.

I hadn't seen Maria since I bumped into her in the hospital cafeteria. When we spoke during lunch I was certain at the time she said her aunt was responding well to her chemotherapy. The funeral date and time were listed for this afternoon, which would allow me to pay my respects while Vickie hung out all day with Lisa at the malls. I empathized for Maria's situation, made a mental note, then moved on to the sports section. I didn't want Vickie to ask me what I was staring at.

Lisa was ringing the doorbell around noon. I knew they would be gone at least six hours, if not longer than that. The malls didn't close until nine. I wished them well and went into the bedroom to get dressed. I stood in the middle of the closet trying to figure out what to wear. I picked out a pair of dress slacks and a casual collared shirt, with a pair of comfortable loafers, deciding to only drop by her house, where I was certain the family would be gathered by late afternoon. I looked in the phone book to determine where she lived, and lucky for me, only a handful of McCorys were listed.

After dialing a couple of wrong numbers I found the right one. I introduced myself as a close friend to whoever answered the telephone, and was given directions.

Her house was only about twenty minutes out but seemed longer because I'd become unsure of myself. How would Maria respond when she saw me walking up to her? I didn't want her to feel uncomfortable, especially given the unfortunate occasion. She had received me well at the hospital, so what would be different now? She'd be glad to see another friendly face. Driving up and seeing the size of her house didn't make me feel any better. It was huge. It looked like something straight out of a *Better Homes and Gardens* magazine. Outside, cars were lined up bumper to bumper. Finding a place to park seemed completely impossible. I drove by the house, turned around, and found a small spot in the grass between a black Cadillac and a gray Oldsmobile.

I turned the car off, sat there for a while, then grabbed the peace lily from the passenger's seat and stepped out of the car, checking my image in my tinted windows, making sure that I was presentable. My shirt wasn't tucked in tight enough, so I smoothed it out and adjusted my belt buckle.

"Here we go," I whispered to myself as I traveled up the long stone walkway. I brushed the front of my shirt again, then rang the doorbell. Someone yelled for me to "come on in!" I pushed the door open to step into the living area, which was full of people eating and chattering away.

"Come on in. If you're here you must be family." A man leaning against the wall with a full plate of food in his hand invited me in like I was a first cousin or something. "All of the food is in the kitchen. Just follow your nose. You'll know where to go." Their conversation didn't stop.

"You know how Maria's mother was. She didn't even care enough about the poor child to raise her!" a short chunky lady whispered in a matter-of-fact tone to an older man wearing an outdated blue plaid jacket and matching pants, who nodded in agreement. "Uh-huh, where she at now? That girl needs her mama."

Judgmental people always amazed me when they spoke. It was just so funny how they could praise one person and curse another in the same breath. That had to be a gift. I tried to make my way through the crowd of people to find Maria. I didn't know a soul and felt a little out of place. I had to find her friendly face. There she was, standing in the kitchen at the island serving food to her guests. Maria was dressed in a beautiful white tank dress; her hair seemed to flow from her head to her shoulders like water. She looked like an angel.

"Maria. Hi."

"Rowan?" She looked really surprised when she turned around and saw me.

"I heard of your aunt's death and I just came to pay my respects to you and your family." I handed her the plant. "This is for you."

She wiped her hands on a dish towel and reached out to take it from me. She read the card, then put the lily on a plant stand below the kitchen window. I was very receptive as she walked over and gave me a friendly hug.

"Well, thank you for coming. That was very considerate of you. Why don't you have a little to eat? There's plenty here." She smiled and motioned toward the dining room buffet filled with everything from fresh-cooked greens to homemade rolls and ham.

"Thank you. I think I will."

Maria handed me a plate. I got a piece of fried chicken and some potato salad. I couldn't help but notice Maria as she moved from one guest to another. *She's such a gracious hostess,* I thought to myself, as I spooned a small helping of gumbo onto my plate. She was courteous and made sure that everyone was comfortable. Everyone around me was just as polite. I joined her family members in the dining room, where they laughed and took turns telling touching, yet funny stories about Bethany McCory. From what I heard she was a wonderful, religious woman who'd give her life and limb for Maria. By the end of the day I felt like I'd known her personally.

Maria sat across from me. I didn't know how she did it despite the circumstances. She laughed and exchanged stories, too. I had never met a woman like her before. Her personality was one of a kind. Who wouldn't admire her? Yes, I had met her in her lowest moment; but looking at her, she didn't even seem like she'd suffered at all. I thought I was coming to make sure that she was all right, but that was completely unnecessary. The woman sitting across from me was strong and resilient. She had to have been the most extraordinary person, male or female, I'd ever met.

I looked at my watch as a group of relatives started saying their good-byes. Man, it was already seven o'clock. The afternoon had flown by. Maria followed them to the door and said her farewells to her aunts, uncles, and friends. There were a few in the living area who were still going strong. Her uncle, the older man in blue plaid, began doing magic tricks and pulled quarters out of the kids' ears. The kids begged him to do it over and over again. Maria didn't spoil their fun and went back into the kitchen. I wanted to help out so I followed her, grabbed a stack of dirty dishes off the table, and took them to the sink. She tapped me on the shoulder to stop me when I started running water for the dishes. I ignored her and squirted dish liquid into the running water.

"Rowan, it's very kind of you to help out, but you don't have to do that." She grabbed an apron out of the closet, put her head through the top, and tied it around her waist. She looked like a petite Mrs. Butterworth. "I can handle everything."

"I want to help, Maria. It's the least I can do. The past couple of months have been hard for you and I know you're tired."

"Yes, they have been, but I've been told that whatever doesn't kill you makes you stronger." She stopped for a second, I guess to think about her comment, then scraped the uneaten food off the dirty plate and into the trash. I washed the casserole dish that had the macaroni and cheese in it as she came around me and slid plates into the hot, sudsy water.

"I really admire your outlook on life. I wish I was able to go through life's ups and downs with the same optimism that you have." I passed her a bowl. She stood with the dish towel ready to dry and put away everything I handed to her.

"Yeah, I got that from my aunt. She would say, 'Baby, life is full of twists and turns, just like one of them roller-coaster rides you kids love so much. But when the ride turns you upside down, you don't panic 'cause that lil' seat belt holds you in place. In life, baby, that seat belt is God!' I used to sit there and just shake my head at her analogies, but I guess she was right, huh?"

I didn't know what to say. I was never really into the God thing. It wasn't that I didn't believe in Him, I just wasn't one who really thought about Him too much.

"Yeah, she was." I handed her another dish to dry. I tried to muster a comforting smile and digest her aunt's wisdom at the same time.

"I must say, you are an amazing person yourself. Thank you so much for the kindness and compassion you have shown me and my family today."

"Oh, that's no problem. No problem at all." I let the dishwater out and watched it run down the drain. She handed me a towel to dry my hands, and then she finally sat down on a bar stool at the island.

"So, what have you been doing with yourself, Rowan?"

I pulled up a seat across from her. "Nothing much, other than working. On my days off I just hang out around the house."

"Hang out around the house, huh? No outside hobbies or

interests?" She leaned her head down and quickly pulled together and twisted her hair into a neat bun.

"I play a little golf . . . nothing to brag on."

"Golf? You don't look like a golf kind of guy." She giggled.

"You wouldn't believe it but, uh . . ." I dusted imaginary dust off my collar as I stood up and took a mock swing. "I'm the next Tiger Woods."

"Did you say Tiger Woods, or you like the woods? I bet that's where all your balls go!"

"Oh, you got jokes." She was even more beautiful when she laughed.

I took a quick look at my watch.

"Oh, I'm sorry, Rowan. I know you probably have to get home to your family, and here I am trying to make small talk."

If she only knew, I wasn't trying to give any clues that I was ready to leave. I only looked at my watch to keep myself from staring at her beautiful face.

"Yeah, I do have to get home soon, but my girlfriend went to the mall with one of her friends, so I have a few more minutes to spare." I wasn't in a rush to get home at all. Maria was a lot of fun and I was really enjoying myself. It felt good just to sit and talk with someone without feeling obligated to do much else. We weren't trying to impress each other with the latest news or career advancements. Just regular conversation and laughs.

"Oh, I was under the impression that you were married with children. You just seem to be the family type."

"I guess you got me all figured out, huh? A nongolfing family man. I don't look like a single, childless Tiger Woods to you?"

She rolled her eyes, then went to the refrigerator and took out a bottle of water.

"Umm . . . would you like one?" She motioned toward

the fridge that was packed with water, sodas, and all sorts of refreshing drinks.

"Yeah, sure," I said.

"Here you go." She pulled out another bottle and handed it to me.

"No, I'm not married and I don't have any children. I would like to have children one day." I opened my water, took a few sips, then placed it on the table. "I just don't think that Vickie and I are ready for that type of responsibility." *Hell, we aren't ready for marriage either*, I thought to myself. It had never come up, even after two years, but I prayed that she would never get the idea of marriage stuck in her head. It wasn't that I never wanted to be married, I just knew that she wasn't the one I was meant to be with. Marriage was just too permanent to choose someone whom you knew in your heart you didn't truly love. I took another drink of water, then looked at Maria. She gave me an odd look, like she was reading my thoughts or something.

"How long have you and . . ."

"Vickie," I offered.

"How long have you and Vickie been together?"

"Almost three years."

"Well, what's holding you back from proposing?"

The question completely caught me off guard. Why all of a sudden was she getting so personal? Maria stared at me with a smile, waiting for my response. Was she quizzing me just to see if I was available? I wanted to tell her the real reason why I hadn't proposed. Yeah, I might be in a relationship, but I was far from being happy . . . just in case she might have been interested.

"We aren't financially stable enough yet." Hmm . . . sounded good to me, so that was the reason I gave instead. Whether it was good or bad I guessed it wouldn't be fair to Vickie to discuss our relationship with another woman. That seemed to be a good enough reason for Maria, because she nodded her head like she agreed with me.

"Yeah, that makes sense. If you aren't where you need to be with your finances, there's no need to commit to taking care of another person. Especially when you are having a difficult time taking care of yourself." Her question suddenly seemed to be genuine. She wasn't interested in me; she was just making small talk.

We talked for another hour before I left to go home. Driving back home, I began thinking of the conversation that we'd had. Marriage is a really big step. I was comfortable with the arrangement that Vickie and I had. *Yes, everything is just fine the way we have it. If it ain't broke—don't fix it*, I thought to myself. There was no need to bring it up or even think about getting married.

CHAPTER 7

People can easily say what they would or would not do.
Have they walked one mile in either of your shoes?

I really liked their nerves; the girls had started the party without me, already lounging around Lisa's pool. All girls needed a night out, you know. Mine was casually referred to as a "monthly candle party." We used this time to male-bash and talk about sex. It was our version of the guys watching Monday night football with lies, beer, and swearing. Lisa's thirty-five-hundred-square-foot lakefront condominium was awesome and directly reflected her substantial tax attorney income. She was my best friend but I hated her. She looked like a runway model: five feet ten inches, 135 pounds, lean long legs with shoulder-length brunette hair she usually kept pulled back. She never went to the gym and could eat whatever she wanted. I couldn't look at a chocolate donut without bloating.

Now Andrea was totally opposite. She had beautiful light brown skin and big brown eyes. Her sandy brown hair was naturally curly and hung loosely around her face. She proudly flaunted her size 12 hips and thought I was nuts for wanting to be so skinny. If she wanted dessert, damn it, she had dessert. Denying herself the simple pleasures of life was a definite no-no. She had a momentum in her stride that simply drove men crazy. Boy, I wished I could walk like that chick. One night when Rowan was gone I put on a pair of high heels and tried to walk like her and damn near broke my neck. She was a married third grade teacher with a four-year-old and a six-year-old. Her husband, Rick, was a gourmet chef for a five-star hotel. She was the Drama Queen and most vocal of our sister circle.

As I walked up, I could tell they were talking about somebody; instead of anyone acknowledging my presence with a simple hello, their conversation continued. My neck snapped because I couldn't believe my ears. They were talking about me.

"Girl, I think it's time for an ultimatum! How long has he been in her apartment?" Lisa questioned Andrea with an attitude. The question was rhetorical in nature and she knew it. She remembered the exact date Rowan moved in. "I think he has a hidden agenda. Why hasn't he discussed marriage?"

"Girlfriend, do you think there's another woman?" I could see Andrea's neck roll from behind as she made the assumption. The thought of her divine revelation and insight made her feel good. She crossed her legs, leaned back on the lawn chair, and waited for Lisa's agreement or rebuttal. Lisa's response to Andrea's statement would determine Andrea's next approach.

"I hope he isn't that bold."

I couldn't believe those two hashing out the details of my personal life behind my back. What else did they say when I wasn't around?

"I wouldn't put it past him. Modern-day men in relationships are scandalous. Girl, do you watch *Lifetime* at all? You know . . . real stories about real women. Lisa, are you listening to me? Just the other day I saw a movie about a man with three or four wives. He was married to them all at the same time and with families. What a greedy bastard. Girl, if my husband did me like that I would cut his—"

"Andrea, you're crazy, girl." Lisa laughed before she took another sip of wine. I couldn't take it anymore, so I cleared my throat and walked up beside them. Andrea turned to give me a quick "hey, girlfriend" and continued to talk.

"Huh! I don't play! If I was ever in a situation like that, it wouldn't be pretty. I'd bronze those bastards myself. Do you hear me?" She snapped the air with her fingers.

"Hell, I know that's right. This is the longest relationship I've ever seen this chick in," Lisa stated, directing her comments toward me. "He's managing to accrue interest before making the investment. I think he's keeping something from her. Maybe his ass really is married." They were being facetious and continued to carry on as if I weren't even there.

"It's got to be something! Why is she holding on to him like that? She's young and can still wear a tank top without a bra. Maybe he's got some serious whip appeal!" Andrea's lips were really loose. She was on her third glass of wine. "Umm, he must work it like a porn star or something. Girl, why didn't you tell us you had it like that? You been holding back."

"Why don't both of you shut the hell up?" I finally said in my own defense.

"Has he asked you to marry him yet?" Their facial expressions were devious as they turned around and waited for my response.

Personally, I didn't appreciate their sarcasm.

"So is tonight let's pick on Vickie night?" I questioned, picking up a glass.

"When is he going to put a ring on your finger? It's going on three years, right?" Lisa said as she rolled her eyes to the top of her head. It wasn't normal for Lisa to instigate, but tonight they both went for my blood.

"Look, I think that's my business. Lisa, who are you to

talk? Your last date was with . . . ? That's what I thought. When you get a ring, then maybe I'll listen to your comments." I tried to be nonchalant with my responses, but already they'd gotten on my damned nerves. I didn't appreciate their attack at all. I poured my wine and took a seat. "I'm sure when he gets ready he'll ask me. He wants to make sure we're financially prepared." I took a sip of wine, hoping they'd find something else to talk about. They didn't.

"Girl, sounds like an excuse to me. You'll never be 'financially ready' for anything. I'm still waiting for Ed McMahon to bring my check to the front door. The envelope did say I was a winner." Lisa slowly rolled her eyes from me to a spot in the middle of nowhere, as if to say "whatever."

"I didn't come here to get harassed by you two 'I want to be a talk show host' impersonators. Maybe I'm not ready to get married. What makes the two of you think it's him? It really could be me. Did either of you think about that?" I cut my eyes at Andrea. "Of course not." Her eyes indicated she was looking for another opportunity to put her two cents' worth in. "You automatically assume it's him. I have my reservations about marriage and children. Andrea, look at how hard you have it sometimes. My life is good. I can do what I want, when I want. I'm not ready to give that up, thank you!" I crossed my legs and nodded my head at both of them.

"Yeah, it's hard sometimes, I'm woman enough to tell you that. But my man is at home waiting on me. Your man is disposable. I mean Schick razor disposable. You use it, then throw it away." She flicked her fingers to demonstrate her point. "He can leave your ass tonight, and there ain't nothing you can do to stop him." Andrea laughed so hard she almost choked. Lisa leaned over and patted her on the back. I wanted her ass to suffocate.

"Why don't you just forget about Rowan?" Lisa broke in. "The new lawyer at the firm is dying to meet you. He's financially prepared and then some, if you know what I mean!" She winked and slapped Andrea a high five.

"How would you know, Lisa, unless you did him yourself?" she cut me off.

"He asks about you at least once a week if not more. He gave me his number to give to you. You should take it . . . you know, just in case you decide to get out of that dead-end situation you refer to as a relationship."

"Both of you know I love Rowan, and being married doesn't prove a damn thing." I was trying to keep my cool, but they'd pissed me off a long time ago.

"Girl, that's the problem. You're being naïve as hell. You're in love with him, right? Well, tell me this. Is he in love with you or is he waiting for something better to come along?"

Lisa was my friend but I wanted to jump up and knock her skinny ass in the pool.

"Vickie, you need to open those pretty little hazel eyes and look around you. You're being used. I guarantee it."

"That's your damn opinion. Our relationship is great. I'm happy and my friends should be too."

"Ohh, we're happy but we'll be elated when he proposes." Obviously waiting on another response they stared at me.

"It's late and I need to leave. I hope I don't get pulled over by the cops like this. They would definitely take my ass to jail." Even with the wine, two hours of roasting and gossip was all I could handle. Because of their cutthroat comments, I'd developed an excruciating headache, which cheated me out of a good time. I got my purse, tucked it under my arm, and headed toward the patio gate with my feelings on my sleeve.

"All right, girl, be careful. Maybe next month you'll have a ring to show us," Andrea blurted out. Lisa burst into laughter. I turned around and gave them both the finger. I knew the details of my love life would be the hot topic long after I was gone.

I was a little intoxicated but not to the point that I couldn't think about what they'd said. Maybe they were right. Why hadn't he asked me to marry him? If he didn't want me it would be nice of him to let me know instead of wasting my time. Andrea made a good point; he wasn't obligated to our relationship and could leave me at the drop of a dime. She had been stern and convincing. Never in a million years would I confess it but both their observations seemed valid. I was in love with him, and I told him nearly every day. He always responded by saying, "Yeah, me too." I'd never heard him say the words "Vickie, I love you." If he couldn't form his lips to say those three words, how would he ever ask me to marry him? Hell, maybe I was being stupid.

When I got home I decided not to go in right away. I had a lot on my mind so I took a walk around the block. As I walked, I thought about Lisa, who was single and had it all. The perfect career. A beautiful home. Andrea had the husband and children . . . security. She seemed happy too. What did I have other than a crusty-ass man lying up in my bed! If he loved me we should be married. I wasn't getting any younger.

I was tired of walking and stumbled over my own damn feet a couple of times. As I walked up the steps I could still hear Lisa's and Andrea's taunting in my head. Why hadn't he asked me to marry him? If they were right how could I ever confess it? Did he really love me? Why couldn't he say it? Was he seeing someone else? Wait a damn minute! Andrea didn't live with my man and Lisa didn't have a man. Entertaining their opinions was silly of me. I tried to let it go.

I took my shoes off and quietly opened the bedroom door. Rowan was sound asleep. The contrast of his dark skin against the pastel sheets sent a warm sensation up my thighs.

Damn, he was so fine. Dismissing my thoughts, I decided not to bother him; I went into the bathroom, unzipped my jeans, slid them down around my ankles along with my panties, and stepped out of them. I unbuttoned my shirt, unfastened my bra, and slid them off together. I turned on the water for a shower, but before I could step in, my mind was again bombarded by all that Lisa and Andrea had said. I took a step back and questioned myself in the mirror. Why couldn't I just simply ignore it? Would real friends provoke me to anger? They'd never been so negative about my relationship with him before. Could there really be someone else? Frustrated and confused, I shut the water off; my unanswered question had to be dealt with. I needed to know the truth.

I stormed across the room butt naked to the bed and poked Rowan hard in his shoulder until he woke up and gave me the attention I wanted.

"Rowan, wake the hell up!" The paramedic response in him caused him to immediately sit straight up in bed like a damned jack-in-the-box.

"What? What's wrong, babe?" he said, slightly dazed.

"I need some answers right now!" I defiantly folded my arms across my chest.

"What are you talking about?" He squinted and rubbed his eyes in an attempt to focus his vision.

"Rowan, we have been living together for ten months now. You dated me a year and a half before you moved in. What's going on? Why aren't we married?"

"What? What the hell is wrong with you? What time is it anyway? You know I have to go to work in the morning." He sat up in bed and ran both hands over his head.

"I don't give a damn about you going to work."

"Vickie, are you drunk? Why don't you take a shower and go to bed?"

"Damn you, Rowan, it's not the wine. I need answers. You lie with me every night. We function like husband and wife but without the full commitment. I refuse to waste any more time. You can't continue to live here like this, so I suggest you make a decision now. I've had enough."

"Vickie, what has gotten into you? Is this going to happen every time you spend an evening with your girlfriends? This fiasco couldn't wait until tomorrow?" He looked utterly confused and irritated. "Our living arrangement never bothered you before."

"Living arrangement? Is that all this is to you? So, is that what I am to you, an arrangement?" I wanted to slap the hell out of him, but I took a deep breath and lowered my tone instead. "All I want to know at this point, Rowan, is do you love me? Right now that is the most important thing you can tell me. If you don't, I'm not going to spend another day waiting on you."

He looked toward the window. The time he took to respond bothered me. I walked over to him, stood in his face, and asked him the same question again.

"Rowan, do . . . you . . . love . . . me?" By this time, I didn't need to hear his answer. His lack of response spoke loud and clear.

"Look, Vickie, when we met I was alone. You never gave me the indication you wanted a husband. So there was no harm in dating you. I've been attracted to you since the first time I saw you. We had chemistry."

"Chemistry . . . and . . . ?" He'd already broken my heart. I moved my hands through the air, signaling for more.

"I love you . . . but not enough to give you my last name." I could feel my lips quiver as his comment echoed in my ear. Oh, hell no! I was infuriated.

"You low-down bastard! You mean to tell me you moved in with me knowing you had no intentions of marrying me?"

"Moving in here wasn't my damn idea. You worried me for months to move in with you. Hell, I never told you I was looking for a wife!"

"If that's how you feel, then it's over! I want you to get your shit and get the hell out of my apartment right now!" I stormed to the closet, picked up one of his shoes, and hurled it across the room. He ducked just in time; it barely missed his head.

"Right now?"

"You heard me, Rowan Miller. Right now!"

"I need a couple of days to find a place to stay. It is one o'clock in the morning."

"A couple of days? You don't even have a couple of minutes!" I spoke sternly, then planted my hands firmly on my hips. "I want you and all of your things out, now!" I stomped back to the closet and started ripping his things off the hangers. My body quivered as hot tears rolled down my face. I was hurt more than anything else.

"So you mean to tell me after all I've done for you I'm out like that?" He threw the covers back, leaped from the bed, and stood naked in the middle of the floor. I could see that his blood had started to boil. In disbelief Rowan stumbled around the bed to the nightstand and picked up the alarm clock. He slammed it back down and turned to look at me. His eyes were bright red.

"And just what the hell is it that you do for me? Huh? I can pay my own damn bills, Rowan! And I sure as hell can find somebody else to screw! You aren't that damn indispensable! Two double-D batteries is all I need." That one cut deep; I saw the shock on his face.

"So *this* is the true you, huh?" He spoke snidely. He stood directly in my face and pointed his finger so close I could have bitten it off with a quick snatch. "I'm glad I haven't married you. What man wants to be married to a woman who'll let her so-called girlfriends dictate her choices?" He threw up both hands, grabbed his blue jeans and T-shirt off the back of the chair, then turned around sharply. "Let's see who caters to you when I leave. Is Lisa going to do it? Is

Andrea going to leave her husband and children at home in the middle of the night to come wipe your tears? I'll bet you money you'll get to know them for who they really are."

"Rowan, I suggest you get the hell out of my house before I make it over there to that phone to call your police friends to help your ass pack." Struggling to put on his jeans, he hopped from one leg to another, tossed his T-shirt over his shoulder, then turned to leave the bedroom. Still shouting at him, I walked up behind him and dared him to walk away while I was still talking. He bit his bottom lip, made a tight fist, and hit the side of the door.

ROWAN

What in the hell just happened? Vickie threw my shit right out the front door and into the grass. For the most part, our neighbors were conservative and kept to themselves, but tonight I saw so many slits in the miniblinds it wasn't funny. I was embarrassed as hell. After one o'clock in the morning I was out roaming the damn streets wondering where I was going with all my belongings stuffed into a few large, black trash bags. I drove around for thirty minutes trying to figure it all out. She went to her girlfriend's house, then came back mad as hell. What did she mean *did I love her*? It was never about love. Moving in was her bright-ass idea. But I guess the "Ya-Ya" sisterhood club brought it to her attention. She asked, so I told her the truth.

When I moved in with Vickie I let her talk me out of keeping my furniture in storage, and had sold or given away everything except my TVs and stereo equipment. Since then we'd made several purchases together that I would rightfully consider mine, but I was so upset it didn't matter. If I bought it once I could buy it again. I had no doubt she and her girl-friends would either sell it or use it for firewood.

I needed a few minutes to clear my head and gather my thoughts, so I pulled into a gas station parking lot. Josh was really my only friend in town. I stared at my cell phone, then dialed Josh's number. I could tell by the raspy way he answered the phone, I'd probably interrupted him making love to his wife. Being startled by the telephone doesn't make you breathe that hard.

"Josh, hey, man. I know it's late, but I really need your help."

"What's up?" He knew something was wrong. I would never call him so late.

"Vickie and I had a big fight and she kicked me out. I need somewhere to stay for at least a couple of days."

"What! She did what? It's almost two o'clock in the morning. Hold on a sec, man." Josh placed his hand over the telephone to mute a few words he mumbled to Jana. Assuming they would say yes I pulled out of the parking lot and started to drive in the direction of his house.

"Yeah, man, it's okay. *Mi casa es su casa!*" Josh said to ease my tension.

"Man, I swear I owe you for this one."

I shook my head when I pulled up to Josh's house. This was humiliating, but other than a hotel I couldn't think of any alternatives at the moment. He opened the front door and walked toward the car with his hands tucked underneath his pajama shirt. He must have seen my headlights when I turned into his driveway. All he said was "damn" when I opened the door. Each of us grabbed a garbage bag. I appreciated his candidness as we walked across the yard and into the house. It was late so he quickly pointed me toward the room I would stay in.

"This is the computer room. You can sleep in here on the daybed. I know it's small. You can use the guest bathroom in the hall and help yourself to anything in the kitchen."

"Thanks, man." We went into the kitchen for a few minutes to talk.

"Rowan, I know you said ya'll might not make it but . . . what happened?"

I felt obligated to let him know why I was standing in his house in the middle of the night. He propped one foot against the kitchen counter and leaned back with his arms folded to hear my response.

"Man, I don't even know. She had 'girls' night out' with those two cackling hens that she calls friends. They sit around drinking wine and gossiping all night. I guess our relationship was the hot topic of the evening. She came into the house, woke me up all pissed off, and asked me why we weren't married. In so many words she gave me an ultimatum."

"What the hell did you say to her for her to kick you out on your ass at one o'clock in the morning?"

"I told her the truth."

"Not what I think." He unfolded his arms, leaned forward, and placed his elbows on the countertop so our voices weren't above a whisper.

"Yeah, man. I told her I didn't love her enough to give her my last name. That's when the shit all hit the fan and here I am." Not believing my own self, I pressed both palms into the countertop and shook my head.

"Damn." He stood up and placed his right hand over his mouth before repeating his comment in disbelief. "Damn."

"Yeah, man, I know. I couldn't lie to her face, though."

"Josh," Jana called like a purring kitten from the bedroom. He looked toward his bedroom door, then let out a slightly embarrassed chuckle.

"All right, man. Well, if you need me you know where to find me." He rubbed his head and moved toward his bedroom.

I went to the computer room and looked around the small

cluttered space. I knew I wouldn't get much more sleep. I had to be to work in less than three hours. With my arms folded beneath my head, I lay on the too-small bed, stretched out as best I could, and stared up at the ceiling. In a matter of minutes, I had been reduced from snoring in a king-sized bed to trying to squeeze myself onto a daybed in my best friend's computer room. Damn.

CHAPTER 8

I can see the sunshine through the rain.
I can feel the warmth of its glow in spite of all the pain.

I could feel a tear forming in the corner of my eye. I reached over and tucked a pillow beneath my head. It sure was quiet now that Aunt Bethany was gone. I had not yet gotten used to her absence and hadn't noticed before how large the house was. Now before I went to bed I'd walk throughout the entire house, look out each window before giving it a slight tug, making sure it was secure. It had become my routine. I knew the neighborhood wasn't dangerous, but being alone in this huge house took some getting used to.

I lay there a few more moments before accepting the fact that sleep wasn't on my agenda. For the past month I'd been taking Tylenol P.M. and leaving the television on in the bedroom to help me fall asleep, but I decided that I was just being silly. Now I wished I'd taken that medicine. I sat on the edge of the bed, wiped my face, and looked around the room. I closed my eyes, then smiled as I absorbed the calming affect Aunt Bethany's room still had on me. This room used to be filled with so much life, and it seemed that when

Aunt Bethany left, she took the lively spirit of the house with her.

Startled by a heavy thumping sound, I tiptoed to the window and peeped out the curtain. I took a quick glance at the grandfather clock. It was a little after ten o'clock and I wasn't expecting company at this late hour. I peeped out the curtain again but still didn't see anything. *Maybe I'm just hearing things.* Satisfied, I turned to go into the kitchen to fix a warm cup of chamomile tea to help me relax.

It was so dark in the kitchen that I reached around the corner and flipped the light switch on before walking in, just like I did as a child. If someone was in there I wanted at least to see them, and get a running start. I laughed at myself as I realized no one was there but me, then walked to the pantry to get the box of tea bags.

Just as I reached into the cabinet to get a mug, I heard the noise again. *Now I know I heard something!* Gripping the mug in my hand, I made my way back to the window, opened the curtain, and looked out again. Still nothing . . . I strained my neck to peek onto the porch to see if I could see someone. Nothing. *What in the world is going on!* I closed the curtain and walked to the front door to look through the peephole. No one was there. I know I heard something bumping around outside. Starting to panic, I backed away from the door, watching, listening, and waiting for any movements.

In my peripheral vision, I saw a shadow dart past the window. The mug I had fell to the floor and shattered as I ran into the hallway. My heartbeat tripled as I leaned against the wall gasping for air and paralyzed by fear. Who could I call to help me? I remembered Rowan writing his cell phone number down and leaving it with me, when he visited after the funeral. I ran into my bedroom, grabbed my purse, and dumped everything in it on the bed. I scrambled through the contents until I saw the small piece of paper he wrote it on. I picked it up, then ran to the telephone. *If he thinks I'm crazy I'll worry about that later.*

"Hello."

"Rowan . . . Rowan . . . this is Maria." My voice quivered though I tried to speak evenly.

"Maria, what's wrong, is everything okay?"

"I . . . um . . . I saw something moving in my backyard," I blurted frantically. "Can you come over and take a look around the house?" A sudden crash caused me to scream out loud.

"Maria . . . Maria . . . I'm on my way over right now! Where are you?"

"I'm in my room." While holding my chest I looked around fearfully.

"Stay there and shut the door until I get there. I'll stay on the phone with you."

"Okay . . ." My voice trailed as I held the telephone receiver tightly and closed the bedroom door, not wanting to make any more noise than what was necessary.

"Try to stay calm," he instructed.

"I'm calm," I lied. I went to the adjoining bathroom and hid in the tub, silently pulling the curtain closed. If anyone was in the house or trying to get in, I didn't want to be standing out in the open.

Rowan maintained a conversation with me until he arrived approximately ten minutes later. I ran to the front door and confirmed it was indeed him by looking through the peephole before letting him in. He closed his flip phone only when he saw me. Boldly but calmly with crowbar in hand he walked in, looked around, then asked for a better description of what I thought I heard or saw. I stood aside and pointed toward the window while he walked into the kitchen. Of course it was dark and I knew he couldn't see a thing if there was anything in the back of the house. He stood silently, watching for any movement.

"Do you have a flashlight?" he asked just above a whisper.

I covered my mouth and pointed to the drawer on the opposite side of the sink. He opened the drawer, found the flashlight, checked it, then moved toward the back door. I was too afraid to say anything as he opened the door and stepped outside. He assured me everything would be okay.

I was moved by his brave efforts, but I held the cordless telephone to my chest just in case. The few minutes that he was gone seemed like an eternity. Finally, he reappeared holding a ripped trash bag and the crowbar.

"What was it?" I asked, holding my breath.

"You might want to secure your trash a little tighter before you set it outside." A warm smile spread across his face. "Looks like a family of raccoons got a little hungry. They knocked the trash can over and had a party."

I let out a huge sigh of relief, throwing my head back. "Rowan, I'm so embarrassed. I'm sorry I called you all the way out here for nothing."

"It's no problem. Your yard is a mess, though. Where are your trash bags? I'll clean it up for you."

"No, I can't let you do that. It's bad enough that I have you out here in the middle of the night chasing raccoons. I'll take care of it in the morning."

He pointed to the broken mug on the floor, then glanced around for the broom. "You were pretty scared, huh?"

I giggled at the outcome, grateful that it was nothing more than what it was. I pulled the broom and dustpan from a small closet and handed them to Rowan.

"Let me fix you a cup of coffee, that's the least I can do." I moved toward the cabinet while he simultaneously moved to sweep the fragments of the mug. His body brushed against me as we crossed each other, and while it sent a tingle up my spine, he didn't acknowledge the contact, above mumbling, "Excuse me." While I rinsed out coffee cups, I watched him clean up the mess I'd made earlier. He looked up at me with a smile.

"Do you feel safe now, Miss McCory?"

I didn't mean to stare but I really couldn't help it. He was wearing a pair of jeans and a wife beater. It was apparent that I had called him while he was relaxing at home. His dark brown skin was so smooth and his wonderful smile accented his big brown eyes. I did feel safe, but part of me wasn't ready for him to leave.

I let my smile suffice as an answer and sat down at the table with our steaming cups. His presence wasn't in the least bit invasive and I was enjoying his company. After emptying his cup, he stood to leave, stretching his muscular arms to the ceiling.

"Guess I better get going."

"No! Please stay." I surprised myself in saying so and immediately wished I could take it back. I suddenly remembered he had a job, not to mention a woman who was probably waiting for him. "I mean . . . umm . . . well, I know you have to go home . . . I would just feel better if . . ." I didn't finish the sentence, embarrassed by my actions. He didn't respond right away, and the silence was uncomfortable.

"You would feel better if I stayed," he stated for me.

I nodded. Again, he tortured me with several seconds of silence. I could feel him studying my face.

"I'll stay."

"But what about—"

"Don't worry about that," he responded before I could finish.

I was relieved. "Thank you, Rowan," I whispered, dropping my head and wrapping my arms around myself. "Let me show you to the guest room."

He followed me down the hall to a bedroom across from my own. Upon entering, I switched on the TV in the corner and flipped to a movie on HBO.

"Oh! I've been meaning to catch the end of this!" he exclaimed. Coincidentally, I'd been meaning to do the same.

We decided to watch the ending together. With no inhibitions, Rowan took off his shoes and sat on the bed. He was so down-to-earth; he stretched out until his toes began to pop. I could only laugh at his frankness and plopped down comfortably beside him.

"You sound like an old man."

"What did you say?"

"I said, you sound like an old man." I laughed while pointing at his feet.

"Oh . . . I dare you to say that again."

"Old Man River!" I chanted while pretending to play a violin on my left arm. He playfully grabbed me and we laughed until our eyes met. Our laughter slowly turned into a capturing stare.

I wanted to kiss him so badly. Hoping he didn't sense the desire in my eyes, I turned my head. With his index finger he turned my head back toward him and looked at me. Ever so gently, he pulled my face closer to his and kissed me tenderly on the lips. My eyes remained closed as he moved his face away from mine.

"You're beautiful, Maria," he said softly. I turned my head and sat up slowly, confused by a battery of emotions. Our budding friendship had become very valuable to me and I didn't want to do anything to jeopardize it. He looked at the expression on my face, then got up from the bed and excused himself to the bathroom. When he left the room, I quickly exited to my own room and closed the door. I held my face in my hands and thought about what happened. A part of me wanted to return and rest in the safety and security of his arms, but the other part of me wouldn't allow it.

I woke up the next morning with a start, leaped out of bed, and tiptoed to the guest room. It was empty. Peeking out the window confirmed that Rowan was gone. He had cleaned the yard and left without saying good-bye. I closed my eyes and traced an outline of my lips with my finger, which intensified the memory of our kiss. I had, obviously, developed feelings for him. When his lips touched mine I wanted to let go emotionally and tell him . . . everything. The truth about my feelings . . . our friendship. How I enjoyed our conversations. How he invaded my thoughts sometimes. Was it more than just a kiss to him? I wanted to call him, but couldn't when I reminded myself that he was involved. What if his girlfriend answered the telephone? I tried to create and justify a reason that would allow me to feel less guilty and more permissive about calling. He left unannounced before I could thank him for his rash act of bravery, which I reasoned I could use as an excuse. Semiconvinced by my own facade, I found his number and stared at it again, contemplating whether or not to dial. One call wouldn't hurt. If he answered, great, if not, I'd be okay. Before pressing the last number I hung up. It wasn't a good idea and I knew it. I threw my hands up at the idea and walked away.

Rather than focusing on Rowan, I showered, dressed, applied my makeup, then sat down at the table to eat a bowl of oatmeal and think through my day. There were a couple of job leads that I wanted to follow up on, and I needed to seriously work out my plans of going back to school. One thought led to another and before I knew it, my mind was on the crisis counseling pamphlet the nurse had given me at the hospital. I hadn't even taken the time to read over it yet, but just the fact I had not thrown it away after four months subconsciously stated that it was something I needed to do. I needed to heal. I got up from the table and walked to a mirror.

The scar was carefully concealed but I knew it existed.

My feelings were also hidden beneath a mask, covered and ignored. Undoubtedly, the commotion my family members brought due to Aunt Bethany's passing allowed me to be pre-occupied and distracted from dealing with what had happened. But now there was no one but me and my reflection.

I got the pamphlet and hurriedly dialed the number before I could talk myself out of it. As the phone rang, I held my breath. Maybe I wasn't ready to make a public confession. I heard the prerecorded message on the other end and I exhaled in relief. A brief introduction was followed by an invitation to attend a session the following Wednesday evening. I hung up the phone, jotted the information down, and felt a sense of both intimidation and accomplishment. At least I'd taken a step, no matter how small it was.

I returned to the kitchen table, and thoughts of Rowan consumed me again. I put my spoon down and decided to call him. *Live a little, Maria. Take a chance*, I thought. *What's the worst that could happen?* After two rings, his voice mail picked up. Disappointed, I hung up the telephone. I couldn't justify leaving a message; not only did I not know what to say, but who would hear it? Maybe he would see my number on the caller ID and call me back. I criticized myself, knowing I shouldn't have called in the first place.

CHAPTER 9

The lies and deception were fun, I heard you laugh.
Just around the corner is a dreadful payback . . .
you'd better recognize and ask.

I was half asleep but overheard a telephone conversation Josh had in the kitchen. Obviously, the company he worked for experienced a major computer meltdown requiring them to call in management and all of their technical support staff. By the time Josh left I was fully awake and heard him give Jana a good-bye kiss. There was no way in hell I wanted to be in the house alone with her, so I threw my uniform, a pair of socks, and underwear into my duffel bag. I could take a shower and get dressed at work, I thought to myself before walking out of the room and into the hallway. Jana's lack of discretion with her appearance in front of me made me highly uncomfortable.

"Good morning, Rowan."

With a devilish undertone I heard my name roll off Jana's tongue. Damn, Jana was doing something in the kitchen. Only the top of her head was visible above the opened refrigerator door. She closed it, turned toward me, and opened her robe. To be sure I saw her red bra and bikini panties she eased her hand inside her robe and placed it on her hip. "I thought you might want to have some coffee with me this morning before you left for work. I made it just the way *I* like it—black." Her eyes fell below my belt, emphasizing that black didn't only describe how she liked her coffee.

"No, thanks. I'm running late. I'll get some at work." Her intentions were obviously clear; I immediately looked away. I knew right then, with or without my paper and morning coffee I needed to get the hell outta there.

"But I have some already made right here, just for you." She spoke slowly and seductively as she rubbed her fingertips along the edge of the counter.

I didn't like where this little charade was headed. If it looked like shit and smelled like shit, it was shit.

"You didn't have to put yourself through any trouble for me." I did everything in my power to avoid eye contact with her. I had the finesse of Iverson when I spun around to pick up my car keys.

She rushed around in front of me, let her robe fall to the floor, and pushed her chest upward toward my face. "Come on, Rowan."

I turned my head and smacked her hand away when she attempted to rub the side of my face. "We can take this opportunity to get to know each other better. Josh never has to know. He could never please me the way I know you can." She turned my face toward her and tried to read the expression on it. "Just touch me, feel it before you say no."

I snatched away and jumped back ten feet when she reached out to grab my hand. She placed her left leg on the bar stool and licked her lips with her tongue as she displayed all she had. "The thought of making love to you is making me wet. Rowan, please. It's just the two of us." I couldn't believe what I was hearing and seeing. She moved her hand along her inner thigh, then kissed her fingertips.

"No! What the hell has gotten into you? Josh is my best friend and he's your husband."

"So, what's your point, Rowan Miller? Don't you think I'm sexy? I see the way you stare at me."

"Hell naw, I don't think you're sexy. Does Josh know who he's really married to? You're a two-faced freak." My steps were quick as I headed toward the door. Awestruck and afraid to look back, I opened the door and slammed it shut.

She opened the front door and yelled, "I don't accept no for an answer." Her next-door neighbor was outside doing yard work. Unless he was deaf, I know he heard everything. "Rowan, if you don't give me what I want, you'll regret it."

I jumped in my truck and drove away like a bat out of hell.

Traffic on Interstate 10 was heavy, which wasn't favorable for the frame of mind I was in. I damn near lost my cool when someone in a red Monte Carlo pulled out in front of me. Moved by anger to give the finger, I pulled into the passing lane but couldn't do it when I looked over and saw four grandmothers in the car. They were probably on their way to a pottery class or something. Out of guilt, I waved, pretending to be friendly. When I got to the station, more drama awaited me. Parker met me at the door.

"Rowan, Vickie has called you every hour on the hour. We told her you worked the B-shift this week, but she kept calling. She sounded pretty upset."

"Thanks, man." I held my composure; I didn't want my personal business discussed around the fire station. Everyone knew Vickie and I were a couple, but they didn't know we had broken up or I had moved in with Josh. I hadn't been there fifteen minutes before the next episode started.

"Rowan Miller, you have a guest at the front. Rowan, you have a guest at the front," the voice repeated overhead. *This better not be Vickie*, I thought to myself as I went to the front door. It was.

Firmly, I took her by the arm to lead her outside before anyone else could see her. Her eyes were red and swollen from crying and her hair was all over her head. She had on an oversized sweatshirt and worn blue jeans. I couldn't believe she left her house and came to my job looking that way.

"Vickie, why are you bringing this nonsense to my job?"

"I just had a box of your things that I . . ." She paused, then burst into a new fit of tears. "Rowan, please forgive me," she sobbed and gasped. "I'm sorry I listened to the girls. I was really stupid and overreacted. What I did was silly and immature. I should never have listened to Lisa or Andrea. Without you I don't have anything. We've been together for the past three years. It took me a while to realize it, but I love you and I'm lost without you." She continued to cry. "Rowan, I want a family and I want it with you. Please, give me another chance. After three years it's the least you could do for me. You owe me at least that!"

"Vickie, I don't owe you anything." I turned my back to the door before I responded to her comments. Last thing I needed was Reverend Fakes reading my lips. "Do you remember how you humiliated me the night I moved out? You didn't love me enough to end the relationship with respect. I apologize but I don't love you that way, Vickie. How could I trust you now that I know how much you depend on your friends' advice? Did you confide in them before you came to see me? Did you ask them if I could move back in or if you should give the relationship another chance? You made the decision, now live with it. And stop making yourself look so desperate. It's not attractive." Not having anything else to say, I turned and walked away.

"Rowan, I refuse to leave. Is there someone else?"

I tried to ignore her comment and didn't turn around to acknowledge it.

"I'm not leaving until you give me one damn good reason you don't want me anymore!" She jumped on me, pounding her fists on my back. I spun around and grabbed her arms to detain her.

"Calm down and get yourself together," I said through clenched teeth. Her hysterical rage embarrassed the hell out of me.

"Have I forced you into the arms of another woman? Whatever I've done wrong I know I can fix it. Please, Rowan, don't leave me like this. Please give me another chance." She squirmed in my arms before grabbing me by the collar. To control her I pulled her arms together tighter. Exhausted, she laid her head against my chest.

"Vickie, if you don't calm down, I'm going to call the police!" She sniffled, then quieted herself and let me talk. "Now, we can talk about this later, but for right now, you need to leave." I persuaded her to go by telling her I would stop by later to talk and get my stuff, but I had no intentions of ever seeing her again. I was wrong for staying in the relationship with Vickie as long as I did; I only did so thinking that I would eventually fall in love with her. Now I realized that the lack of emotional involvement was evident and wouldn't be produced by time. I knew that her putting me out was the best decision for the both of us.

To be certain she'd left I watched her get into her car and stood in the parking lot until she drove away. I walked back into the station as though nothing had happened. I wasn't surprised that Fakes was standing by the front door pretending to be on the telephone. My glare dared him to say anything; he turned and went on about his business. Refusing to be the topic of the day, I continued my normal routine, fixed a cup of coffee, and grabbed the morning newspaper.

ROWAN

Things were pretty slow for a Saturday afternoon. A transport of an elderly patient from the hospital to a nursing home was our only call. Looking for a good deterrent from my thoughts about the fiasco with both Jana and Vickie, I noticed that the floors needed to be cleaned. I maneuvered the mop bucket from the utility closet and got to work. As I swished the mop up and down in the water I thought how badly Vickie's immature display embarrassed me. The guys knew who she was. We'd dated for three years and she attended both Christmas parties with me. They were certain she was "the one," but there was no doubt in my mind that she definitely wasn't. I lifted the mop, wrung the excess water, and started on the floor. Then, I didn't know *what* to do about Jana's attempt to have me all tied up. I needed to call the apartment complex to see if they could expedite my move-in date, ASAP! Since Vickie was storing some items for me, I made a mental note to pick up whatever she was trying to drop off at the station, along with a few items I would need for my new place, like a TV and a stereo.

My mind began to rest as I started to plan for my place. Staying with Josh had gotten old; I needed my own place to call home. The first thing I was going to do was prepare a nice dinner for Maria. I was sure it had been a while since anyone had shown her the attention she deserved. I chuckled, thinking about the startled look in her eyes as she stood in the doorway afraid that an intruder was in her backyard, and then the look of relief that followed.

I rested the mop against the wall and considered calling her. If for nothing else but to say hello, and let her know I was thinking about her. Would she be forgiving and receive my call? I felt guilty for leaving unannounced after the kiss I so passionately delivered. Had I been too forward? Did I blow my chance? I couldn't push the issue, but I wanted to let her know how I really felt. I wanted to be more than her friend. She was under the impression that I was still in a relationship. The truth of the matter was Vickie was history and I wanted to let Maria know I was available. I should have gone home instead of staying the night; but then again, she did ask me to stay. I didn't know whether I should call her or not.

My cell vibrated twice from the holster on my hip. I reached to unclip it from my waist and the damn thing fell into the bucket of mop water. I quickly fished it out, but in the two seconds it spent submerged in the soapy water, it had been ruined. I'd be damned . . . I hadn't even had that phone two months, and now it would have to be replaced. I didn't remember reading a clause in my contract covering acts of carelessness. The caller ID display was distorted, then completely faded out, preventing me from viewing my last call. Hoping to restore the service, I took the telephone into the kitchen and wiped like mad. I mumbled obscenities beneath my breath. From mere frustration I kicked the edge of the counter with my foot.

Luckily, the remainder of my shift was uneventful. I regretted going back to Josh's house when I got off. How could I look him in the face knowing his wife made a pass at me? What would she try next? Also, I was afraid Vickie might show up at his door looking for me. I couldn't deal with any more drama and decided to spend the night at a hotel. What a day!

MARIA

Wrestling with my thoughts, knowing I couldn't hide behind makeup forever, I bolted myself into an upright position. The demons in my past had to be dealt with. Maybe the time was now. Convincing myself it was a good idea, I put my shoes on, checked my purse for the pamphlet, and left the house. The group met every Wednesday night from six until eight o'clock. It was only five thirty and if I hurried, I could at least make a good portion of the meeting.

I got inside my car and was overcome by a moment of

doubt. I held on to the steering wheel and rested my head as I took a couple of deep breaths. With my right hand I reached over and pulled the pamphlet out of my purse. I set it on the console and read through it briefly while emphasizing the bold print saying all meetings were confidential. I scorned myself for being silly, then started the ignition. The sessions could only prove to be beneficial.

As I drove into the parking lot I estimated fifteen cars . . . if that many. I found a parking spot and located the front entrance before getting out of my car. By this time it was six fifteen. Good, I thought to myself. I walked through the double glass doors and looked for an activity posting. On an easel to my left, there was a yellow flyer announcing the small group sessions. With my index finger I found the one I was looking for, turned around, and proceeded down the wide hallway of the recreation center to the appropriate room. The farther I walked, the eerier the hallway became.

Ready to convince myself to leave, I heard voices at the end of the hallway. There wasn't a number above the room, so I peeped through the small window. I could only assume it was the right room. About ten ladies ranging from the ages of maybe fifteen to I would say thirty were sitting in a circle. A member of the group was talking. Afraid to interrupt I cracked the door only enough to slip inside and hear the conversation before making my late entry.

"Yes, I'm a recent rape victim . . . but I've realized it wasn't my fault. No matter what I was wearing or doing it wasn't my . . ."

Shocked, I let go of the door. The group was startled and turned around after the door slammed. I stood speechless inside the room . . . now afraid to move forward and make a public confession. I understood that all of us were victims in some form or another of the same crime, but that didn't make me ready to open up about it. The leader of the group looked up and asked if she could help me. Without saying a word, I held on to my purse strap tightly and turned to leave. I realized I wasn't ready. Before I got out the door, a soft-spoken voice stopped me, although I refused to turn around.

"Ms. . . . Ms. . . . don't be afraid. All of us were once victims of the same crime."

I stood frozen in place.

"When you're ready to be healed we'll be here in the same place next Wednesday evening."

I looked towards the group and acknowledged her invite with a nod of my head, then turned around and walked away.

Panting desperately for my next breath as I walked as fast as I could to my car, I fumbled through my purse for my keys. Hearing them rattle in the bottom only made me exert more energy to find them. My hands trembled as I searched the key ring for the key. The loud clatter from my keys startled me as they landed on the ground. Before bending down to pick them up I leaned against my car and took a deep breath. I closed my eyes, then took another deep breath, hoping to open them and see another reality. I did open them and gasped, knowing that this was my reality and it was up to me to deal with it. I couldn't ignore my past and sweep it under the carpet like two-day-old dirt. I had to deal with it one way or another. If not I would never have a fulfilling relationship with a man—ever.

I sat inside my car, too embarrassed to go back inside, re-open the same door I'd just closed, sit down, and introduce myself as Maria, a recent rape victim. I convinced myself there was always next Wednesday.

CHAPTER 10

No need to lose sleep at night.
You don't have to worry about the battle or the fight.

As I turned the corner I could see two boxes overflowing with clothing, side by side on the curb by Josh's driveway. Something in my gut told me that this wasn't good at all. Maybe the boxes were goodwill donations, or items from an attic or garage cleanup. What in the hell had gone on? Those were my things in the driveway! Josh had stuffed my belongings into boxes and was throwing them out! After my encounter with Jana I could only imagine his reasoning. Thank God he used boxes. I pulled into his driveway, stopped my truck, then opened the door slowly. I walked toward the curb to identify and confirm the contents in the boxes as my things.

Josh came out of the house with another box, and bit down on his bottom lip when he saw me. He immediately dropped the box, gave me a piercing look, then kicked it swiftly across the cement. I had never seen Josh so angry, and I was willing to bet Jana had everything to do with it.

"Josh, man, what the hell is going on?"

"You know what's going on. Don't play innocent with

me! There are thousands of single women in New Orleans. Why, Jana?"

"What are you talking about?"

"Man, I've known you for years. I never thought you would come on to my wife. Not only is she married, but she is married to *me*, your supposedly best friend. You stood beside me at my wedding, man!" His eyes were dark and his body seemed to tense up with every word he spoke. He clenched both his teeth and his fists as he continued kicking my belongings toward the street. "She told me everything. She has been living in fear for the past three weeks. This is her home and you've violated it! I had no idea when I was at work you were tiptoeing around the house watching my wife." He intermittently emphasized his words with more kicks.

With the last one, the box tipped over and the contents spilled out onto the sidewalk. It just had to be the one with my drawers in it! I bent down and scrambled to stuff my clothes back in before anyone else could see the boxers with the little hearts that Vickie bought me for Valentine's Day. Josh made a horrible scene; it would be only a matter of moments before the neighbors would come out to see what was going on. I was embarrassed enough at the accusations he was spitting at me, I couldn't let them see my underwear too. That would add insult to injury.

"I don't want you anywhere near my house ever again. So, get your things and get the hell away from me and my wife!"

Obviously, she kept her promises. Her trade had been mastered; a woman with a deadly sting. She'd threatened me and promised to make my life miserable if I didn't give in to her requests. I ignored her, thinking she would never want Josh to hear the truth about her. During the entire charade I never saw the culprit's face and hoped I would never see it again. I only had two seconds to formulate in my mind the best way to handle the situation. I knew she was somewhere watching and I refused to give her the response she was looking for.

"Josh, man, think about what you're saying. That doesn't even sound like something I'd do, man! Calm down, this is me, Rowan. You know I would never put our friendship in jeopardy like that." He *couldn't* believe what Jana told him. If I could just calm him down just a little, I could talk some sense into him.

"Me, Josh?" I mustered a halfhearted chuckle as I stood to my feet. Josh was now heading my way and at a dynamic speed. "Come on, Josh!" I yelled, backing down the driveway, almost tumbling over my own feet. This man had lost his mind! He charged me like a raging bull! "Damn it, Josh! What exactly did she say I did? Talk to me, man! What the hell did I do?" Josh looked like he was going to kill me. His fist was already formed and poised to knock the shit out of me. I shielded my face and braced myself for the impact. To my surprise and relief, he didn't swing. Instead, he got right in my face. I came face-to-face with Satan himself as I uncovered my face and looked into his eyes. All of hell showed clearly through. He might not have hit me right then, but I could see that it took every bit of willpower he had not to.

"You know what the fuck you did! How are you gonna try to sleep with my wife, Rowan?" he hissed through clenched teeth. "You were my best friend. That was the only reason why she didn't tell me immediately. In her mind she assumed her verbal threats would eventually scare you off. But you kept on, didn't you, Rowan? You sick son of a bitch! You touched my wife!"

"Josh, I . . . I . . . I didn't do anything. That's a lie. I never . . ." I couldn't believe what I was hearing. If that was what he was willing to share with me, I could only imagine what the whole story must have sounded like. Her execution of the plan was stellar. The look on his face and the drastic measure he pursued proved it to me. "Man, listen to me. She made it all up. Hear my side, man, please. She had coffee ready for me the morning your job called you in to work . . . she flaunted herself half nude in front of me, man! She did everything except lie down on the countertop. She initiated everything. She told me if I didn't have sex with her she would—"

"You're standing in my face, looking into my eyes and telling me my wife cornered you?"

I searched his face for any indication of what he was thinking.

"Yes, Josh, I swear she—"

Before I could finish my sentence, Josh knocked the hell out of me. He didn't want to hear or believe the truth.

"Rowan, you're a lying son of a bitch and you know it! I trust Jana. She would never cheat on me with my best friend!" Damn! He had a terrible left hook! I tried to look up at him but everything was so blurry. I could see Josh times three. My head was spinning and my only option was to focus on the man standing in the middle. He continued yelling and screaming as I rubbed my jaw. I couldn't even hear what he was saying anymore. My attention was now demanded by the horrible throbbing I felt in my face and neck. Did he break my damn jaw?

"Get the hell out of here, Rowan! I mean it. You sitting there rubbing your damn face, get up, get your shit and go!" he yelled as he stomped back up the pathway to the house. "And I mean now!" With that he slammed the door. Once I got up off the ground and steadied myself, I loaded up my truck and left. As I drove down the street, I shook my head in disgust. He wouldn't believe it if he saw her seduce me himself. I couldn't believe how she told him I initiated everything. What a snake. She proved to be shrewd and cunning. Damn, where did I go from here?

I went and checked into an efficiency suite, which would have to make do until my apartment was ready. Then I hopped in my car and wasted gas driving around the city, thinking it would help me evaluate my options. Even then my thought process was slow and unclear. My family was in Dallas. My best friend no longer existed and hated my guts. Vickie would love for me to come running back to her with this story. Finally, I thought that the riverfront would be a good place to sit and think things through. Well, after three hours I had no bright ideas. I finally drew the conclusion that staring at the water wasn't going to solve my dilemma.

Overwhelmed by my lack of options, I failed to pay attention to my route. I looked up and realized I was only a couple of blocks from Vickie's apartment. No better time than the present to stop by and pick up the rest of my things. I parked my truck and gained my composure before I got out. I knocked, then visualized several scenarios but wasn't prepared for what met me at the door. Lisa opened the door scantily dressed in a lacy blue Victoria's Secret bra trimmed in black ribbon, a matching thong, and a garter belt complete with thigh highs and five-inch stilettos. Yes, Vickie's best friend, Lisa. My jaw must have hit the ground. I thought about Fakes. For him that would have been the perfect situation. I thought it was ludicrous.

"Rowan, what a lovely surprise to see you. Has it been . . . three weeks since you broke my girl's heart? I'm sure she'll be delighted to see your face." She traced her finger between her breasts to down below her panty line, then placed it in her mouth and pulled it out slowly.

What the hell? I thought to myself. This was definitely not what I'd expected. Another man, maybe. Definitely not another woman camouflaged as a "girlfriend" waiting on the perfect opportunity to provide a shoulder to cry on.

"Lisa, baby, who is it at the front door? I wasn't expecting anyone. Were you?" While putting on her bathrobe Vickie came out of the bedroom with a huge smile on her face. Her steps were brisk before she saw my face. She slowed down as she got closer to the front door.

"Rowan! I wasn't expecting you. I guess you remember Lisa?" She didn't show surprise or embarrassment. I guess she didn't give a damn her little secret had gotten out.

"Rowan, don't look so surprised. Love surrenders itself and surfaces in many different forms." Lisa spoke dramatically as she embraced Vickie from behind and nibbled on her neck. Vickie's expression seemed blank, but Lisa gloated in the moment. "Vickie told me about the judgmental comments you made when the two of you broke up," she said, sliding her hands up and down Vickie's thighs. The same thighs that I used to grip and hold tightly in a fit of passion.

"You were so wrong. There's always someone willing and ready to pick up and mend the pieces of a broken heart. Even by the one you least suspected." Vickie's blank look disappeared as she closed her eyes in response to Lisa's touch.

"You two can quit your display. Vickie, I only stopped by to pick up the things you said I left behind."

"Oh . . . well, let me go and get them for you." As though they were going to be separated for hours they locked lips again. Lisa gave Vickie a hard pat on the ass as she flung her head before walking away. I didn't know how to respond when Vickie came back to the door carrying a small box.

"Vickie, you've got to be joking. This is what the commotion at the fire station was about, this little-ass box?"

She fluttered her eyelids, then returned to Lisa's embrace. Had I stood there any longer, they would have made out right in front of me. Disgusted, I looked at them both, turned around, and then walked away. My assumption was wrong; her friends were there to support her when I left. This really took me on an emotional spin. It all became clear to me that I should have seen it all along. Best friends. Single. Great careers. No husbands . . . the long shopping sprees and late-night dinners. Then it all made a lot of damn sense.

CHAPTER 11

Have our spirits journeyed into the future?
Have our souls forgotten the hurt of the past?

The day after Thanksgiving represented an anticipated phase of our family tradition. It was customary for us to decorate Aunt Bethany's huge artificial Christmas tree, along with the fireplace mantel, and hang our wreaths. Aunt Bethany's home always came to life for the holidays. She followed a hard-driven ritual to decorate and prepare our holiday meals during the entire season with pride. On the morning of Christmas Eve she'd wake up very early to prepare her ingredients and start her meal. Her organization and timing were amazing. First, she would dice up her celery, onion, and bell pepper to be used in her dressing and vegetables. My job was to peel the sweet potatoes she used in her pies. While her pies were cooking she'd prepare the batter for her cakes. Five minutes before the pies were done she'd pour her cake batter into the cake pans, making them ready for the oven. Like clockwork she'd remove her cakes, then place her turkey in the oven and allow it to cook slowly for the rest of the evening.

The aroma from the kitchen would make me beg her for just a little piece of pie or cake. When I was a teenager, I'd sneak up behind her and get a small piece of sweet potato pie. She would catch me every time. I remembered one year taking the entire pie off the counter. When she noticed, my slice was already gone. She found me sitting at the dining room table smiling with a mouthful of her hot pie. As a threat she shook her spoon at me.

Grudgingly, I went into the upstairs storage room to retrieve the boxes. One by one, I slid them down the steps and into the living room. As I rustled through them I realized my attitude needed to change. Before I sat down on the floor beside the box to coordinate the color-coded limbs and place them in their appropriate slots I counted my blessings. My situations and outcomes could have been a lot worse than they were. Amid my reflection, I almost lost my balance as I stood up to attach the large preassembled topper. Out of breath, I sat on the floor and stared at the beautiful angel with the golden wings on top of the tree.

I laughed as I blew the dust off the faces of the three tiny wise men and shook their miniature robes. The nativity scene had its own special place on the mantel. I was never bold enough, even as an adult, to move it or arrange it differently than what she thought was best. She remained faithful in her display of the true and biblical meaning of Christmas. Lastly, I strategically placed the empty gift-wrapped boxes beneath the tree. There was the box covered with the red Santa Claus paper with a white bow, another with bright gold shiny paper that read *Merry Christmas,* and a large green box with a stiff gold bow. Aunt Bethany had loved her annual gimmick of leaving unlabeled gifts. From the smallest to the largest, no one could guess whose gift was whose or what was inside.

This year I declined an invitation to Thanksgiving dinner

at Clara's house. I didn't have the strength to put on my artificial smile and answer one thousand and one questions. "Maria, how are you doing? What are you doing with your life? Why haven't you called us? Are you dating? Is there a special someone in your life right now? Are you lonely? You know you can call us if you ever need us. We're just one phone call away. Are you in school and so forth and so on?" I spared myself the stress.

I looked at the clock on the wall. I'd been caught up in my decorating frenzy for more than three hours and had almost forgotten the weekly counseling session scheduled to start in twenty-five minutes. I knew that if I didn't start counseling I'd only sink into a mode of depression and would never be able to move on with my life. I convinced myself to try to attend the session again, slid the empty decoration boxes into the hall closet, dusted my pants leg, and went to freshen up.

MARIA

This evening there were more cars in the parking lot than before. It was so crowded, I had to find a spot in the rear. Before I could give myself time to ponder the decision I grabbed my purse and headed for the door. It must have been family recreation night. Before I could open the double glass doors I could hear screams and laughter coming from inside. I didn't let that distract me, but kept my eyes straight ahead. This time I couldn't be a coward and leave. I picked up my pace as I got closer to the end of the hallway, but once I saw the door I stopped. As though there were a steel barrier in front of me I couldn't move. The door opened and a woman smiled and extended her hand, inviting me inside. I assumed it was the same woman who had attempted to stop me the last time. I made an effort to walk inside the room but still couldn't move. I took a deep breath. She discerned my tension, held on to my arm, and guided me into the room. Everyone smiled and gave affirming nods as she escorted me to an empty seat. I wasn't forced to speak, but everyone in the circle took turns and introduced themselves to me. I stared at the floor, inhaled, then made my introduction using my first name only for the sake of privacy.

"Hello . . . my name is Maria."

"Maria, welcome to our group," the group leader responded before coercing the group into another discussion.

Not ready to participate, I slid back in my chair. With an open mind I listened to their scenarios and the counselors' affirmations. Before long I realized we all shared the same pain and desire to be healed. I could feel my back lengthen as I leaned forward to participate in the discussion. The members of the group were very receptive as I shared my experience. In turn the lady I guessed to be in her late thirties sitting beside me reached out to hold my hand. Her grip tightened as the details of my story became difficult for me to share.

"Maria . . . it's all right." Using a calm tone the counselor placed her hands on her thighs and leaned toward me as she spoke.

Tempted to look down, I maintained eye contact.

"All of us have been there, including me. You don't have to rush. Take your time. Healing is a process and it will not happen overnight."

After another hour, I was relieved knowing that I had made it through without running. To end the session, the members gave each other assuring hugs and vowed to see each other the following week. No longer intimidated, I hugged other participants before leaving the room.

Coincidently, the lady sitting next to me was parked beside me. Before getting into our cars we made eye contact. She walked over to get my opinion about the meeting.

"I'm so glad you decided to come back and join us this week." As she walked closer to me she extended both hands with the palms up.

"Yes, so am I," I replied before placing my hands inside hers to accept her kind gesture.

"Well, tell me, did you find the session helpful?" Before releasing my hands she grasped them firmly, then paused for my response.

"I think it's a start. At least I talked about it." Remembering a simple affirmation from the meeting, 'In all things be true to thyself', I looked her in the eye and answered honestly.

"Yes, you did and you did a great job. You should be very proud of yourself. It may be a little uncomfortable at first, but you'll soon get used to the other girls." She looked toward the door as two other group members exited.

"Thanks." The positive interactions during the session and now coupled with her genuine concern had only confirmed my decision to attend next week.

"Well, I have to go. I have class first thing in the morning."

"Class? Where are you going to school?" I held up my hand to stop her and possibly get more details as she turned to leave.

"The University of New Orleans."

"Really?" I had attended classes at night; the unfamiliarity of her face on an exceptionally large campus didn't surprise me.

"Yes, I'm taking my prerequisites for nursing school."

"I was enrolled there but I . . . I wasn't able to finish the semester after . . . the . . . rape and the death of my aunt." I looked away before I could finish my statement. "I plan to reenroll next semester."

"I tell you what . . . I'm going to give you my number. Call me sometime. There's no reason you shouldn't finish your education."

"Yeah . . . I know."

"If I can survive the college experience at thirty-eight, I know you can. Girl, from what I can tell you're younger than me. It would be nothing for you to readjust."

I smiled slightly, feeling encouraged.

"I'm not kidding. Did you know the school offers an excellent counseling program? You may find it to be very helpful in addition to the weekly sessions here at the center."

I took the paper with her name and number on it. "Wow . . . thank you so much." Honestly I knew the on-campus services existed but never thought I would need them.

"Remember all hope isn't lost, girl. There are other women who are overcoming with help." She stopped me as I turned to unlock my car door.

"Are you in a hurry?"

"No . . . not really."

"Would you like to grab a cup of coffee? I know a little place that has the best cappuccino. I can tell you more about both counseling programs." Unlike me and in no way exemplifying characteristics of a recent rape victim she seemed so confident and sure of herself.

"Sure, that would be great." Interested to hear how counseling had obviously helped her interact with society and overcome any obstacles from the rape, I agreed to go.

"Follow me. The place is close by."

I eagerly followed her to a small bookstore less than fifteen minutes away. She parked and waited for me to get out of my car. As we walked toward the door she told me it was her place to unwind. We ordered our cappuccinos, then had a seat at the counter. Juanita, who had been married to her high school sweetheart for fifteen years, was now an outgoing single mother and divorcee of five years. Her daughter was a seventeen-year-old high school senior who would be attending Louisiana State University in the fall. Juanita's divorce allowed her to take advantage of a window of opportunity and achieve one of her lifelong goals, getting her college degree. Listening to her caused my curiosity to get the best of me.

"Juanita . . . how can you get a divorce after fifteen years?"

"Girl . . . let me tell you, it really hurt."

She was married to her first love, her high school sweetheart. His job as a long-distance truck driver required him to be away at least five days a week, leaving her alone to raise their daughter. She explained that it had been her birthday and he was gone, so her best friend at the time invited her out for drinks. Excited about one night on the town, she found a babysitter and prepared for her night out. Juanita received a call from her friend, who was running late and asked to meet her at the bar for the sake of time. Not foreseeing a problem, Juanita went alone and for whatever reason the friend never showed. Disappointed, but still wanting to celebrate her birthday, she treated herself to a drink instead of leaving. Unfortunately, on her way to the car she was pulled into a dark alley and assaulted by someone who followed her from inside the club. She managed to crawl back to the main street where a passerby stopped to help and called 911. Unable to overlook the innocence on her behalf, her husband blamed her and offered no means of support or forgiveness. He walked away from everything, leaving her devastated, alone, and with her child.

"And if I can do it after all of my drama . . . girl, I know you can."

"Well . . . I . . ."

"Well, no excuses. You have my home and cell phone numbers, use them."

Juanita helped me realize that any situation in life was conquerable, including mine. I promised to see her at the next session and let her know when I reenrolled in school.

As I drove home, I noticed how relaxed and light I felt. It had been a long time since I confided in anyone; our conversation was therapeutic. A huge burden seemed to be lifted as I foresaw a bond developing into a friendship. God, a power far greater than me, used her as a hand on earth to encourage me.

ROWAN

I stayed in an extended-stay hotel two weeks before I landed a lease on a one-bedroom apartment that would suit my needs as a bachelor. Nothing too big, low maintenance, and easy to keep clean. I needed a fresh start, a completely new beginning. No connections or commitments, just me against the world. I stood on my balcony and looked over the lake. I stepped back, turned around to look inside, and nodded to myself in approval at the floor plan. My being a man, details didn't mean much to me, but I did notice two things: the Italian marble fireplace and the awesome view of the lake. Wanting to enjoy more of my view, I leaned back over the balcony and noticed a young lady jog past. When she got closer I saw Maria's face and had to shake myself. I shouldn't have been seeing images of Maria. "She still thinks I'm in a relationship with Vickie anyway," I mumbled to myself. To her I'd only become a "big brother."

The large delivery van coming over the hill got my attention. Oh yeah! It was the company delivering my furniture. I would need a shrink if one of those burly guys with beer guts reminded me of Maria. I watched them carry the pieces from the truck into my apartment; then I fantasized as they, piece by piece, assembled my bed. Sleeping in my own bed, in my own crib without the stress would feel good. When they left I got a beer out of the fridge and fell asleep on my new bed thinking about my accomplishment.

I woke up the next morning in the same spot I fell asleep in. I stood up, stretched my arms to the ceiling, and cussed when I got a good glimpse of myself in the patio door. Damn, I'd turned into a fat ass and needed to start my cardio and ab routine pronto. Eating pancakes and double meat cheeseburgers for the past two months had caught up with me. In the middle of the floor I jogged in place and did a couple of kick and jab moves from Tae Bo. I had to sit down to get my breath before changing into my workout clothes. I grabbed a bottle of water, and draped a towel around my neck before heading out the front door to the gym.

Hyped and psyched out, I walked in and went straight to the incline bench. My ego was too big to let the brute on the next bench lift more than me, so I put twenty-five more pounds on each side of my bar and huffed and puffed with the best of them. When he left I sat up and rubbed my shoulders, hoping no one really saw me squirm from pain as I stood to leave.

When I walked through the door at the station, I could hear Fakes and stopped dead center because I couldn't believe his topic, "single women in the church." He called himself opening the door to broaden our horizons, categorizing churchwomen by type, characteristics, and availability. Footnote: Knowledge on the topic was articulated from first-hand experience. I found it hard to believe he invested the time to make his assessments. I grabbed my newspaper and coffee because I knew his conversation would get on my nerves quick. I refused to go to church to win lost souls to Rowan; the day I ever did that would be the day that the world would know that I was a desperate man!

I sat away from where Fakes was holding his conference, to read the paper. The news was the same . . . murder, theft, and deception. I drank my coffee as I glanced at a few articles, but before I could get through the sports section, Parker interrupted me.

"Man, what's going on?" he asked, sitting down beside me. "I know you broke up with your girl, but you're too damn quiet. You're not speaking to nobody. What's up?"

"Hey, man, you know, just one of those days. I decided to go to the gym after three years and it kicked my ass, but I'm okay." I frowned and rubbed my shoulder while I blatantly lied to my coworker. I was too ashamed to admit my ex-girlfriend was in love with her best friend; my best friend's wife tried to seduce me, then lied to her husband and got me kicked out of the house, and that I was in love with someone I might never see again. My life sounded like the drama of a soap opera . . . like a woman's. I didn't even want to think about it.

"Female, unconscious . . . possible . . ." The broken tones from the overhead speaker system skipped around the room. As usual before the call was complete we were headed to the scene. Obedient drivers yielded as we scurried through heavy lunch-hour traffic. It was the week after Thanksgiving . . . the busiest shopping season of the year. Shoppers in full defensive gear were swarming in the malls in search of the "perfect deal." Our call led us to the parking lot of a local department store. My heart competed with deep raspy breathing as I maneuvered my way through the crowd of curious onlookers. On the ground from mere exhaustion we found a lady in her midforties. In her state of unconsciousness she maintained a strong hold on her shopping bags. She gave literal meaning to the statement "shop until you drop."

I noted her case as "severe dehydration" and administered treatment according to our standard protocol as I held my breath, trying not to laugh. I couldn't look my partner in the face it was so damned funny. Once we determined the situation was of minor cause we excused ourselves and left.

CHAPTER 12

The mystery of a woman is so easy for me to say;
I walk in her shoes every day.

My present to myself—a college degree. I decided to give the University of New Orleans Office of Admissions a call this afternoon to schedule an appointment. The time had come for a little self-preservation. Completing my college education would be yet another step toward achieving that goal. My time alone had proven to be very beneficial; I'd grown and matured. Most of all I stopped depending on outside sources for the answers and learned to depend on God. Daily my goals were becoming a reality as I slowly regained my self-esteem and developed a very positive outlook on life.

After all of the storms and tragedies I realized there was hope for me. At first I questioned the obstacles in my life. *Why did it have to be so bad? Why me?* Not realizing once I set goals, there would be a process. A refining process. I had to be purged and cleansed in order to appreciate the benefits I was preparing to receive. No one ever said it would be easy or the sun would always shine. When it did shine I accepted its goodness, thankful for the light it provided. Ultimately, I realized the sun never set but constantly provided light even though I couldn't always see it.

Ready to put my plan into action, I woke up with a renewed sense of self. I arrived on campus and made confident strides toward the counselor's office. After a couple of light taps on the door, she asked me in. A full-figured woman with short gray hair stood behind the desk. With an extended right hand she moved enthusiastically forward to greet me.

"Hello, I'm Mrs. Tate. Welcome back to the University of New Orleans. I'm assigned to be your counselor."

"Thank you. I'm glad to be back." With the same fervor, I responded to her greeting with a firm handshake.

"If you would, please have a seat." She gave me a few seconds to sit down and get comfortable before speaking again. "My primary task is to work with returning students like yourself."

"Great." I watched her manipulate a few manila folders on her desk, then open her drawer for an ink pen.

"We should have no problems with your paperwork or registration." Her job knowledge, expressed through clear and distinct words, gave me the confidence I needed. She wiggled her computer mouse, adjusted her reading glasses on her nose, then asked for my Social Security number. After a few keystrokes and a click of her mouse, the printer generated several documents.

"Since your last date of attendance a few things have changed around campus." She took another glance at her computer screen, thumbed through the documents, then passed a copy to me.

"Really?"

"Definitely . . . we've added two more programs and several degree incentive plans. Our college has become more oriented toward working individuals, like you, who want to attain a higher education." Briefly, she reviewed the changes, discussed new opportunities, then wished me luck.

Next there was the registration process. Students migrated toward each other as they shared exciting news about their winter breaks.

The entire process had been exhausting and I'd worked up quite an appetite. It was before eleven o'clock. I didn't exactly know what I wanted for breakfast, so I got into the car and drove. The way I felt the corner Waffle House sounded fine. Before getting out of the car I checked my pocket for my money, then took one final look at my face. I walked inside and chose a seat in the corner. The restaurant was empty except for three seniors having coffee while reading their newspapers. For me that was perfect. I only wanted a quick bite to eat and thought it would be a good time to review my pamphlets from registration. A few minutes later I looked up because I heard a couple of guys laughing at the counter. The hearty laugh sounded very familiar. Oh my God . . . it was Rowan. Our eyes made contact at the same time. What was he doing here? He did have a way of showing up unexpectedly. He got up and walked toward me. I sat up straight and inconspicuously ran my fingers through my hair and moistened my lips.

"Maria . . . hi . . . what are you doing here?" His smile was warmer than ever.

Me, I gloated; someone I knew and admired had shown up unexpectedly.

"A girl has to eat. I should ask you the same question." When Rowan got closer to the table I looked up and tried to hide my blushing cheeks. Honestly, I was ecstatic and couldn't believe he was standing beside me.

"Hey, it comes with the job. We may end up eating breakfast or lunch anywhere."

"I guess you have a point."

"All jokes aside, it's really good to see you. You disappeared on me."

I was receptive as he leaned down to hug me. "I disappeared? I made an honest attempt to call your cell, but I got your voice mail." Wanting to see his reaction, I folded my pamphlet and looked into his eyes.

"My voice mail? Why didn't you leave a message?" he questioned, standing in an upright position.

"I couldn't."

"You couldn't? Why?"

"I didn't want Vickie to get it. Ruining your relationship was never my intention."

"Maria . . . I don't believe you. You called and didn't leave a message. You should be ashamed, but I think I can forgive you." For someone in a relationship he seemed really bothered by my missed call. His concern surfaced as tight wrinkles formed in the middle of his forehead.

"I'm sorry. I didn't think to ask if I was interrupting you. I see that you're reading."

"No, I was only looking at these brochures from registration." I hadn't started to read yet, so I placed them on the table.

"Registration?"

"Yes, I reenrolled this morning. Classes start in two weeks."

"Congratulations."

"Thanks."

"You know you don't have to eat alone. Especially not today, we have to celebrate. Come over and have breakfast with us. No need for a beautiful lady to eat alone when she can be accompanied by two men in uniform." He winked his eye as he tugged jokingly on the sleeve of my sweatshirt.

"Mmm . . . I'm okay. I don't want to be a third leg." I looked at his partner, suggesting I didn't want to impose.

"Are you sure?"

"Yeah . . ."

Rowan stepped back and folded his arms. Mischievously, he snatched my menu off the table and stuck it under his arm.

"Maria . . . you owe me this for not leaving that message on my cell. I promise I will not let him bite. He's totally harmless. We've got a lot to catch up on."

I laughed, accepted his offer, and joined him and his coworker for breakfast.

"Parker, this is my friend Maria. Maria, this is my partner, Parker."

I sat down in the booth and slid next to the wall. Rowan sat down beside me and waved the waitress back to the table to take my order.

"How have you been doing?"

"Fine."

"No more raccoons?" He nudged me lightly on the arm.

"No more. I've learned a lot about properly securing my garbage." Rowan and I both took turns letting his partner in on the story as we laughed together.

"Tell me, are you excited about school?"

"Whew, I'm a little nervous. It's only been a little over six months but it seems like I've been out forever."

"Believe me, you'll fit right in again. You don't look two days over eighteen."

"Well, I wouldn't go that far but thanks. I'm really going to be taking some tough courses this time."

"Don't worry, sit next to the student with the glasses and pocket protectors. That's who you ask to tutor you."

"I'll keep that in mind." I chuckled at his bluntness when he nodded at his partner, who wore glasses and looked like he owned a couple of pocket protectors. Ashamed of his naughty behavior, I shook my finger at him. Rowan made circular motions on his stomach with his hand when he saw the waitress walk toward our table. We moved our elbows to give her room to put our hot plates on the table. Before putting butter and syrup on my pancakes, I whispered a silent prayer. Even though selfish in nature, I was glad to see Rowan and hoped he'd broken up with Vickie. I looked at him and smiled when I said amen. Our conversation continued while we ate, but I was soon disappointed when our breakfast was interrupted by a call on his radio.

"Maria, sorry but duty calls." He looked let down as he accepted his call. "I have to leave."

Of course I understood. "Thanks for breakfast. I really enjoyed the company." He lifted my hand as he stood and kissed it gently. Inconspicuously, I covered it to conceal the area and contain the warmth from his kiss.

"It was good to see you, and good luck with your classes. You know my number if you need help finding that tutor I was telling you about." He winked and tilted his head toward his partner. With a smile he rubbed gently across my chin with his index finger, took my check, then walked away. I couldn't help but stare as he hurried to pay before leaving. I finished my meal, laid a tip on the table, then left.

When I opened the front door I could see the red indicator light blinking on my answering machine. Hoping it was Rowan, I quickened my steps, pressed the button, and let out a heavy sigh when the caller left no message.

ROWAN

"Dude, I didn't want to be rude in the restaurant. You never told me the two of you had become friends." Parker looked at me with a smirk as he secured his seat belt and put the keys into the ignition.

"Didn't think I had to."

"Please, I mean you never mentioned her or the day we

made the call at her home again. So, when did all of this take place?" He started the vehicle, then leaned forward on the steering wheel as he drilled me and waited for answers.

"I was concerned and went to visit her during one of our runs. Are you satisfied?"

"Oh yeah, I'm satisfied. Man, she's beautiful. Is she married?"

"No!"

He knew I wasn't going to volunteer personal information; he turned up the corner of his mouth as he checked the traffic before pulling out into the street.

"I thought we were closer than that. Why didn't you give a friend a better intro? You know I'm a single man."

I looked at him, then pointed at the traffic ahead of us. He needed to keep his damn eyes on the road. He was a good driver but couldn't talk and drive at the same time.

"Hell no. She's not married and she really don't want yo' sorry ass."

"Hey, just asking. Don't get so personal." He attempted to turn his head to look at my expression, but I pointed forward again. "Damn, man, you're acting like she's your girl or something. I thought she was just a 'friend.'"

I couldn't argue as he pushed the issue and overemphasized *friend*. "Man, keep your eyes on the road. You know you're half blind anyway."

Trying to be funny he made a sharp right, then a left onto the street of our call.

"All right. Keep playing and hurt me. I'll have your ass on *The People's Court*."

"Yeah, yeah . . . sure you will."

"Try me." When we pulled up, a woman was outside with a blanket wrapped around a man's shoulders. We assumed he was being chastised, because she was cussing and he had a look of anguish on his face.

"Parker, another day in the life of a paramedic." He silenced the sirens while I placed a call into dispatch.

"You can say that again." Putting all jokes aside, Parker and I jumped out and ran around to the back of the ambulance to get our equipment. Before we got close enough to hear the wife blurted out, "I told yo' ass to stay off that damned ladder." The husband frowned as he reached toward us in pain. Seeing he needed immediate medical attention, Parker secured the gurney while I attempted to get background information.

"Ma'am, can you tell me what happened?"

"Every year this time he has to compete with Mr. Richardson across the street. Well, he saw some new design on *HGTV* and wanted to try it out. I told him to stick with the usual and just hang them damn lights around the edge of the house and be done."

"Okay?" I was trying to get the nature of the incident but had to be a psychologist in the meantime.

"He's so damn hardheaded and got his old ass up there anyways."

"Oh . . . ?"

"Well, you see what happened, don't you? He lost his footing and fell off the ladder. He can't move and I think his leg or something is broke." She went on and on and on.

Finally, in between fits I was able to get enough information to transport him. I advised her to get a neighbor or friend to drive her to the hospital. I didn't want her to cause another casualty and break his other leg. I tossed my clipboard in our duffel bag and went to help Parker secure the patient. As we lifted the patient onto the gurney, my mind reverted to the Waffle House. Despite his wife's cussing and screaming I could see Maria's smile.

"Rowan? You ready?" Realizing I hadn't been much help at all, I summoned my strength to help Parker. Together we lifted the injured man into the back of the ambulance. I jumped in and Parker shut the door. I patted my cell phone, debating whether or not to call Maria, if for no other reason than to apologize for having to leave so abruptly. I removed the telephone from my hip and attempted to dial her number. I cursed when I realized I couldn't remember it.

MARIA

The first day of class I decided to sit next to a student much younger than myself. He had his assortment of pencils and black ink pens on the desk. I glanced at his shirt pocket. Yes! He had a pocket protector and twitched with anticipation, showing how eager he was to learn. I laughed to myself remembering Rowan's advice and made a mental note to let him know I'd somehow managed to follow it.

The professor introduced himself then began carving archaic algebraic equations onto the chalkboard. He explained each one but never paused to assess our comprehension. This display of higher knowledge lasted one hour and fifteen minutes. The entire experience was mind-blowing and quickly reminded me how much time I would need to spend in the school library studying. After class I couldn't wait to get home, kick off my shoes, and take a hot shower. I rushed to open the door, my telephone was ringing.

"Maria McCory please." I hesitated before responding. I didn't recognize the voice on the other end, and the telephone number on the caller ID wasn't familiar either. As I thought it was a telemarketer, my first reaction was to hang up the telephone.

"This is she."

"My name is John Hodges with Hammerstein and Associates." He was one of the legal assistants from the law firm that handled all of Aunt Bethany's legal matters. I found it odd to receive a late telephone call from their office. To my knowledge, I finalized all of her legal business regarding her estate before the funeral.

"Yes?"

"Mr. Hammerstein would like to see you in his office at your earliest convenience."

"Okay?"

"May we schedule a time now?"

"Can you tell me what this meeting is about?" From the tone of his voice it sounded serious, so I sat down on the couch to brace myself.

"Ms. McCory, we need you to come in and settle some unfinished business and sign a few legal documents. That is the extent of my knowledge. I'm sorry, I can't provide you with more information."

"Well, I don't get off work until four thirty tomorrow."

"Can you be in the office by five?"

"Yes, I can."

"We look forward to seeing you at five. Have a good evening."

After giving it a little thought, I decided I wouldn't worry about the telephone call. I was sure it was as simple as a missed signature.

MARIA

I rode around the parking lot and noticed a car leaving a spot close to the front door. I got out and entered the three-story brown brick building, then took the stairs to their office on the second floor. I opened the intricately designed wooden door and was greeted by the receptionist. "The attorney will be with you in a few minutes. Would you like a cup of coffee or a soda while you wait?" she asked courteously after ending a telephone conversation. I wasn't thirsty so I declined the offer and had a seat on the leather sofa. Before I could browse through the *U.S.A. Today* she called my name.

"Ms. McCory, Mr. Hammerstein is available."

"Thank you."

"Maria, good to see you. Please come in and have a seat." He was smiling and didn't seem anxious. He picked up a brown folder, opened it, and scanned the pages before having a seat in his huge brown leather chair. "I'm sure the telephone call from the office was unexpected."

"Yes, it most certainly was."

"Again, I would like to express my sympathy." I thanked him for his kind words. "However, I have some good news to share with you."

"Good news? I can handle some good news."

"Well, Maria, this is actually better than good."

"Really?" He turned several pages in the folder and pulled out three documents.

"Maria, a few weeks before the initial diagnosis of your aunt's cancer she came into the office and changed her will." He passed the documents to me.

I looked down at them, skimmed through a few pages, but really couldn't interpret the legal jargon. I placed them on his desk and waited for an explanation.

"In so many words your aunt modified her will, leaving the house, land, and her savings to you."

"Oh my God. She did what?" From disbelief, I covered my mouth as tears started to form in the corner of my eyes.

"Before you were born, it was their request to have the land sold and the money donated to charity, preferably homeless shelters. But after she reared you she wanted you to have everything for your future family."

"Aunt Bethany was always full of surprises."

"My office has taken care of the deeds. All I need you to do is sign some final paperwork." He thumbed through the thick stack of papers inside the folder, then placed them in front of me on the desk. One by one he went through their contents, indicating specifically where I needed to sign. Thirty minutes later everything was signed, initialed, and dated.

"If you have any questions don't hesitate to call the office. Any of my associates will be more than happy to assist you."

"Thank you, Mr. Hammerstein." He extended his right hand and escorted me back to the front door. I thanked him again and turned to leave. In disbelief I repeated my assets over to myself as I exited the building and walked to my car. I owned a house, forty acres of land, and the remainder of their savings. I opened the car door and barely sat down before I started to cry again. "Aunt Bethany, I know you're looking down from heaven with a smile. Words will never be able to express how thankful I am to God for your years of devotion and the influence you had on my life."

CHAPTER 13

Observe the strong and question the weak;
take inventory; which of the two do you want to be?

Becoming reacclimated to the entire college experience was easier than I thought. During registration I was reminded by my first conversation with Juanita to take advantage of the counseling services provided by the college. My inquiry proved to be constructive; I was advised to contact the Women's Center and schedule an appointment.

My first session was basically a getting-to-know-you session. The counselor asked questions about my childhood, my parents, my aunt, and any particulars I thought were a mental hindrance in my life. He rephrased questions while emphasizing many of those factors that played a major role in my current thought process. Oddly, I did most of the talking. My sessions at the recreation center were interactive and heightened my expectations from a professional counseling session. His final comment was, "If the issues aren't dealt with, you will continue to hold yourself accountable for everything that happened to you." Expecting solutions, not suggestions, I didn't feel better or worse. As a matter of fact

I felt somewhat disappointed. That might not have been the answer I was looking for.

I seriously contemplated whether or not I would attend the second session. Why should I attend if I was going to resolve the problem myself? To the contrary I attended only with lower expectations. He told me after reviewing the notes from our first session he decided to take another approach. He asked me what hurt me the most about my childhood. Several things hurt me as a child, so I responded hesitantly, deciding to finally talk about the rape.

He listened to me as I shared the most private details. In response, he gave me an assignment for the next week. Write down on a sheet of paper three things during my life that hurt me most, rank them one to three, tear it up, and throw it into the garbage can.

Throughout the week I thought about my counseling assignment. Three things that hurt me: the rape, feeling abandoned, and mental abuse. By the week's end, I had jotted them down and thought through each one. The mental abuse left me wounded internally and prompted me to go through life with low self-esteem. Being abandoned forced me to constantly look for approval whether from family, friends, or strangers. The rape only validated my low sense of self, making me feel like I was unworthy of anything other than the best. I looked at the list one last time, shredded it into small pieces, then threw them into the garbage.

While admitting my initial impression of the campus counseling sessions was negative and perceived prematurely, I decided to start reading a book he recommended. As I was anticipating the end of the chapter titled "Calming Your Emotions to Listen to Your Inner Voice," the sound of the doorbell interrupted my reading. I frowned, then placed my finger on the page to hold its place. I wasn't expecting company and couldn't imagine who would be ringing my doorbell other than a salesperson. I ignored the doorbell and reopened my book to the last page I'd read. The doorbell rang again. To prevent an echo from my steps I eased off the couch and tiptoed to the door. At first glance I couldn't recognize the face through the small window in the door. As I got closer the facial silhouette became clearer. It was my sister, Jamilia; I hadn't seen her since Aunt Bethany's funeral. How did she find me? I didn't realize she knew where I lived. I very seldom talked to my father anymore and I never talked to her. To think about it, the last time I had a conversation with him was two weeks after Aunt Bethany died. Saying hello to her through my father was our only attempt to communicate. Following a deep sigh I opened the door.

"Jamilia?" I was surprised but tried not to reflect it through my tone. If she had taken the time to find me, there was either something wrong with her or my father or she was running some kind of scam. Aunt Bethany left me a substantial inheritance, and Jamilia's sudden appearance made me certain that it was no secret among my family members. Managing to acquire several tricks of the trade, theft, wild parties, and alcohol, Jamilia proved to be no different than my father. A few years ago she was involved in a scandal that made the daily newspaper. She stole credit card information from customers at an upscale clothing boutique near downtown. How she did it was very clever. As customers used credit cards she'd memorize their account numbers, then write them down at her first opportunity. Finally, a dedicated employee who feared the privacy of the customers as well as other employees reported her scheme to management. Without her knowledge cameras were installed throughout the store, eventually catching her in the act. I'd heard blood was thicker than water. For a thief does that hold any truth? I rubbed my forehead to refrain from more of the same negative thoughts. The ethics from my counseling must be applied to my daily life.

"Hey, girl." Out of courtesy I reached out to give her a hug. She shrugged me off nonchalantly as though she was in pain. I could see a small tear form in the corner of her eye. She let herself go, then cried profusely. I stepped back to prepare for her dramatization. If she was crying she needed either money or a place to stay.

"Come inside and have a seat." She pushed past me, took a quick glance around the room, then sat down on the edge of the couch.

"It's . . . my man, T.Q., our relationship . . . he hit me in front of all of his friends." She cried hysterically with small sniffles between syllables. She didn't look like someone who had been hit. I didn't see any visible bruises and she didn't seem the least bit shaken.

"Did you call the police?"

"No! How . . . how could I?" Through her crocodile tears she continued. "I barely got outta there alive. I don't have anywhere to go and I'm scared. I know you can help me."

"Jamilia, I never even see or talk to you. How did you conclude that I could help?"

"You're right, I know I don't come around much and, uh . . . I knew where you lived, but I'm never on this side of town. Can you forgive me? I know I been a sorry-ass excuse for a sister but I really need your help."

While attempting to play on my emotional heartstrings, did she think looking into my eyes would convince me her plea was sincere? I decided to beat her at her own game.

"You can call the police and wait safely here." With my arms folded I leaned back to observe her reaction to my comment. Her response was the first red flag.

"Ahh . . . well . . . I'll be okay. I just wanna talk about it right now."

"We can talk about it, but the details should be reported to the police while they're vivid in your memory."

"No . . . ahh . . . just listen to me."

"I'll listen but when you're done I'm calling the police. Would you like anything to drink?"

"Yeah . . . what you got in there?"

"I have bottled water, juice, or Coke." She turned up her nose at every choice I gave her. I assumed she wanted alcohol.

"If that's all you got I'll take a Coke." Before taking her first sip she gave it a few large swirls. She shook her head as though she was too ashamed to look me in the eye. "I'll be honest with you. Do you remember Pops? Well, I started dating his worthless-ass son . . . I mean his useless son T.Q. about eight months ago."

I always knew she was vulgar and didn't know why she tried to cover it with apologies. I looked at her to let her know I was an adult and had heard profanity before.

"The chances he took excited me. He gave me everything I dreamed of . . . cars, clothes, and money. You know, for Christmas, girl, he bought me all name-brand clothes and a pair of diamond earrings. See . . . look."

I squinted to look before she jerked her head around.

"It was no secret T.Q. slept around, but he slept with them to support me. Damn it . . . Maria, how could I argue with him? I was too involved in the relationship when he fessed up. He told me it was okay and I was his 'Boo.'"

The way he explained his hustle did something for my ego. He was making ends to support me. Maria, I believed him." She took a gulp of her soda before speaking again.

I leaned my head to the side, crossed my left arm in front of me, and cupped my chin in my right hand.

"I can't believe his ass sold me out like he did and wanted me to dance in front of his boys." As though disappointed she shook her head.

I listened but I couldn't believe the extent of her story. Well, yes, I could believe it. I nodded my head so she could tell me more. I knew to stay composed for the remainder of her story when she reached for my hand.

"T.Q. decided to invite his boys over to watch a football game . . . right? You know, they had chips, dip, and beer. I was the only female there at first. I was used to the parties, but it got out of control. Before I knew it 'D,' his boy, called his girls over to join them."

I watched her hands flail through the air as she restlessly shifted from side to side in her chair. I could only envision what was really wrong with her.

"The music started before T.Q. opened the front door. Five of them showed up dressed to throw down and get paid. They had no problems switchin' their tight asses around before they stripped. After that every man was for himself. No one, not even my man, was left out. I got my shit and was gettin' ready to leave the apartment. I knew about his parties but I ain't never wanna see it. He got pissed when he saw me standing at the door with my purse.

"'Hey, you too good for us now? Don't ever disrespect me in front of my boys again. You get yo' ass back in there and enjoy the party.'

"'Wait one damn minute . . . you ain't gotta push me.'

"'What the hell? Now you tellin' me what to do?' he yelled. 'Hey, ya'll! Guess what? My girl is gonna give you a private performance on the house. I mean all of ya'll, including me.' He was serious about what he said. 'Go ahead! Take it off. You owe me.'

"Maria, I couldn't believe he wanted me to dance for his friends. I told him hell naw. I wasn't gonna dance for his friends. I told him straight out, get his nasty girls to do it. All I really remember after that was him making a fist and hitting me hard as hell. I fell down in the middle of the floor. I could hear everybody laughin' at me. They all left me right there in the middle of the floor after they went into the other room to keep the party goin'. I was hopin' you could kinda help me through this."

"You'll be safe with me until the police arrive and take a report. T.Q. should pay for what he did to you." I watched her twirl her thumbs around each other.

She wiped her face with the back of her hand and the tears disappeared. "Well . . . well . . . I don't wanna call the police. You don't know him and his low-down friends."

"I don't have to know him or his friends. He's obviously hurt you and you need some help." I watched her become a bundle of nerves. I knew within seconds she would come unglued.

"Maria . . . look . . . I'll be honest with you. I've hit some hard times. I got kicked out of my apartment and all I need is a few hundred dollars to find another place to stay. Ya know what I mean?" Well, there it was. She didn't disappoint me. She needed either money or a place to stay.

"You're my sister. You can stay with me until you find another place."

"Well . . . okay, girl . . . ahh . . . what about the money?"

"Don't worry about the money. You won't owe me anything."

"I . . . really need the money. I'll find my own place to stay."

"Don't stress yourself. There's more than enough room. I've been in this house alone since Aunt Bethany died."

"Ahh . . . yeah . . . can I use your bathroom? Whew, that Coke has gone straight through me, girl." To demonstrate the urgency she squirmed, then crossed her legs.

"Sure, it's down the hallway and to the right."

She looked over her shoulder nervously as she strolled down the hallway. The door shut and I heard the locks tumble. I returned to the living room and started watching television but adjusted the volume when I heard her mumbling. She wasn't singing and I knew no one else was in the house. I re-adjusted the volume and listened to what sounded like a con-versation. My curiosity got the best of me so I tiptoed to the door and leaned against it to listen. She was on her cell phone, obviously talking to T.Q. in what she thought was a low whis-per. As a deterrent she turned on the water faucet while she talked.

"Man, she ain't falling for it. I asked for a coupla hundred dollars and she asked me did I wanna place to stay until I could get back on my feet? I don't need no damn where to stay. I need somma that damn money."

I stood against the door and listened to her conversation with her boyfriend. Did she think I was that naïve and hadn't realized her entire fiasco was a lie? I shook my head and re-turned to my seat in the living room. The water ceased and a few minutes later I heard the door open. I met her in the hall-way with the telephone.

"I've called the police and they need an account of your story." The air in the hallway became stiff as she stood speech-less. She snatched the telephone from my hand and slammed it on the base. Quickly she regained her composure. "Jamilia, charges should be brought against T.Q. for hitting you."

"Ahhh . . . well . . . I . . . if you just give me the money I can find a place."

"Jamilia, stop the charade!"

"I really don't know what you're talkin' about." Her eyes widened as she placed her hands on her chest. She didn't have a clue I was standing on the other side of the door while she talked to her boyfriend.

"Sure you do. You know exactly what I'm talking about. Your boyfriend didn't hit you and you never needed a place to stay. You're my only sister. If you're experiencing hard times I would have loaned you the money. Honestly, I would have given it to you." Without saying another word or looking at me she threw her hands up in the air and hurried toward the living room to get her purse. I followed her to the front door, opened it, and shut it with no regrets. Did she think she could deceive me? Surely not?

CHAPTER 14

Are we listening to the warnings?
Are we paying attention to the signs?

"Josh, I can't take the notes or telephone calls from the school anymore. Junior's behavior is totally out of control. I just finished having a conversation with his homeroom teacher, who called to schedule a meeting with us either this evening or first thing in the morning."

I tossed the computer cable to the side, moved a stack of loose papers, and turned off the speakerphone. Dale reminded me of a gossiping woman when I noticed him inch closer to my desk, probing for the details of my conversation. The guys already heard her yell, but I was determined to be discreet. I found my headset, put it over my ear, and looked at my coworkers, who pretended not to hear a word.

"Jana, honey, I'm busy. Can you call me back later?" Someone had downloaded a music file with a virus on their office computer. Their infatuation with free music shut us down for hours.

"Do you see what your long hours at the office are doing to our son? When was the last time you spent any quality time with him?" I frowned as her sharp tone reverberated in my ear.

"I'm busy. Now isn't a very good time." The guys snickered as I sang my words to keep from yelling back.

"I take him to all of his practices, Boy Scout meetings . . . you name it and I take him there. No one even knows he has a father." I adjusted the headset on my ear, making certain they couldn't hear anything else she said.

"Really?"

"I'm tired of doing for him what you should."

"Uh-huh . . ." Silently evaluating the damage done to the entire operating system, I tuned Jana out.

"When will you stop spending so many hours at the office? When, Josh? Tell me when."

"Yeah . . . sure . . . dear."

"Josh, are you listening to me? Have you heard a single word I've said?"

"Ahh, yes, that will be good." Dale stood in front of me and pantomimed a question with his hands. Responding nonverbally to his question while delegating tasks was frustrating with her shouting in my ear.

"I need to talk about our son and you're ignoring me. While you work, have you ever thought how difficult it is for me to discipline him alone? I need to vent."

"I'm sorry, but now really isn't a good time. I'm in the middle of a computer crisis." Requiring more privacy I apologetically held up my hand as I turned my back to Dale.

"Go to hell!" Jana slammed the telephone down in my ear. I was occupied and didn't have time to deal with an issue at home.

Three hours and many curse words later the virus on the main server had been quarantined and the hard drive reformatted. After work the guys wanted to meet at a sports bar for a couple of drinks to unwind and relax.

"Count me out, I need to go home." After seeing them for twelve hours I wasn't in the mood for socializing.

"Oh, Josh-e-poo can't go with us for drinks. The boss wants him to report home immediately." To illustrate his sarcasm, Dale stood at attention and saluted me.

"Hey, screw all of you, you got that?"

They laughed and cracked jokes the entire time we waited in the hallway on the elevator. Needless to say they didn't stop when the doors opened and we got on. Even with their taunting I opted to go home, drink a cold beer, and take a hot shower.

The house was dark, so I stood in the doorway and took off my shoes and jacket. I blindly felt my way into the kitchen, tossed my keys on the counter, and drank my beer solely by the light of the refrigerator. I was extremely tired and it only took three large gulps to satisfy me. Bad luck to waste good beer, so I returned the half-empty can for later use. I cursed as I turned around and stumbled over a toy truck. I was too damn tired to bend down and pick it up, so I kicked it to the side. I hadn't seen Junior all day and wanted to check on him before I went to our bedroom. From his room I was pleased to hear a soft snore.

Jana didn't flinch when I opened the bedroom door. The night-light was on in the bathroom; I could see she was tucked in tightly. Before going into the bathroom I walked to her side of the bed and kissed her on the nose. She curled up in her blanket, then changed positions, obviously still upset with me. Careful not to disturb her sleep, I closed the bathroom door before turning on the light. Tired and fidgety I did totally the opposite and dropped everything I picked up. I finished my shower and tumbled into bed beside her. Within minutes I'd fallen asleep.

Rolling over in bed and finding an empty spot at 2:45 a.m. bothered me. I rubbed my eyes with the back of my hands before closing them and attempting to go back to sleep. Still restless I looked at the time again, kicked the comforter off my body, sat up, and slipped on my pajama pants. I stood up and looked toward our bathroom first; the door was open and the light was out. My next thought was Junior's room. When I realized Jana wasn't in there and he was sound asleep, I backed out and pulled the door shut. *Hmm, this is weird*, I thought to myself. Why wasn't Jana in bed at three o'clock in the morning?

I walked down the hallway, stopped when I saw the light shining beneath the door of our computer room, then stood close enough to hear any movement in the room. Standing still, I really didn't hear anything and assumed Jana left the computer monitor on by mistake. When I turned to walk away, I heard fingertips tapping on the keyboard. The keystrokes were consistent like she was typing a letter or something. *Okay what type of business is transacting on the computer at nearly three o'clock in the morning?* I leaned closer to listen. Then it stopped a few seconds before starting again. My instinct told me to slowly peek inside. Her back was facing the door, so I only opened it wide enough to get a glimpse of what she was doing. My eyes became wide when I saw the dialogue box on the computer screen. I leaned in a little closer to see who she was talking to and read any parts of the conversation.

Did you like the way I made you feel yesterday?
Evan . . . I'm still fantasizing about my climax. At this very moment I'm burning inside.
Tell me, what did you enjoy most, the appetizer or the dessert?
The appetizer. Couldn't you tell? Didn't you hear me moan from pleasure?
I owe you for the risk you took. When are you going to let me make up for it?

Soon, baby, it will be soon. Until then it will be sweet
dreams.

*What the hell? Is she doing what I think? I squinted my
damn eyes and held my breath while I attempted to read
more of their conversation.*

Jana, I know there's a hot spot between your legs waiting on me. Touch it and think about the time we've
spent together.
Promise me the passion will never end. I can't wait to
be with you again.

I was at a loss for words and didn't know what to say
when I saw her rub her breasts. By that time my vision
started to blur and my head was about to explode. Damn, I
couldn't believe her! That slut was chatting online and fantasizing about sex with another man with me right there in the
house. *What a freaking bitch.* I made a fist but stopped myself from smashing it into the wall. Unable to believe what I
saw, I pushed the door open. "Jana, what in the hell are you
doing in here at three o'clock in the morning?" Stunned, she
turned toward me with widened eyes, then in one smooth
move minimized the computer screen.

"Josh, baby . . . hey . . . I couldn't sleep . . . so I . . ." Her
body became stiff as she tried to fabricate a lie.

I interrupted her midsentence. "You couldn't sleep, huh?
So you decided to sneak in here and make love with another
man online?"

She spun around and tried to turn the computer off, but I
grabbed her by the wrist and moved her hand before she
could touch the power button.

"Josh . . . baby . . . what are you talking about?" *Deceitful
bitch* was the only thought that ran through my mind at the
time.

"You know what the hell I'm talking about. Who were you chatting with?"

"Don't be silly. I wasn't chatting with anyone." She maneuvered her wrist back and forth to loosen my grasp while struggling to move her chair in front of the computer to hide the screen.

"So now I'm blind and stupid? This morning were you pissed about our son's discipline problem or the fact you couldn't set up another date?" When I pushed her chair to the other side of the room she jumped up and tumbled backward onto the computer desk. I maximized the computer screen, reopened the dialogue box, and printed two copies. One for me and one for the lawyer I was going to retain. She covered her mouth with her hands as though she couldn't believe she'd been caught and was ashamed. I grabbed the copies off the printer and pushed the monitor onto the floor. I'd be damned if she'd talk to him again that night. I watched the screen shatter into pieces while I pushed by her and went into the kitchen to finish my beer I desperately needed. She stumbled over the broken monitor and followed me down the hallway.

"Josh . . . please we need to talk."

"So now you want to talk? Save it for that jerk you were talking to on the Internet!" The opened beer spilled on the floor when I tugged on the refrigerator door to open it.

"Please . . . I can explain everything," she pleaded between her spontaneous sobs.

"I don't want to hear shit you've got to say. Just get the hell out of my face." I drank what remained, then crushed the empty can on the counter.

"It's not what you think. I was . . ." Frantically, she wiped her eyes and rubbed her fingers through her hair.

"You were what? Anything else you have to say, speak to my attorney! I have the proof in my hand." I held the copies up and snapped them in front of her face.

"Josh, please. What about our son? What about the future? Our future?"

"You tell me. Were you thinking about Junior or our future when you were screwing another man?" She made an attempt to walk toward me. I held my hand up, daring her to take another step. She covered her face and ran halfway down the hall toward the living room while I stormed toward the bedroom.

Rowan's voice and the look on his face suddenly popped into my head. The day I kicked my best friend out he told me Jana made a pass at him, but I didn't believe him. She had blatantly tried to seduce my best friend. I turned around and forcefully called her name while walking toward her. "Jana! Was Rowan telling the truth? Did you try to screw my best friend, in my house, while I was away?" She stopped, turned around, and looked at me with a blank stare. "Well . . . did you?" Infuriated, I reached out and grabbed her around the neck.

Her mouth fell open as she stuttered. "Rowan . . . no . . . I . . . he . . ."

I knew she was lying to me. My fingers tightened around her neck while she moved her hands in circles in an effort to find air. I let go of her, shook my head in disbelief, and backed away while she grabbed her neck and coughed repeatedly until she caught her breath.

"You know what, Josh? I did make a pass at Rowan." She arrogantly overenunciated each word, pointed her finger, then placed her hands on her hips. "I tried my damn best to give him some."

I slammed my fist on the countertop and stared at her in disbelief.

"I've tried everything with you. I joined the health spa, lost weight . . . started buying new lingerie. Still, I got nothing from you. You haven't touched me in six months. So tell me, who's meeting your needs? It sure as hell isn't me."

I grabbed her by the arms and pushed her against the wall.

With her eyes she deliberately dared me to lay a hand on her. "Are you gay now, Josh? Is it one of your office buddies?"

I couldn't believe my fucking ears. I became furious as thoughts of her standing naked in front of Rowan ran through my mind. Moved by anger and resentment, I snatched one of our wedding pictures off the wall, threw it down on the floor, and crushed it with my foot. She flinched but stood her ground in front of me with a glaring stare. This time she stormed down the hallway into our bedroom, and I went into the living room and sat on the couch.

Damn, Jana had balls, I thought as I leaned my head back and held it to suppress the horrible thoughts of being humiliated and disrespected in my own house. She had me totally fooled the entire time Rowan was here and I never saw it. *Who else has she slept with during our marriage? My coworkers? A neighbor? The UPS man?* I spent long hours at the office. If she was bold enough to chat with me in the other room, what in the hell did she do when I was gone? Knowing the truth not only embarrassed me but made me really feel like shit inside. In so many words he'd tried to tell me, but instead of halfway listening I immediately took her side. She cost me a relationship with my best friend. My best friend? Damn, I owed him a major apology for kicking him out on his ass when he needed me. I dialed Rowan's first five digits, then hung up the telephone. Hell, after what I did I was the last person he'd want to talk to.

The following morning Jana never came out of our bedroom, and everything in our house was quiet. Instead of sleeping in I woke up to take Junior to school myself. I was surprised to see him dressed and sitting on the side of his bed when I opened his door.

"Good morning, Son." Like a normal morning I walked over to give him a high five and rustle my fingers through his hair.

"Hey, Dad."

"Are you hungry?"

"Oh yeah. Dad, I'm a growing boy. I'm always hungry." He grinned as he flexed his pretend biceps and inhaled to make his chest swell.

"Son, I can't disagree with you on that. We'll stop and have breakfast on our way to school."

Assuming I meant the three of us, he leaped off his bed and skipped toward the door. "I'll go get Mommy."

"No, Mommy is tired and will not be eating with us this morning."

"Oh." He sat back down on the edge of the bed and lowered his head. "Is she tired from yelling at you last night?"

His comment caught me off guard. Other than lying I didn't know how to respond. "No. No one was yelling."

"Yes, you were. I heard you." With a puzzled facial expression he looked up and searched my eyes for an honest answer.

"Like I said, she's tired and will stay at home."

"Whatever you say, Dad, but I know the real reason she's tired."

"I'll be ready in twenty minutes, so wait for me in the kitchen."

"All right."

Expressionless, I turned and left his room. There was a possibility he heard everything. With a major situation on my hand I went into the kitchen to call the IT manager and requested a few days off for an emergency. I needed time to regroup before I made any major decisions regarding the end of my marriage to Jana and how I'd share the details with my son. I didn't have any major projects pending and was confident he could handle the technical support calls while I was off. If nothing else I owed Junior an explanation.

CHAPTER 15

I'm a rose, a black rose.
Who will acknowledge my beauty and
testify of my strength?

The bank was closed for Martin Luther King Jr.'s birthday and I didn't have class. Wanting to take advantage of valuable free time, I called a local bookstore to reserve another book my counselor recommended. Fortunately, they had one copy left in stock; I left my name and telephone number with the salesperson and made plans to pick it up later. Not really excited about my routine trip to the grocery store, I went into the kitchen to take a quick inventory. Of course, I had almost depleted my supply of basic essentials, including paper towels and toiletries. I grabbed the next to the last roll of paper towels out of the closet, removed the plastic wrapping, placed it neatly on Aunt Bethany's wooden holder, then turned to toss the old cardboard dowel into the trash. Aunt Bethany had bought household supplies in bulk and would frown at the idea of using her last. On that note, I smiled as I leaned against the kitchen counter and prepared my to-do list for the afternoon: bookstore, then the market.

The weather forecast predicted cold weather and sunshine. For a spark of natural energy I opened the curtains and allowed sunlight to fill the room, turned on the stereo, and did the two-step to R. Kelly before I took my shower and got dressed. I left home casually dressed in a pair of Gap jeans, a University of New Orleans sweatshirt, no makeup, and a ponytail.

While I was driving, avoiding thoughts about the remainder of my week was difficult. Working in the bank, I'd developed a strong sense for details, which later turned into a need to plan, organize, or itemize all of my activities. To deter those thoughts and focus on a day void of stress and serious obligations I pulled out my cell phone and called Juanita.

"Hello."

"Juanita, hi." Shocked she was even at home, I turned down the radio to hear her clearly.

"It's so ironic that you called. I was in the middle of my thoughts about how you planned to spend your one-day break from class."

"Believe it or not I'm going to the bookstore."

"Really? Well, that sounds exciting." The sarcasm in Juanita's voice made me laugh.

Certain an afternoon at the bookstore wasn't her idea of a break, I responded with a comparison to justify my choice. "It's better than the college library."

"I guess you have a point." She chuckled in the background.

"What's on your agenda? Anything exciting?"

"I'm going on a date."

"Oh, a date, who's the lucky man?" Her comment heightened my curiosity. I saw her every Wednesday night and she'd never mentioned anyone special to me.

"Denzel Washington! I'm going to see his new movie *Out of Time*. He's so fine."

"You're crazy and will say anything." As though Denzel would be sitting next to her himself, she spoke with such passion.

"Ha, I'm only telling the truth."

"Okay, I'm driving into the parking lot now. Enjoy your date. I'll see you Wednesday night."

"Take care, girl, and don't have too much fun."

"Talk to you later."

Inside the front door was a discount table. All titles, regardless of genre, were fifty percent off, so I stopped to browse. The vegetarian cookbooks caught my eye; I chose one for my collection, then spent almost thirty-five minutes reviewing the top twenty best sellers displayed directly in front of me. Overwhelmed by endless class assignments, I realized it had been several months since I purchased a novel to read for personal enjoyment. With time to spare, I also wanted to browse the self-help section in the rear and look for titles recommended by my counselor. I made a final choice, went to the front counter, requested my reserved book, and paid for them.

Persuaded by the aroma of fresh-brewed coffee emanating from the center of the store, I bought a cup, then decided to have a seat in the small area set aside for eating and skim through my new books. Apparently, a small book club was having their monthly meeting nearby. I was drawn into the conversation taking place at their table about a book I'd recently read, Toni Morrison's *Love*. Wanting to participate, I eagerly turned around and asked if I could participate in their discussion. By the end of the meeting, I'd joined the group and suggested a nice coffee shop for their next meeting.

Excited as I was from the interaction and ready to start the book for next month, stopping by the corner market to pick up a few things for the rest of the week almost slipped my mind. Seeing an advertisement for milk on the billboard suddenly reminded me to stop at the market only three blocks away. I walked through the automatic doors, got a shopping cart, then veered to the left, avoiding eye contact with a conservatively dressed gentleman standing inside the doorway.

As I was following my usual shopping routine, a list wasn't necessary. I first looked at the selection of fresh vegetables to my left and chose from an assortment of lettuces, cucumbers, celery, and bell peppers. My taste buds were brought to life by the smell of fresh fruit along the back wall of the store. The light reflected bright yellows, reds, and oranges off the mirrors behind the produce displays. I took my time making the perfect selection, shifting, plucking, thumping, and squeezing various fruits. When I turned to put my choices in the basket, the unfamiliar gentleman was there. His crisp starched jeans, white pullover shirt, and caramel blazer accentuated his strong facial features and his dark flawless skin. At first glance he appeared to be about five feet eleven. He stood tall with broad shoulders and long, lean legs. He was obviously older than me, in his late thirties I assumed. "Hello. How are you doing today?"

"Hello," I said, but he was still no comparison to Rowan. In canned goods, there he stood. On the sugar and flour aisle he passed by. I passed him on every other aisle of the store. It soon became obvious it wasn't a mistake.

He used my food choice to initiate a conversation. "You have a very healthy choice of foods in your basket. Apples, pears, celery, squash . . . are you a vegetarian? I've been trying for years to modify my diet. Maybe you can give me some pointers on disciplining myself to maintain such a strict diet. That is, only if your husband doesn't mind." He slyly observed my left ring finger for indications of a husband or fiancé.

"Yes, I'm a vegetarian," I responded nonchalantly as I turned around to leave.

"So does that mean you'll talk to me about starting a healthy diet?"

"I'm sorry, but I'm not—"

"Excuse me please." The ringing of his cell phone interrupted my response to his question. The concerned look on his face convinced me the subject of the conversation was serious and took precedence over the details of my diet. Still on the phone, he lifted his hand to excuse himself, handed me a business card, then rushed toward the exit. I glanced at the logo, inquisitively read his name and title, slightly impressed to see he was a physician at the neighborhood clinic. Contemplating whether to discard it or not I held the card in my hand a few seconds longer before placing it in my pocket.

CHAPTER 16

The mystery of a woman is inside the man;
above his heart . . . at the touch of his hand.

The guy exercising next to me left before I finished my last set. I don't know what in the hell possessed me to compete on the bench press with him. He had me by thirty-five pounds; I felt obligated to keep up but soon found out I wasn't the man I used to be. Gasping for breath, I covered my face with my towel to wipe the sweat.

"Yeah?" I spoke through my towel in response to the tap on my shoulder. I forgot how possessive gym rats were and was sure someone wanted me off the equipment. Guessing I didn't move fast enough, the person tapped me on the shoulder again. Before looking up to respond, I removed the towel from my face. Instead of a man standing behind me, there was a gorgeous, well-defined woman; five feet five inches tall, 120 pounds all in the right places.

"Excuse me . . . are you done with this bench?"

"Ahh . . . yeah . . . as a matter of fact I just finished." I stood up, moved to the side, and continued to wipe my face and neck. She sat down, wrapped her towel around her neck, and put on her workout gloves.

"Enjoy your workout." I took a final glance, picked up my bottled water, and turned to walk away.

"Are you in a hurry?" she said innocently while placing her hands behind her on the bench and leaning back.

"I have a few minutes." Hell, I hesitated, knowing I didn't have anything to do all day.

"Do you mind spotting me a couple of sets? My partner never showed up." She looked up at me as she tightened the velcro closures around her wrists.

"I don't mind." I threw my towel over my shoulder, looked at her small frame, and removed the heavy weights from the bar but leaving ten pounds on both sides. She positioned herself and did two sets of twelve reps.

"Thanks for your help." She sat up, shook her arms out, and wiped her forehead; I didn't see a drop of sweat.

"Yeah . . . sure." Ready to leave I grabbed my water and looked at my watch to check the time.

"By the way, my name is Lynn and your name is . . . ?" She batted her eyelashes and tightened her abs as she spoke.

"Rowan . . ."

"Well, Rowan, it was a pleasure having you stand over . . . I mean spot me." She stood up and moved closer to me. Hardly impressed I took a step back.

"Anytime . . ." I knew exactly what she meant. As I turned to walk away she spoke again.

"Hey, before you leave I have a confession to make. I wasn't waiting on my partner. I noticed you from my treadmill on the other side of the room." With a cunning smile she moved her eyes up and down my body.

"So you did, huh?"

"Yes, I did. I'm not letting you leave without my telephone number." Her comment was very matter-of-fact as she rolled her head.

"Lynn, what if I'm married?" I stepped back and folded my arms across my chest.

"You're not wearing a ring and I don't see any tan lines on your ring finger." She seductively leaned against the bench and pointed at my finger. The gym atmosphere hadn't changed at all. What happened to all of the people really trying to lose ten or twenty pounds?

"Take my number and give me a call." She reached into her fanny pack and pulled out a business card. She was a real estate agent. "I hope to see you in here again."

I took it and waved good-bye. I looked at her card, chuckled to myself, and put it in my pocket as I walked toward the locker room.

Before I opened the locker to get my gym bag and clothes, my phone started to ring. I cussed when I went three numbers past my combination and had to start over again. I scrambled to answer it before my voice mail picked up.

"Hello."

"If this is a bad time I can call you back. You sound out of breath."

"Oh no, I'm at the gym." It was Maria. I glanced over and laughed when the guy bench pressing next to me walked by. "I tried to compete with a guy ten years younger than me. He kicked my butt," I confessed, slightly embarrassed. "Maria, are you okay?" Her silence behind my humor was unusual.

"The detectives handling my case contacted me about five minutes ago."

"Well, did they have an update on your case?"

"Yes, they've made an arrest."

"His arrest should be closure and allow you to move on with your life." Concerned and not wanting to say the wrong thing, I paused to let her respond and to gauge how she was feeling.

"Yeah, I could only hope it would be that easy. They'll be coming by in about an hour to talk with me."

I slumped in my shoulders when I heard a deep sigh. "Would you like for me to come over?"

"If you're not busy I'd really appreciate it."

"I need to shower and change clothes. I can make it to your house within forty minutes if not sooner."

"Rowan, thanks. Your support means so much to me." She sounded relieved.

"Hey, just remember I'm here for you." I closed my phone, thinking she shouldn't deal with her situation alone. I tried to imagine how she felt but I couldn't.

When I got inside my truck and started to drive, the love I felt for Maria hit me like a ton of bricks. Telling her how I felt became imperative even though the circumstances weren't ideal. I'd already blown several opportunities to confess: my second visit in the hospital, the hospital cafeteria, definitely after her aunt's funeral. I'd be damned if I would miss another one; I vowed the day wouldn't end until we talked. When I pulled into Maria's driveway, through opened curtains I could see her standing in the window with a solemn facial expression. She wasn't smiling or frowning when she opened the door and motioned with her hand for me to come in.

"Hi."

"Hey, I'm glad I arrived first," I responded before giving her an assuring hug.

"I'm thankful you were able to come over. I thought about calling Juanita, a lady from my group session, but changed my mind."

I watched as she locked the door, then turned slowly and folded her arms in front of her. As though confirming her thought she shook her head and leaned against the door frame. The fact that she called me before a girlfriend showed a potential trust factor.

"Would you like something to drink?"

"No, thank you."

In silence we sat down on the couch together and stared at the television but completely ignored the sitcom. She tapped her foot nervously as she watched the front door. Fifteen minutes later, I was still debating whether or not I should talk to her. Maybe, knowing how I felt would strengthen her. She needed to know I'd broken up with Vickie, had moved on, and my feelings for her were sincere.

"Maria." I turned her face toward me, then gently cupped her hands in mine. I didn't have a dramatic presentation with a dozen roses and a live band, only my openness and honesty. "I know the circumstances were unfortunate when we met, but I—" The doorbell rang, interrupting me. Wanting but unable to complete my thoughts, I rubbed her hand, placed it on her lap, then rose to answer the door, prepared to console Maria as her assailant was revealed.

"I'm Detective Peter Sturges and this is my partner Detective Renee Madison. Maria McCory, please." Both detectives showed their identification.

"I'm Rowan Miller, a very close friend. Please come in." I stepped back as Maria stood to greet them and offered them a seat.

"Ms. McCory, hi, thanks for letting us come by on such short notice." They stepped forward to shake her hand while I moved to take my place by her side.

"You look well," Detective Madison said before having a seat. Detective Sturges stood in the small space between the chair and the wall.

"Well, yes . . . considering the circumstances and all." Maria smiled as she nodded.

"Your case had become top priority. Putting offenders behind bars is our job and we take it very seriously." He rubbed the back of his neck before putting his hand in his pocket.

"Knowing that is reassuring. With limited details, I was certain my case would take some time." Maria clasped her hands together and rubbed them gently.

"One detail you gave us may have been insignificant to you, but it eventually led us to him."

"What was that?"

"When you gave us the make and model of the car, you mentioned there was a dent. When we left we placed calls to all of the local body shops within a one-hundred-mile radius. At first, we found nothing." Detective Sturges spoke with his hands as he moved from behind the chair. "About a week ago a fella called us about a car in the repair shop fitting our description, said the shop owner wouldn't report the dent, didn't want to get involved. When his boss left he waited on us at the shop."

"Really . . . what did you find?" I leaned closer to Maria and held her trembling hands.

"It was a dead ringer. We guessed after several months that scum figured we'd given up on catching him. So he finally took his car into the body shop for repairs. We got the license, which was identical to the first letters you gave us. Then we went from there."

"From the injuries you sustained, minute traces of dried blood and skin were left on the door handle, dashboard, and steering wheel of his car. We have one of the best forensics laboratories in the United States. With samples from the rape kit, PCR testing proved the blood was yours."

Excited, Maria sat on the edge of her chair as Detective Madison spoke.

"DNA helped us get him hands down. I wish we'd gotten him sooner." Detective Madison nodded her head in agreement to Detective Sturges's frank statement.

"Now that you have sufficient evidence, what will be done to guarantee a proper indictment and arrest?" Her brow turned into a frown before she blinked her eyes, then looked down at her folded hands.

"We'll need you to come into the station and make a positive identification."

"Sure, no problem." She placed her hand on my knee, then turned to look at me. "Rowan, do you mind going with me?"

"No doubt, Maria." I grasped her hand, then firmly embraced her around the shoulder.

"The two of you can follow us if you like," Detective Madison said before excusing herself and removing her cell phone from her hip to make a call.

Vaguely, I could hear her say, "Yeah . . . she's coming in."

"Thanks. We will."

Maria was nervous and tense, judging by her facial expression. As she walked toward the car her nerves were unraveling.

"You have my support. I'm sure everything will be okay."

"Is my uneasiness that obvious?"

"Maria, I'm here. We'll get through this together. You can trust that I'm not going anywhere." I stopped her, turned her face toward me, then hugged her tightly to confirm my statement.

"Thank you. That gives me peace."

Maria didn't say two words as I drove; I played my Maxwell CD to break the silence, then reminded her not to worry. We turned into the parking lot and parked beside the detectives. They got out of their car and waited on us.

"Maria, we know you're skeptical but everything will be okay. The worst part is almost over."

Maria parted her lips like she wanted to ask the detectives a question but didn't know what to ask. We followed them inside the old brick building, down a long hallway and through two double glass doors, into a small room with gray walls. They asked Maria to have a seat in front of a two-way mirror. She turned to look at me, then reluctantly faced the mirror. I stood behind her and placed a hand on each shoulder for support.

"Before we let them in, we want to assure you that none of these guys will be able to see you. We are going to have your friend go into the room for a demonstration." Detective

Madison nodded toward the door, asked me to go on the other side and wave back when I saw Maria wave. After a minute or so the detectives' voice came over the intercom asking me to come back inside.

"Rowan, what did you see?" Sturges asked.

I assumed he was a habitual smoker when he pulled a toothpick out of his pocket and stuck it in his mouth.

"Nothing at all, not even a shadow or silhouette."

Maria seemed confident as she told them she was ready.

"All right, boss, let'm in."

Everyone in the room watched the door on the other side open as four guys walked in. Initially, I wasn't looking at the suspects but the expression on Maria's face when they turned around. "That's him, the man on the far right."

I looked up and damn near passed out. *Oh, hell no.* It was Josh.

"Ms. McCory, are you certain?" With a raised eyebrow, Detective Madison looked at Detective Sturges.

"Yes, I'm positive. It's him. Never in a million years will I forget those glaring blue eyes."

I was there to support Maria. In turn I needed support my damn self. How in the hell could this be? Josh, a rapist? I looked at her as she confirmed his identity again with a head nod. The small room suddenly got very hot and smaller.

"Rowan, are you okay?" Maria asked, looking up at me.

Quickly, I pulled myself together and answered, "Ahh . . . yeah . . . sure, I'm fine." I couldn't believe it; Josh was in the lineup. I stepped back, took a deep breath, looked at Maria, then looked at his face.

"Ms. McCory, thanks for your cooperation. That's all we need from you today. You'll be hearing from us again in a few days."

In no way could my facial expression or body language show my emotions as I helped Maria stand up and put on her coat. Before leaving the room, I turned back to stare at Josh again to confirm without a doubt it was him. I wanted to lose it but remembered Maria desperately needed me.

"The front door is this way."

I followed Maria down the hallway and out the door. When we got to the truck, I walked around to the passenger's side and stood there still dumbfounded.

"Rowan, are you going to unlock the door?"

"Yeah, it was just hard for me to look at him knowing what he'd done to you. And if it was hard for me, I can only imagine how you must have felt."

She was silent for a moment, wrapping her arms around herself and looking into the distance. "I definitely feel better knowing that he's behind bars . . . and you being here with me made it a lot less difficult."

I saw true appreciation in her eyes as one corner of her lips turned upward into a half smile. I gently pulled her into my chest, giving her a comforting embrace while I rested my chin on top of her head. As I held her, she released a heavy sigh that seemed to take months of tension away with it. She sniffed as a few silent tears slid down her face and moistened my shirt. My mind raced with various thoughts, including the way I had found her on the bathroom floor. Before I could come up with a solid plan to get revenge on Josh, Maria stepped back, letting me know that her tension had been eased. With my thumb, I smudged her last tear away and lifted her chin to look into her eyes. I wanted to say something, but I knew the right words were too far away for me to make an attempt of saying them. The more I looked, the more I loved her and hated Josh. Knowing it was my best friend shed a different light on the situation, creating an obstacle I'd have to deal with or completely dismiss. Could I love her unconditionally, knowing the truth? With this thought on my mind we rode in awkward silence back to her home.

"Rowan, thanks a million for going with me to the station."

"Ahh . . . it was no problem at all . . . that's what friends are for, right?"

"Would you like to come inside, have a cup of coffee or a soda?" She sounded relieved, yet I was overwhelmed.

"Hmmm . . . no . . . thanks." I was going to head straight to the jailhouse to pay Mr. Stephenson a visit until I glanced up and saw the disappointed look in Maria's eyes. I had to remember that this wasn't about me; I needed to be there for her.

"You know what? I think I will stay for coffee."

"Thanks, I appreciate you staying."

"No problem at all." For the sake of my sanity and our friendship I pulled myself together and went inside.

"Knowing he's behind bars will help me rest much better at night."

I sat down at the kitchen table and shuffled the salt and pepper shakers, putting forth every effort to remain supportive.

"Identifying him in the lineup wasn't difficult at all. There were certain features, like his eyes, I could never forget."

My eyes followed her as she walked to the sink, washed her hands, then reached into the cabinet beside the stove to get the coffee.

"Both detectives seemed very committed to your case, leaving me with no doubts they're going to pursue him aggressively."

She set a cup of coffee on the table, then braced herself before speaking again.

"You being there meant a lot to me. I didn't want to be alone."

I was sure she noticed the blank stare as I said nothing but placed my hands on top of hers. I took two sips of coffee, then apologized to Maria before telling her I had another obligation. Together we walked down the hallway; she hugged me and thanked me again. Unaware how long I could contain myself in front of her, without looking back I walked briskly to the truck and got in.

Unable to maintain my composure any longer, I left Maria's house like a bat out of hell. Just that fast, my entire perspective on everything had been changed. No wonder his wife accused him of cheating. Maybe that would explain why she was a freak her damn self. Her husband took advantage of innocent women. Thinking about it pissed me off. I was on the interstate and punched the gas harder the more I thought about it. I weaved in and out of traffic, slammed on brakes when I almost ran into the back of a pickup truck, and cussed and flipped off anybody who slowed me down. Approaching my exit, I hurled my truck across three lanes to get off the interstate.

Literally on two wheels, I turned into the parking lot and parked in a spot reserved for employees only. I was there on official business and didn't give a rat's ass. The doors vibrated when they slammed against the wall. I showed my identification and signed in as I told the officer whom I was there to see. A guard led me into a large room with tables and told me I could have a seat while I waited. To hell with a seat, I was too damned mad to sit down. I paced back and forth, watching and waiting for Josh to come in.

When the door opened, I folded my arms, completely beside myself with anger. He walked toward me with his arms extended for a hug. I held my hands up and told him to stop.

"Hey, man, I owe you a huge apology. Jana told me everything."

"I didn't come here for a damn apology." He had assaulted and raped the woman of my dreams. What made him think I was there to hear an apology about his low-class-ass wife? "Josh, how in the hell could you do it, man?"

"I said I was sorry. If it makes you feel any better we're separated and I'm filing for a divorce."

"Man, I don't give a damn about Jana, I'm talking about the innocent woman you raped."

"Those allegations against me are false, I swear, man. It's not true, some black woman said I invaded her home and raped her. Can you believe that? Hopefully my lawyer will have me out of here in a few days." As though swearing on a Bible, he held his right hand up and gestured with the other. He was more delirious than I was.

"You're a liar." Maria didn't just make Josh up.

"How long have you known me? You know I'm not a rapist. You know how those people are."

When he said that I bum-rushed his punk ass. "Those people? What in the hell do you mean, those people? Did you forget I'm one of those people?"

"Rowan, what the hell?" He was caught off guard by a blow to his stomach.

"That 'people' you're talking about is Maria."

"I don't know a Maria."

"I know you don't, you low-down son of a bitch." Three security guards came from the corners of the room and pulled me off him. I got one last punch in before I let him go. I struggled to get free of the guard who'd grabbed me from behind, picked up a chair, and hurled it across the room. I wasn't sorry at all when it caught him squarely on the jaw.

"Shit, Rowan, you hit me with that damn chair."

"And you raped the woman that I love. You better be glad all I could get was a chair!"

"Sir, you have to leave the premises immediately!"

"Yeah . . . I'm leaving! I hope your ass rots behind bars," I spat.

"Sir, we need you to leave right now." Two security guards, one on each side of me, lifted me by the arms and escorted me from the room.

"Josh, you'll see what it feels like to be somebody's bitch. Just wait! You're gonna get yours."

CHAPTER 17

Have our spirits journeyed into the future?
Have our souls forgotten the hurt of the past?

I was disappointed that I hadn't heard back from Rowan in two weeks. At the same time I concluded that I should be grateful I hadn't gotten too emotionally tied up, only to be let down. I couldn't ignore the fact that I knew he was in a relationship. He'd been honest and told me that right up front. When I panicked like a damsel in distress he rushed to my rescue. Maybe I misinterpreted his actions and assumed he wanted more than a platonic friendship. I secretly wished the night he stayed over was an indication he was no longer involved. Again, the day I identified my attacker he responded without hesitation. Suddenly, his demeanor changed and he left abruptly. Reluctantly, I tucked him away in a corner of my mind and focused on getting myself together.

Resolving a last-minute problem at work, I was delayed twenty minutes and late for my final counseling session at the university. Since their fifteen-minute grace period had already been exceeded, I called the receptionist from my cell phone to reschedule.

"Campus Counseling Services, how may I direct your call?"

"This is Maria McCory. I had a five-thirty appointment and was delayed due to last-minute work issues. Can Dr. Irving still see me today?"

"Ms. McCory, let me check Dr. Irving's appointments. Hold please." Until she returned I listened to the soothing music. "Ms. McCory, still there?"

"Yes." Ready to reschedule, I readjusted my headpiece.

"Dr. Irving said he can still see you today. You were his last scheduled appointment."

"Great, I'll be there in fifteen minutes." While maintaining a safe speed and respecting fellow drivers, I arrived on campus twelve minutes later. There was no need to cause an accident during evening traffic; I was already late. Before getting out of the car I thought it was necessary to check my bag, making sure it contained all of the books for my evening class. When the sound of a siren echoed from behind, resisting the temptation to look over my shoulder seemed difficult. *Don't be ridiculous, it's not Rowan,* I thought to myself before locking my doors and following the long walkway that led to the building.

Dr. Irving's receptionist told me he was waiting as she prepared to leave. I knocked on the door and opened it when he said, "Come in." He leaned back in his large leather chair, placed his fingertips together, and told me to have a seat.

"Ms. McCory, according to my records, this is our final session together."

"Yes, it most certainly is." Feeling a sense of accomplishment, I clasped my hands together and placed them on my lap. Preparing to take notes, he turned to a blank page in his legal pad, then asked my opinion about my last assignment.

"Afraid society would stereotype me, I resolved within myself to keep the rape a secret and move on with my life.

Other than the scar, there were no visible signs. Physically, I looked like everyone else. Several months later the death of my aunt Bethany propelled me into an emotional tailspin, forcing me to accept the fact that I needed professional guidance."

"Well . . . Ms. McCory, would you like to expound?" He leaned back in his chair, lightly pressed his ink pen to his chin, and waited for me to continue.

"Originally, I didn't see how listing and categorizing my previous hurt or pain would benefit me at all. In comparison to my experiences the exercise seemed menial, offering no valid benefits or consolation. Creating a list, enumerating the contents, then throwing it away wasn't how I visualized my healing. However, one of the books you suggested highly recommended the same exercise, and the content was very interesting. I read the book in its entirety, then completed the task thinking it could only help me sort through issues that hindered me." Then I listened perceptively to his summary.

"I'm very pleased. Maria, half of the battle has been won, the rest is up to you. According to my documentation you've progressed and I don't see the need to recommend additional sessions." Prior to ending he made a final recommendation: using a journal as a tool to candidly express my deepest emotions. He shook my hand and wished me the best of luck. I hurried to the bookstore to make my purchase—a blank journal to use as an outlet. As I walked across campus to my car, I revisited each session and concluded they did promote healing.

Relieved to be home, I couldn't wait to sit down, kick off my pumps, and massage my feet. I stretched out, making myself comfortable in the recliner, then reached for the remote. *Soul Food* was a repeat; I'd already seen the episode where Teri confided in a psychologist for her panic attacks. Disappointed there was nothing else on that interested me, I turned the television off, decided on listening to my favorite Grover Washington CD and taking a hot bath. I took a final glance around the room, turned off the light, and went into my bedroom to relax and take a hot bath. Feeling myself drift to sleep in the tub, I pulled myself from the warm water, slipped into a silk gown, and cuddled beneath my covers to read a good book but reached for my new journal instead and flipped through the blank pages. Not really in the mood to write, I closed it and studied the cover. The image of the woman reaching upward seemed to visually represent one who'd overcome and was celebrating her freedom. Now inspired and motivated, I turned to the first blank page and began to write.

15 April

In spite of the blind twists and turns my life has taken after the rape, I'm on a better path. The same journey, only another path. Along the way I'm learning valuable lessons about myself.

Numerous times I questioned the negative occurrences in my life. Making a proclamation to no longer be a slave to my past, I took the time to search deep within myself. In retaliation to deep hurt and pain, my freedom would be openly confessed as I loved and admired myself.

I am a rose, a black rose . . . its mystery to yet unfold.

Others have yet to understand me . . . they question my strength and integrity.

No other flower compares to me; I am a rose, a black rose, a mystery.

I am a rose, a black rose . . . the beauty is in my petal; the strength is in my stem.

No other flower possesses my beauty and strength.

I am a rose, a black rose, a mystery.

I am a rose, a black rose . . . no one knows the field
where I grow; it is too
    mysterious, yet it is spiritual.
No other flower compares to me; I am a rose, a
black rose, a mystery.

I ended my thoughts with a prayer of thanksgiving and supplication, closed my journal, laid it on the nightstand, then tucked myself tightly between my sheets.

MARIA

The sun shown brightly through the bedroom window and directly into my eyes, making it impossible to sleep any longer, so I sat up, slipped on a pair of jeans and a T-shirt, and went into the kitchen for a cup of hot tea. The warmth of the cup soothed my hands as I looked out across the property and reflected on the day before. Completing the counseling session was the end of one chapter and journaling had become the beginning of a new one. In addition to peer support received from my weekly counseling sessions my options to heal had broadened. With the proper resources, one day at a time, hurt and pain could be overcome.

Our postman delivered the mail at the same time every day; I walked outside and to the end of the driveway to receive it. Between work and classes I hadn't seen him in several weeks.

"Maria, good morning."

"Good morning, Mr. Taylor. How are you?"

"Doing well."

"I'm glad to hear that."

"Yeah, you know I miss seeing that ole gal walkin' in the morning. She'd always stop and talk to me." He used his hand to shield his eyes from the morning sun.

"I know. She loved to talk."

"Yeah, and I loved every second of it." He thumbed through the mail, rechecked himself, making certain it belonged to me.

"So, is all going well with you and yours?"

"Yes, I won't complain." At the same time we both looked toward the house and smiled, reminiscing about Aunt Bethany.

"All right, Maria, I won't keep you any longer. Gotta finish my rounds. Have a good day now."

"I will. Be careful." I looked through the small stack of weekly sales papers and bills he'd handed me. As I walked toward the house I opened an envelope from the hospital, apparently an unpaid bill for services provided to Aunt Bethany. I knew to investigate the extensive list of services and charges before picking up an ink pen to write a check. The hospital suggested I call the insurance company. The insurance company suggested I call the hospital. Well, in both instances, customer service had me on hold for what seemed like an eternity. I was too impatient to wait any longer so I ended the call.

The gentleman I'd met at the corner store was a physician; maybe he could recommend someone to explain the charges on the bill before I paid it. I found his business card, dialed the telephone number, and was somewhat surprised, imagining how busy his day could have been, when his receptionist immediately transferred me.

"Dr. Simmons speaking."

"Good morning, this is Maria McCory. I met you a few weeks ago at the market." I looked at his card, rubbed my fingers over the raised letters, then placed it on the table.

"Yes, I remember."

"I understand you're a physician, not a billing clerk, but I have a concern."

He laughed. "Well, some days I'm both. How can I help you?"

"I received a hospital bill for my aunt who is now deceased. Before I pay it I need some of the charges and services explained. I tried calling both the insurance company and the hospital to no avail. Do you have anyone on your staff who could help me sort through it?"

"Sure, it's not a problem at all. Someone in billing will be more than happy to review the charges. Actually, the office lunch hour would probably be a good time. We're closed from noon until one o'clock."

"Thank you. I'll be there before one o'clock. I really appreciate it."

When I entered the office I empathized with a mother as she talked to one child and rocked the other. Their little noses were running and she had dark circles around her bloodshot eyes. The contents of her diaper bag were dumped out in the chair beside her. She seemed distraught so I offered to assist and repacked her diaper bag. Temporarily organized, she put the bag on her shoulder, grabbed the toddler's hand, and said thanks as she maneuvered through the exit door. Dr. Simmons saw me when he passed by the window at the clerical desk and waved me to the back. I walked toward him and admired how professional he looked dressed in dark pants, white shirt, and lab coat.

He was cordial and introduced me to a billing clerk, who after one telephone call and a few questions clarified everything. I thanked her for the assistance and wanted to thank Dr. Simmons for the professional resource and let him know everything had been resolved. From her desk I followed the hallway to the end; his office was the last door on the right. His door was open but I apologized when realizing I'd interrupted his lunch.

"Maria, come in." I walked in and had a seat in one of two chairs directly in front of his desk. "My next scheduled appointment isn't until one thirty." It was one o'clock, giving us a few minutes to talk.

"Did all go well?" He covered his lunch and moved it to one side.

"Ms. Robinson was great and explained that the insurance company had several unclaimed files." Grateful the entire bill wasn't my responsibility, I placed my hand on my chest.

"I can't blame you, medical billing can be difficult to decipher."

"Not meaning to disrespect your profession but without health insurance, care is unaffordable."

He frowned and nodded his head in agreement. "Would you like to share lunch with me? Rita bought enough food for two."

"No, thank you, but I appreciate the offer."

"Would you consider Friday afternoon?"

"I'll consider it once we become better acquainted. We only met a few weeks ago."

"You have my card. Getting to know me is possible," he said while sitting forward and pointing at the business cards on his desk.

"I'm flattered, but no, thank you. I will think about communicating by telephone first." I picked up a business card, wrote my number on the back, and placed it on his desk before leaving.

During the next two weeks I received several telephone calls from him. Our brief conversations were mostly questions about my day, making him seem kind and genuinely concerned. Spending time with him could be a way to momentarily take my mind off Rowan. I finally agreed to lunch and an early movie.

Like having any first date, we spent the majority of the evening asking and answering questions. "Tell me something interesting about Maria. Are your parents natives of Louisiana?"

"Both of my parents were born in New Orleans."

"Do they live here now?"

"Yes, they've never lived anywhere else."

"Great, I'd really like to meet them. I'm sure they wouldn't mind showing off some off your old elementary school pictures."

"Well, I don't think that's possible. As a child I lived with my father's aunt." He listened patiently as I told him about my aunt Bethany and uncle Brewster, and honored my non-verbal request not to talk about my mother or father. He read my facial expressions and didn't press for answers to questions that made me uncomfortable.

"Dhilan, we don't want to spend the entire afternoon talking about me. Tell me about yourself. I'm sure your childhood was very interesting."

"I was the younger of two boys and reared in a small town outside of New Orleans. My father was a surgeon, which afforded my family a very secure lifestyle."

"So, tell me, do the children of physicians have reputations like those of preachers?"

He laughed before answering my question. "I'm sure we were considered spoiled, but my father managed to equip us with good basic fundamentals."

They attended private schools and knew the importance of a quality education at a young age. In the midst of a hectic schedule and long hours at the hospital their father taught them by precept and example. He never wanted them to take their lifestyle for granted and assume achieving their goals would be easy.

After a great evening, we mutually decided to end our date when he mentioned several early morning appointments. He was chivalrous and walked me to the front door.

With a hug and a noncommittal kiss on the cheek and in no way ready for what the look in his eyes insinuated, I thanked him and went inside. I shut the door behind me, leaned against it, and listened while his car drove away, then sat down on the couch to slip off my shoes. While I'd had a nice time, I realized it was too soon for a relationship of any sort.

MARIA

"Dhilan, what are you doing here?" I'd briefly mentioned my place of employment to him, and to my surprise he showed up during the busiest hour of my day, stood patiently in line, and smiled as he advanced, finally becoming my next customer. I tried to act irritated that he'd shown up unannounced, but his finesse made me smile instead. "We're swamped. It will be at least twenty minutes before I can take a break." I could sense my peers stealing glances.

"I'll wait," he responded nonchalantly before moving to the side and having a seat in the small lobby.

Thirty-five minutes later I joined him in the lobby during my break. He turned slightly toward me and smiled as I sat down beside him.

"Maria, I've called you several times. Why haven't you returned my telephone calls?"

I wasn't ready to become emotionally involved and had maintained limited contact for the sake of a friendship, but more so tried to stay to myself.

"My work schedule has been keeping me very busy." Wanting to avoid the question altogether, I offered him a cup of coffee. He only stared, sensing that I was making an excuse, and waited for me to answer a second time. "My course schedule is hectic," I said more adamantly. He looked at his watch and turned to look me in the eyes.

"Maria . . . nothing would mean more to me than for us to

become better acquainted. But I can't do it alone. I need your help in the process. Now that I know you're doing well, call me when you're available." Not allowing time for a response, he stood and walked away.

I picked up a magazine while blatantly ignoring the stares and whispers of my coworkers. Still surprised by his visit, I turned my head toward the window and pretended to read.

No one said a word as I walked behind the counter, removed the small partition, and waited on the next customer. A man moved forward and set twelve shoe boxes full of loose change on the counter. Convinced it would take me the remainder of my shift to feed it through the counter, I paced myself accordingly. Six hundred eighty-five dollars and ten cents later he was gone, two minutes before my shift ended.

CHAPTER 18

The mystery of a woman resides in her soul;
its value can't be measured in platinum or gold.

While walking across campus I thought how my friendship with Dhilan had developed during the past month. His
surprise visit at the bank was followed by the delivery of a
fresh mixed floral bouquet and telephone calls. My attempts
to be rude and continuously avoid him seemed immature.
Though I wasn't ready for an intimate relationship, ignoring
my desire for adult male conversation seemed unrealistic.
Reasoning no harm could be done, I chatted with him on the
telephone.

Realizing I'd put unnecessary pressure on myself, I decided casual dating seemed harmless. With him a simple
walk in the park became an unforgettable adventure, making
it a challenge to ignore occasional thoughts of Rowan that
entered my mind. Even though I was a native of Louisiana
he shed a different light on the abstract culture and rich her-
itage that surrounded us.

My cell phone started to ring so I reached inside my
purse to answer. "Hello."

"Hi, beautiful."

"Dhilan, hi." As though someone else were looking I covered my mouth to hide my smile.

"Do you have plans for the weekend?"

"Well . . . none other than studying for a huge exam on Monday."

"Do you think you could pencil me in for tomorrow evening?"

"Maybe for a couple of hours. I need the entire weekend to study." Did I really believe our date would only last two hours? Surely not.

"Okay, I can respect that. Wear something casual. You need to be very comfortable."

I smiled as I looked at my telephone, closed it, and put it into my purse.

With comfort in mind I looked for something to wear. It was late September so I decided on an airy light blue linen sundress and sandals. I removed the dress from the closet, spread it over my bed, and took a shower. As I wrapped myself in a towel and smoothed on some scented lotion, I tried to imagine what the evening would bring. What more could we do? I started singing a few verses of Alicia Keys's "If I Ain't Got You" as I slipped into my dress and slid my feet into my shoes. My doorbell rang promptly at six o'clock. Excited, I danced to the front door, but quickly checked my hair and makeup before opening it and inviting him inside.

"Good evening, beautiful." He was holding a picnic basket, flowers, and a bottle of wine. "Are you ready for our date?" He brushed past me as he smiled. "I thought you would enjoy a picnic beneath the oak tree in the backyard. Come now, my sweet. I have everything we need in the basket."

With confidence, he led the way up the hallway into the kitchen and to the back door; I followed. There were no questions to ask; his plan was in motion. He extended his left hand as he held the door with his right hand. Together we walked down the steps leading to the backyard. He looked around to find the perfect spot and put his basket on the ground. I watched as he carefully spread the blanket and asked me to sit down.

"Maria, I want this evening to be very special." He took out two place settings, fresh vegetables, fruit, and a variety of wine cheeses. He poured me a glass of wine, then fed me bit by bit until I was satisfied.

"Take your shoes off." He removed a lightly scented oil from the basket and gently massaged each foot. The enjoyment was definitely in the moment. "Turn around, let me finish my massage." With firm circular motions he started at my temples, and then moved to my neck and shoulders.

Although I started to relax, I couldn't let my guard down.

"Dhilan, please stop." I shrugged my shoulders and quickly moved away from him.

"What is it? Am I hurting you? I can be very heavy-handed sometimes." Oblivious, he looked down at his hands and rubbed them together.

"No, you aren't hurting me."

"Then what is it?" He leaned back on the palms of his hands and positioned himself to listen.

I could only respond to his puzzled stare with the truth.

"I . . . can't . . . I'm not comfortable . . ."

He never questioned my scar, making the rape a topic never discussed.

"Oh . . . I'm sorry. Is it the outdoor picnic?" He looked around, then placed his hand on top of mine.

With regrets I had known this time would come. "No . . . Dhilan. Intimate touches still make me pretty uncomfortable."

Dhilan paused, then removed his hand.

"I was the victim of a horrible crime." I inhaled as I assumed our romantic date would be over.

"I had no idea. Please accept my apology. It was never my intent to make you feel uncomfortable." He looked at me, then stared at the oak tree as he spoke. His eyes moved back and forth across the property as he searched for something to say.

"I'm sure you didn't, but I have several issues to overcome before I'll become intimate with a man." Each week at the end of the session we repeated our affirmations. We affirmed to forgive our offender and eventually move on. But healing was a process that couldn't be taken lightly. Dhilan seemed to be nice, but for me intimacy wasn't going to be that easy. "If I'm ever able to be intimate with a man."

My last comment seemed to bewilder him. He stood up and walked toward the oak tree. Knowing my revelation was a shock, I couldn't blame him. Just like Rowan he had a decision to make. He turned around and asked me to join him. I stood up, smoothed the back of my dress, and walked toward him. He reached for my hand.

"Maria, please don't say that . . . I care for you. If there's a session available for companions or close friends I can come with you. Better yet, I have an excellent colleague who'd be more than happy to counsel us privately. We can make it through this as partners . . . a team. I respect your feelings enough to wait . . . I promise."

Did he understand the implications of his promise? I was speechless. While I didn't doubt the sincerity of his statement, I couldn't reciprocate the feeling. I knew he expected a response from me. I didn't have one to give. He broke the silence as he wrapped his arms around my shoulders, held me to his chest, and rested his chin on my shoulder.

ROWAN

Were my feelings for Maria that strong? Just that quick my mind drifted to the day Maria had identified Josh at the police station. The look on her face was still vivid in my memory. If I wasn't so damned tough I think I would have shed a tear. Time had proven I couldn't ignore Josh's betrayal or my feelings for Maria. He was evil enough to leave a per- manent scar on the side of her face to remind her and anyone she loved. How could it be? I loved her and couldn't deny it from the first time I saw her.

I pulled out a chair from the kitchen table, sat down, and just laid my head on top of my arms. Now what should I do? Should I pick up the telephone, call Maria, and say, "Oh, by the way, that punk that raped you was my best friend. I've known him for years but I never knew he was a per- vert"? No, I couldn't do that, but in order for me to move on, it had to be resolved. I couldn't leave her guessing for- ever why I left and never called or came back. She called me over to support her. What if her friend went and I never found out who did it? What if our relationship got in- volved and I was in the courtroom with her when Josh walked in?

Using my arms for support, I stood up, went inside the bedroom, looked at the telephone, knowing I owed her an explanation. I sat down on the edge of my bed and held my head each time I looked at the telephone. Really wanting to see her and hear her voice, I picked up the phone and just held it. Frustrated, I slammed the phone down. There was no way around this, one way or another she'd soon find out Josh and I were acquainted.

I snatched my cell phone and keys off the nightstand, drove to the corner convenience store, and picked up the first thing I saw on the cooler shelf, a Bud Light. I paid the cashier and didn't wait on a bag. I jumped into my truck, leaned my head back, took a big gulp, then put the can in the cup holder on my console. What next, should I confront Maria with the truth or just ignore it forever? Packing up and leaving town sounded a helluva lot easier. I looked around, put my transmission in reverse, and backed out of the parking spot.

Calling her would be a way to relieve my conscience. I opened my cell phone and dialed her number. She answered on the third ring.

"Hello. Hello . . . anybody there?"

I held the phone and listened to her voice on the other end. "Hello . . . Hello." Dumbfounded, I ended the call, closed my telephone, and made an attempt to throw it out of the window. Lucky for me the window wasn't down and the telephone fell on the passenger seat instead. Driving and driving, I ended up on her street. The first time I rode by her house I assumed she was awake because the light was on in the front room. I circled around the block and drove by her house again; the light was still on.

While I was slowing down, the thought occurred to me to stop and knock on her door. Her car was the only one in the driveway. No, I couldn't, so I stepped on the accelerator and sped away. Feeling uneasy, I made another damn circle around the block, this time stopping in front of her house. Unlike my "best friend" I wasn't a punk, but a man, and a man confronted his problems head-on. I wasn't going to let anything stop me from loving Maria, not even this. I had responded to the call, and I knew she'd been raped. Hesitantly, I opened my door and got out. After seeing my reflection in the door I straightened my shirt and dusted my pants. Now embarrassed by the smell of beer on my breath, I reached inside my console to get a mint.

All the way to the door I mumbled beneath my breath, rehearsing what to say. My finger felt like a brick when I lifted it to ring the doorbell; her footsteps echoed as she walked toward the door. I stuck my hands in my pockets when she looked through the small window and opened the door.

"Rowan, oh my God." She reached out to hug me. With a puzzled look on my face I hugged her back. Why wouldn't she be surprised to see me after I disappeared and never called back? "Wow, I never thought I'd see you again. Come in."

I barely stepped inside her door and stood. She moved me to the side to close it. My hands remained in my pockets while I looked at her, then around the room.

"Rowan, are you okay?"

Speechless and void for words, I took a hand out of my pocket and made a weird up-and-down motion.

Her right eyebrow shot up as she stared. "Have a seat."

I didn't move.

"Tell me, what brings you to my part of town? I haven't seen you in months."

I looked at her radiant smile and shook my head.

"Let me get you something to drink."

"No, Maria, listen."

With a disconcerted look she stood back and folded her arms. "What is it? What's wrong?"

"Everything is wrong. Timing, circumstances, this whole situation is wrong."

"I'm confused. What situation?"

"Maria, look at me and listen." She looked startled when I held her by the arms and pulled her closer to me. "Josh Stephenson was . . . I knew him . . . he was my best friend. I swear I never knew he was capable of rape." I couldn't wait on her response, so I let go of her and bolted out of the front door.

"Rowan . . . Rowan Miller. Rowan, *wait*!"

I didn't stop or turn around when she called my name. Prepared to leave all of my memories behind, I got into my truck and drove away like a coward.

CHAPTER 19

The origin of our beauty; the field where our sweet smell grows; the light source that makes us glow.

Five o'clock Christmas morning the alarm clock buzzed in my ear and irritated the hell out of me. It sounded too much like being at the fire station. I rolled over, smacked the Off button, and kicked one leg from beneath the cover. Feeling like a disoriented five-year-old, I sat up, put both feet on the floor, and staggered into the bathroom to take a shower. I stood beneath the hot water and rubbed my face to wake up. I hadn't been in Texas for Christmas Day in three years. Mom insisted I come home and called every day to make sure my plans hadn't changed.

After my shower I wrapped my towel around my waist and stood in the mirror to shave. Disappointed as hell, I pressed my knuckles into the sink and leaned forward to look in the mirror. *Damn, Josh, damn.* I closed my eyes and shook my head at the thought of not spending Christmas with Maria. This should have been our time, but Josh jacked it all up. *Ro', let it go. The past is now the past.* I couldn't look at myself, and turned my back toward the mirror with my arms folded in front of me. *Nothing stopped you from turning around when she called your name. Not a damn thing.* I turned around to shave; that chapter in my life was over.

I wanted to be comfortable in the truck so I wore my gray Sean John jogging suit and tennis shoes. Making sure nothing was left behind, I double-checked my apartment, set the alarm, then left for my parents' house. I could smell Mom's steaming hot sweet potato pie from Texas. Dinner would be ready when I got there, and Mrs. Charlene Miller wouldn't allow a fork to move before I arrived.

Thinking about "Charlene" made me laugh. My father was about six feet three inches tall and very muscular. Her height, five feet seven inches, was above average for a woman, but she was still much shorter than my father. Ironically, her sons were all above six feet tall. As teenagers we had played with the thought of flexing our manhood, but she let us know who held the lifeline, her, then God. It only took one time for each of us to step out of line.

I remembered when Edward Jr. broke curfew his senior year in high school. Mom and Dad were already pretty liberal, but Junior's dumb ass tested fate two days after his eighteenth birthday. This particular evening Junior was given permission to attend a school dance. I don't know what demon in hell convinced him to stay out past his one o'clock curfew. I couldn't sleep and stayed awake to hear the action.

Junior thought he was slick, but Mom and Dad were slicker. Before he pulled into the driveway I saw the headlights go off. Slowly, he parked the Camaro, then eased out. I moved to the edge of my bed and peeped out my window. Without making a sound he closed the car door, then lightly bumped it shut with his hip. He thought the situation was under control when he took off his shoes outside the front door to walk in. So far so good. I could hear his key turn in the locks, then . . . silence. The door creaked. I started to pray for my stupid brother. *"Dear God, my name is Rowan Miller and I'm eleven years old. If you can hear me please help my big brother Edward Miller Jr. I love him. I know he can be a jerk, excuse me, God, sometimes, but he is like that to everybody. He has done something very stupid and stayed out past his curfew. It's quiet in the living room and I'm very scared. Please, God, don't let my father kill him dead to-night. Amen."* Before I finished my prayer I heard the house come to life. I leaped out of bed and crawled to the edge of the stairs to look through the banister. Mom and Dad had chairs directly in front of the door to block him in.

"Well, Son, good morning."

Mom echoed Dad's "good morning."

"It's one forty-five in the morning, right? Charlene, look at your watch and tell me, what time do you have?"

"My watch says it's one forty-five."

I could see the side of Mom's face and heard the attitude in her voice as she amened my Daddy's comments with her mm-hmms on the sideline.

"I'm human and humans do make mistakes, so correct me if I'm wrong. Your curfew was one o'clock, correct?"

"Yes, sir."

"Do you have an explanation for staying out of my house past your curfew?"

"Ye . . . ye . . . yes, sir. The boys and I hung out in the parking lot after . . ." He was dead meat. His story lacked any creativity. I knew we weren't supposed to lie to our parents, but in the case of life or death a little white lie had to be exceptional. He might have done better if he'd tried the "I left my watch at home and lost track of the time" lie.

"That's the best excuse you got? Oh, so now it's you and the boys? If the boys jumped off the bridge would you jump? If they jogged over hot burning coals would you?"

"No . . . no, sir."

"After tonight, yes, you would! By the way, your name isn't 'the boys.' Your name is Edward Duane Miller Jr. You got that? Give me your car keys."

He was scared as hell, I could see his hands shaking from upstairs when he gave Dad the keys.

"You're grounded for one month. You better cushion those shoes you're holding in your hand. They'll be your primary form of transportation. Do you understand?"

"Y . . . yes, sir."

I jumped up and ran back into the bedroom before they saw me. My prayers were answered when my parents took his privileges and not his life. Junior had crusaded for the Lord since that night and accepted his divine call into the ministry his junior year of college. He's still alive and has two sons of his own now. To this very day talking about it embarrasses the hell out of him. I still think it's very funny.

Tony was lighthearted and fun to be around like my mother. As a child, he loved games and taught all of us how to play his favorite, Monopoly. No one really knew all of the rules, only the ones he told us. It was only a game, so Michael and I never thought to read the rulebook behind him. He cheated his little ass off and won every time we played. His payoff was better than a loose casino slot machine in Vegas.

Michael was the bookworm of the family. After work my Dad would sit in his favorite recliner and read the evening newspaper. Michael, probably three, would pick up anything, move his fingers across the make-believe pages, and pretend to read. His fascination with the written word developed into a keen interest in language arts and history. He graduated from college with a major in history, attended graduate school, then became a history professor. Mom and Dad were especially proud when he spearheaded an adult literacy program two years ago at a local community center.

I didn't realize how long I'd been driving and was about twenty miles from Shreveport. Stopping for gas and coffee would give me a chance to get out of the truck, enjoy some fresh air, and stretch my legs. My job required me to be in and out of a vehicle for the majority of my shift. On my off days I'd rather spend them at home on the couch and not driving.

I was happy to see the large green sign that read DALLAS and called Mom.

"Hello."

"Mom . . ."

"Hey, baby. I'm so glad to hear your voice."

Her tender, loving tone made me smile. "I'll be there in thirty minutes."

"Praise God! I'll see you when you get here."

Hearing Mom's voice was comforting. I could only hope being home would help me clear my head.

The tradition continued. I laughed at the sleigh with the uneven reindeer when I turned into the driveway. Mom still had guts. Daddy would cuss below his breath every year as he climbed the ladder to hang her lights and decorations. It would irritate him more when she would stand back, with her index finger on her chin, and look at everything as if to say something wasn't exactly right. His eyes would dare her to say a word. Whether the reindeer were straight or not, damn it, that was how they would stay.

I could see someone with a black shirt and shiny red pants peeping through the front door. Oh, damn! It was Uncle Buddy with his loud and country ass. My brothers were conservative and wouldn't be caught dead in that outfit. Before I could park my truck and get out, the front door was wide open.

"Hey, baby boy." I was a grown-ass man and he still called me that. "I'm glad to see ya, but the family is hungry. Get on in here so we can eat. Ev'rybody is in the dining room."

Some things would never change. Uncle Buddy, my mother's oldest brother and the family comedian, was always the first to arrive and the last to go home. He was our family's version of Madea's Mr. Brown. He laughed as he gave me two hard pats on the back.

It was so good to see my family around the table, my mother, father, brothers, their wives, my two nephews, Uncle Buddy, and his wife, Joyce. Junior had two children, Edwin and Kenard. Edwin was a sophomore in high school and Kenard was in the sixth grade. The bass in Edwin's voice startled me as he greeted me. "Uncle Rowan, hey."

"Rowan, welcome home." My father nodded as my mother stood up and walked around the table to give me a hug. "I'm so glad to see you. You can get your luggage later."

"Mmmm . . . Mom, you don't know how much I miss your southern cooking." I rubbed my stomach, gave Dad and my brothers a high five, hugged and kissed everyone else, then pulled out a chair to sit down. Mom had cooked smoked turkey, honey-glazed ham, corn bread dressing, collard greens, macaroni and cheese, sweet potato casserole, green beans, fresh rolls, pumpkin pie, and chocolate cake. Eating so much food at one time had to be a sin. I closed my eyes, asked for God's forgiveness, then took it all in.

"Now that Rowan is here we can say grace and eat. Buddy, would you . . . oh Lord, never mind. Junior would you lead the family in prayer, Son?"

My mother made a gesture with her hand and shook her head. We knew better than to let Uncle Buddy pray. Except for funerals and weddings, he never went to church.

"Gracious Heavenly Father, we are gathered to give thanks. Thank you, not for the holiday or the benefits it has to offer, but for the gift of your dear son, Jesus. We would like to thank you for this blessed unit—our family. Thank you, dear God, for divine health and most of all your grace. Bless

the food we are about to receive for the nourishment of our bodies. Amen."

The amens echoed around the table as Junior finished his eloquent delivery. Of course, Uncle Buddy was reaching for the ham before we could open our eyes good. Mom smacked his hand and he snatched two slices anyway.

"So, nephew, how is it in 'NOLA'?" He pinched a piece of his ham and stuck it in his mouth. "I heard the city was something to talk about. Is it true about the naked women swingin' out the windows on Bourbon Street? Tell me, is it true about—"

Aunt Joyce popped him on the thigh and rolled her eyes. If he hadn't changed in twenty-five years he would never change.

"Uncle Buddy, we have a minister and two children present. I'll talk to you later." I chuckled.

"Yeah, we can talk later." He reached for the green beans, then looked at me again. "But is it true?" He nudged me playfully in the side and winked his eye. "I may be gettin' old, but you know what they say, everything dead needs to be buried. Ro', I'll talk to ya later. Don't think I'm gonna forget either."

"Okay, Uncle Buddy." I put my finger over my lips to sshh him. "Tony, would you please pass me the dressing?"

Mom was getting very uptight as she rolled her eyes at her brother, then pointed at Aunt Joyce to shut him up. After all of these years he still got on her nerves.

"Tony, you look great. I understand marriage is agreeing with you." I laughed as I pinched his stomach. In high school he could eat anything and would never gain one pound. Now to see him as a married adult carrying a few extra pounds around the waistline was so hard to believe.

"Hey, man, can you tell?"

"It looks good on you. Jovita needs something to hold on to."

"I've put on a few pounds since the last time I saw you."

Her promotion in management at Saks two months ago had warranted an extended celebration. He laughed as he hugged and kissed his wife.

"Does this celebration include children? I need another niece or nephew."

"I think we'll give it another year. The first year or so Jovita will have to travel a lot. But I think we're almost ready. What about you? What's taking you so long? We're waiting to meet Ms. Right."

"Time . . . Tony, give it time."

"Time? You ain't getting no younger, little brother. The biological clocks are ticking."

Mom started to laugh as my brothers joined in to harass me. "No comment. You all know how I feel." Forks rattled against the plates and our small talk continued during the meal.

After dinner Uncle Buddy and Dad fell asleep on the couch while the women and children watched *The Preacher's Wife* for the tenth time. My brothers and I went upstairs to bond and talk. Two hours later everyone was ready for dessert and migrated back into the kitchen. We all stood around and talked.

"Look at my Charlene. Boys, I tell you, your mother doesn't look a day older than she did the first time we met at the mall in Virginia." It never failed; every year after dinner Dad would get all sensitive while he told us old navy war stories and how he met Mom. Must be something that came with age. "Norfolk, Virginia, was my first duty station after boot camp."

Mom smiled and joined the conversation. "I was at the mall with my girlfriend. Your daddy was with his friend."

Dad looked at Mom and winked his eye. "I know you wouldn't believe it but I was shy back then. My friend noticed the girls first, then pointed them out to me. I nodded and continued to walk. Well, my friend turned and walked toward their table."

"Yeah, his friend was almost your father." From my mother's viewpoint Dad wasn't your typical ladies' man.

"Carlos gave me the eye and then I walked over to join the conversation." Dad knew he was attracted to Mom and decided to join them.

"Sons, you know your mother tried to act stuck-up and wouldn't give a brother no play." Oh, hell no. My Dad had been watching entirely too much television. When did he get hip? "That's why I sent Carlos to do all of the talking for me."

"Your daddy had to say something quick. His friend was a little mack." Oh no, not Mom too!

"You ain't kidding, Carlos was sharp when it came to the girls. Almost took my date."

"You knew when to talk, didn't you, honey?"

"Sure did. I asked her out on a date that Friday after class."

My mother dated him but knew better than to fall in love with a military man. They were too unpredictable. My father always hoped she wanted to be more than just friends but was too ashamed to ask the guys for help. While he thought of a game plan she focused primarily on her major in elementary education.

"Baby, go get the letter I wrote to you when I proposed." He had received his overseas orders when she was a junior in college. He had to go public and soon. She didn't know my father had fallen in love with her. Three weeks before he left Virginia she received a letter in the mail. I couldn't believe how fast Mom found the letter. It was still in the original envelope. She unfolded it and read it to us again.

Dear Charlene,
Listen before you judge me. Growing up in Virginia, you have seen men come and go. Many times leaving

behind girls with broken hearts. This time is different.
During our friendship you have done most of the talk-
ing. I have enjoyed listening. Your outlook on life is
fresh. Your future dreams are attainable. If you would
let me I want to be with you for the rest of my life. Will
you consider becoming my wife?

Love,
Edward

"This letter still makes me cry. I wish you could have seen me the day I got it in the mail. I was speechless, picked up my purse and keys, turned to open the door, and there he was."

"For the first time since we met she didn't have anything to say."

"That window of silence gave him the opportunity to tell me how he really felt. Your father stammered on for hours, sharing his future plans and dreams. We both agreed to marry before he left on his Mediterranean tour. One week later we confessed our love before a justice of the peace."

The grandchildren fell asleep on Dad's trip down memory lane. Everyone else had gotten bored and started to yawn. Junior was the first to say good-bye. "All right, Mom, dinner was excellent as usual. Wouldn't miss it for the world. Thanks."

Mom kissed the grandchildren and hugged everyone else. I couldn't believe it when Uncle Buddy said he was leaving too.

"Ro', I didn't forget. Ahh, you thought I forgot, didn't you?"

"No, Uncle Buddy, I know you didn't forget!"

"I'ma take Joyce home and see if I can get her to swing for me."

I was grossed out when he patted her on her wide ass.

Mom just shook her head and Dad laughed. When everyone finished their good-byes and left I took my luggage upstairs to my old bedroom.

"Rowan, someone is at the door to see you."

Who knew I was at home? I didn't remember telling anyone. It hadn't taken me long to change into my jogging pants, T-shirt, and socks. From the top of the stairway it sounded like my best friend, Montel, from high school.

"Hey, man! My mother will never change. Come on in and have a seat." I hadn't seen him in years. We shook hands and gave each other a brotherly hug. I couldn't believe he damn near looked the same except for his thinning hairline. I rubbed his head and laughed. He rubbed his head and laughed too. "I know, man."

"This is a good surprise." Seeing him brought back so many memories.

"I apologize for being so late. We all crashed on the couch after eating all of that food. You know how we do, but I promised Mrs. Charlene I would make it over today."

I gave him a hard pat on the back before we went into the kitchen for more of Mom's sweet potato pie. He snatched the knife out of my hand, cut himself a huge slice of pie, and straddled the bar stool.

"Man, tell me what's been going on since I last saw you." I asked him about old classmates, friends, and girlfriends.

"Rowan, I hate you couldn't attend our ten-year class reunion. Man, so much has changed. You gotta see the pictures."

"I know."

"I'll bring them over tomorrow."

"Montel, don't leave me hanging. Tell me about it. Give me all of the details."

"Do you remember the pretty 'little' cheerleader you always had a crush on?" He stuffed a spoonful of pie into his mouth.

"Yeah, man, she was so fine! A Coca-Cola bottle had nothing on her." I closed my eyes and outlined the shape of a bottle with my hands.

Montel choked and nearly fell off the bar stool. He patted his chest and cleared his throat. "Ha, man, picture a two-liter. You remember her high school sweetheart? They got married one year after high school graduation and had three children."

"Man, you lyin'."

"Ain't kiddin'. I believe he went to college, majored in accounting, and is working for the IRS now."

"How disappointing. Oh, I know. How is our old quarter-back, Dederick, doing?"

"I guess Mrs. Charlene didn't tell you. He got a full scholarship to Texas A and M. The professional scouts had him on lock. He even started as a freshman."

"Really? He did have an arm."

"He was doing good before he injured his knee his junior year and never finished getting his degree. He gave up on life, man. If you wanna see him, he works at a warehouse about four blocks away."

"Damn, man, that sucks. Guess I don't have nothing to complain about."

"But dig this. Do you remember the little brown-skinned girl from our senior English class?"

"Hmmm, the little brown-skinned girl?"

"You know, the one with the glasses. The nerd. You remember, she never said anything and made the highest grades in class?"

"Yeah. Hell yeah, the little one that kept our grading curve all messed up."

"That's the one. She is *so fine*! She's beautiful now. If I knew then what I know now she'd be mine. Guess what? She's a dentist. I thought I was gonna lose it, man. Too late, though, she made my dumb ass pay for ignoring her in school."

For the most part everyone was doing okay. It did hurt me to know two of my classmates had died over the past year. I also realized I wasn't the only one who decided to make a living in another state. Montel finished his second piece of pie and called it a night. Mom and Dad had gone to bed, so he promised to check back before I left town.

Being home reminded me of times past with my brothers and how much I really enjoyed being around my family. I sat down on the edge of my old full-sized bed and looked around the room at my old ribbons and trophies from school. Mom might have been right. Moving back home might be a good thing.

MARIA

Bad memories of Rowan's disappearing act had no place in my heart and wouldn't confine me at home on Christmas Day. They wouldn't be allowed to disguise themselves in pleated black pants, starched pin-striped shirts, and little pointed bow ties to deal me a bad hand. I dictated who held the winning combination and vowed that person would be me. The aroma from my coffee soothed me as I sat down to look at an activity planner I had picked up the day before. "Christmas in the Grove" sounded great. A local trumpeter and his band would keep the New Orleans tradition alive at Le Petit Theatre du Vieux Carre. I grabbed my coat, purse, and keys and headed to the car.

Observing the children at play in my neighborhood had a positive influence on my attitude. They seemed happy and carefree as they jumped and ran around with no rhyme or reason. At the four-way stop I saw a little girl playing with a group of children much larger than her. The little knit ball on the top of her cap wiggled as she played. From looking at her size I guessed she was about six years old. By mistake one of the larger children bumped into her and made her fall. Without hesitation she looked at her little mitten-covered hands, brushed the dirt off her knees, then got back up. She was okay, so it was time to move on. Maybe that was my lesson to be learned before driving away. After an inconvenience, evaluate the situation, shake it off, and move on.

The French Quarter was exquisitely decorated and pleasing to the eyes. As I walked through the doors of the theater I inhaled deeply to become one with the moment. The white angel hair, lights, and ornaments formed a canopy while Christmas trees lined the lobby, giving the illusion of a Christmas paradise. I walked through, slightly glancing at myself in the many mirrors, proud of my accomplishment. I was alone and I enjoyed the feeling of falling in love with myself.

"Hello," I said to the perfect reflection of myself in the mirror.

"Hello!"

"Let me introduce myself. My name is Maria A'Twanette McCory. And you are?"

"You."

"Well, it's a pleasure to finally meet you, 'You.'"

"No, believe me, the pleasure is all mine."

"So tell me, where have you been hiding such a beautiful smile?"

"To be honest with you I don't know."

"What a shame."

"I know. I'm ashamed to confess the truth."

"Oh no, never be ashamed. Would you like to join me for

a delightful Christmas brunch? We need to become better acquainted."

"Yes."

The moment was monumental when I opened myself to every good thing due to me and dedicated Christmas Day to Maria A'Twanette McCory. I'd come too far to give up.

CHAPTER 20

*You are a diamond about to be; still in the rough...
being carved and shaped by life, you see.*

"Rowan, it's me. Are you awake?"

"I'm up, come on in."

"Breakfast is ready. I want you to eat before the biscuits get cold." After all of these years her habits hadn't changed at all. Mom walked over, leaned down, gave me a big hug, and kissed me on the forehead. She was my mother so I couldn't refuse her baby kiss. I pulled the covers over my head and turned on my stomach when she opened the curtains and started singing old Mahalia Jackson songs. After a few yawns and stretches I got up, put on my robe, then flopped down in the old beanbag I'd left beside the bed.

"Rowan, I'm so glad you could make it home for Christmas. Your dad didn't let me get any sleep last night. He went on and on for hours about the four of you and how proud you've made us. If we had to do it all over again we wouldn't change a thing."

"So you wouldn't have traded me in for a fourteen-day Alaskan cruise?" I laughed when she put her finger on her chin and looked toward the ceiling.

"Hmm, no, not for a fourteen-day cruise, but I would have traded you for . . . I'm just kidding, just kidding. So, how are things really going in New Orleans?"

I could tell by that question, as innocent as it seemed, where the conversation was headed.

"Everything's okay, good job and three hot meals a day. For a bachelor I can't complain."

As an excuse to stay in the room and continue the conversation, she made up my bed. I wanted to see just how long the charade could last before anything else was said. She shook my sheets, placed them back on the bed, and tucked them neatly between the mattresses. I handed her the comforter and watched without saying a word as she inspected it for the white DO NOT REMOVE tag on the bottom right-hand corner. Ahh, she couldn't take it any longer. Before she could place the pillows on the bed she stood up straight to look at me.

"Rowan, talk to me. You're my youngest son." Before walking over to me she fluffed and arranged the two large pillows. That form of interrogation couldn't take place with her on the other side of the bedroom. "I know you better than you think you know yourself. Have you fallen in love or did someone break your heart?"

I cleared my throat after her assumption. "Hmm . . . I really don't know what you're talking about. I'm an adult and we shouldn't be having high school who-do-you-have-a-crush-on conversations anymore."

"You can call it high school if you want to." She stepped back, put one hand on her hip, and waved her finger at me. "Whether you're thirty-four or sixty-four, I'm still your mother. Don't you know I can look into each of my son's eyes and tell when something is not quite right?"

It's amazing how a mother's stern conviction could humble a grown man.

"Mom, you need to start a psychic network and get paid for your skills."

She pretended to rub a crystal ball before looking at me again. "I foresee you never quitting your day job as a paramedic, your jokes are lame." Dang, even her Ms. Cleo accent was impressive.

"Now that was harsh, and I thought I was funny."

She picked up a pillow and tossed it at me. "Anyway, back to my question. Is it love or did someone break your heart?" Reaching for the pillow she threw at me, she sat down on the side of the bed and nestled it in her arms.

"Honestly, I think it's both. Mom, it's a long story and I really don't want to talk about a dead issue."

"An issue isn't dead if it still bothers you."

"Oh, it's dead, believe me."

"I have all of the time in the world, now talk."

I shook my head, thinking she really wouldn't understand. "Mentioning my two-year relationship with Vickie to you was unnecessary because the attraction was completely physical. When I met Maria I realized how uncommitted I really was." I closed my eyes, let her name roll off my lips, then visualized her warm smile. "Mom, I can't describe my experience. It sounds so crazy, so irrational."

"Rowan, love isn't crazy: Keep talking."

I struggled to get out of the beanbag, opened my suitcase, and tossed the clothes around, looking for something to wear. "If it's okay I really don't want to talk about it anymore. I need to get dressed for breakfast. I'm sure Dad has eaten all of the biscuits by now." Trying to convince her to leave it alone, I pinched her on the cheek.

"What makes you think you can change the topic of our conversation?"

"Please believe me, the details are like an HBO special and I don't want to talk about it."

"Try me. It's obvious this is something you need to get off your chest." She stood up, took the clothes out of my hand, and laid them on the bed.

Hell, Mom knew when she looked into my eyes and touched my shoulder, that would get to me. Without any resistance I sat down on the bed beside her.

"I responded to a 911 call at her home. When we arrived, the crime scene was awful, making it hard to imagine the brutality. We stabilized her, then transported her to Tulane University Hospital, where I left feeling completely empty and emotionally drained. Two weeks later another call was transported to the same hospital. I made a complete idiot out of myself knowing I would find her. When I made it to the room she was gone and somebody's grandmother was in the bed. I'd never been so humiliated in my life. Later, the hospitalization of her aunt caused our paths to cross again. Over time we became friends. I was able to deal with the reality of the situation until they arrested the creep that did it." Unable to believe I was pouring my heart out to her, I stared across the room to avoid eye contact. "It was my best friend from college, Josh." I moved away from her and leaned against the headboard.

"Oh my Lord . . . tell me it isn't so." She covered her mouth with both hands, then reached for mine. "Honey, I'm so sorry."

"If you only knew how sorry I was."

"Had she met him before? Did she know he was your friend?" Shocked and concerned, Mom rattled questions off the top of her head.

"No, she didn't know anything. When she called to tell me her attacker had been arrested I was at the gym. Knowing she shouldn't be alone I offered to go to the precinct for support. Everything from the conversation on the telephone to the trip downtown went well. I came unglued inside when I looked up and saw his face. I kept my cool long enough to get out of the room and take her home. When we made it to her house I didn't have the courage to tell her that I knew him, so I left. Day after day, no matter how I tried to ignore it, I couldn't stop thinking about it. My guilt got the best of me. A few weeks later I went back and told her everything."

"When you talked, was she receptive?"

"I don't know if she could look me in the face or not. How would you react if someone told you they watched Monday night football with the man that violated you? There are not enough psychiatrists in the state of Louisiana to prepare you for that. To avoid her total rejection, I left before she could respond." Disappointed, I lowered my head and stared at nothing on the floor.

"Right now it seems bleak, but if you really love her it isn't too late."

"Mom, believe me, it's too late. How can I love or be intimate with the woman my best friend raped? How?" I covered my eyes with both hands and shook my head when I visualized Josh's grimy hands all over her body. She hugged me, then held both of my hands as she spoke.

"Rowan, God doesn't give me the answers to everything." She made circular motions with one hand as she held my hand with the other. "I do know one thing, never let love go. Hold on to the moment you first fell in love until it finds you again. No, you didn't make a fool out of yourself. For once you searched for what you knew was true to your heart. I look forward to meeting Maria. Remember, a mother knows."

Before standing to leave the room, Mom rubbed my hand and lovingly looked into my eyes. For a few moments I sat in silence reflecting on what she said, *Never let love go.*

ROWAN

"Excuse me, sir, are you waiting on someone?" I set my wine down on the bar and turned to answer. Mom was optimistic and understood when I wanted to spend my last night in Texas alone, so Tony recommended Avanti Ristorante, an Italian bistro downtown.

"No, tonight I'll be eating alone. Thank you for asking." *Alone. I'm alone,* I thought as I followed her to a table in the corner. There were beautiful women all around me. Tonight would be about me, all about me. I ordered another glass of Merlot while I looked over the menu. Hmm . . . chicken limone or Brazilian lobster tail?

One by one I forced myself to let go of my memories of Maria. I was ready to step into the arena and face any challenges a relationship with her might or might not have presented. But before I could the game became lethal and my ammunition was too weak when I looked up and saw Josh's face on the other side of the mirror instead of a stranger. Like a coward, I bobbed, weaved, then retreated, knowing I couldn't deal with that one truth.

I was thirty-four years old and ready to settle down. Was it asking too much to have the desire to go to bed and wake up with the woman that I loved every day? Was it selfish for me to want the love and affection of one woman all to myself? I didn't mean a situation of convenience; I was talking about one true love. I never meant to hurt Vickie, but I knew early in our relationship she wasn't the "one."

Yeah, my relationship with Vickie threw an inconvenient jab to my chest. I took it like a real champ and moved beyond that particular scenario. Whew, both Jana and Josh proved to me you never know what's going on inside a person's mind. For the sake of sanity I'm glad I never totally found out.

Since the last time I saw Maria, I was almost certain she'd made a one hundred percent recovery and moved on with her life. If we hadn't crossed paths by now I was convinced it was never meant to be. After my talk with Mom this morning I made the decision to move back home. My parents weren't getting any younger and my father could use the extra help around the house. What did I have to lose? Actually, when I thought about it, there had to be more to gain.

The outcome of my future was totally up to me, I thought to myself as I leaned back in my chair. I'd lived in New Orleans for thirteen years. The time had come for me to open myself to new options. Josh had been there for me in college but blindsided me with a betrayal of another sort. Never in a lifetime did I think he was capable of something so cruel and hideous. With Vickie I'd experienced a short-term relationship . . . two years.

"To Josh and Vickie, New Orleans, and my decision to move back to Texas."

CHAPTER 21

The mystery of women will bewilder the minds of men;
until they realize we are one of a kind.

"Ooh-wee, did you see that pass?" I laughed when Parker jumped up and shouted. The college football games attracted us to the television like a magnet all day. Our support coaching staff yelled out play after play to lead our favorite teams to victory.

"Hell yeah, I saw it," the flamin' chef yelled back across the room.

This would be the last holiday season I would share with the guys at the station. Now that I'd worked with them for six years I realized that I was really going to miss them. My decision had been made and I knew it was time for me to move on. I hadn't told anyone because the rumors would spread like a wildfire through the forests of California. One by one and then collectively each of them would talk to me and make me feel guilty about going back home to my family. I'd worked with them long enough to know the approach they would take.

"If he'd listened to me he could've scored another touchdown." Disappointed in the failed pass, Chef paced back and forth on the other side of the room. Failure of the team to listen forced our animal-like instincts to take over. How could we condone our irrational behavior in those circumstances? Team division wasn't tolerated on our shift.

"Damn, Parker, let go of the popcorn bowl. Didn't yo' mama teach you any manners?" Fakes's wayward ways would truly be missed.

"Hey, don't go there today. You don't want me to start on yo' mama."

A few bowls of microwave popcorn and chips with a few two-liters of Pepsi sadly represented refreshment vendors, who hailed in the stands, with their fresh popcorn, beer, and pretzels. Reaching too slowly for the bowl of popcorn only guaranteed you golden kernels and hot butter. The cheers and screams from the college football games didn't put a damper on Fakes's philosophical input about New Year traditions.

"Guys, did you know New Year's wasn't always celebrated on the first day of January?"

"Oh, really? You've got to be kidding me." Only the new guy in the corner responded. We chuckled because no one had taken the time to school him about Fakes.

"No, I'm not. Everyone should know in the years around 2000 B.C. the Babylonian New Year began with the first . . ." His audience of listeners was scarce and inattentive as the majority of us watched the game and shushed his crazy ass.

"First responder! Shot wound, lower abdomen, victim unconscious. First responder! Shot wound, lower . . ." This frantic announcement interrupted our version of a day at the stadium. Parker and I jumped up but backed out of the room, anticipating a touchdown during the last thirty seconds of the quarter.

We high-fived each other, then verified our location as the dispatcher continued the announcement. The call sounded domestic in nature. Only a couple of seconds behind on our response time, the sound of our sirens alerted traffic of our immediate need to depart from the station. Like a bolt of lightning, we whipped into the street and made a sharp left.

"Damn, Parker, you trying to give me whiplash?"

"If we hurry we can make this call and see the beginning of the next game."

"Hell, step on it, then."

The bright red lights reflected and bounced off the buildings in our path. We weaved in and out of traffic, proceeded through two red lights, and hooked a right, then a left. I wouldn't recommend a job in emergency medicine for someone who had a faint heart. To stabilize a critically injured or bleeding patient the pace at which we worked was fast and very stressful.

What was usually a nice quiet neighborhood, composed mostly of widows and retirees, had experienced a slight shake-up. Parking was a problem as we maneuvered between two squad cars parked at an angle against the edge of the yard and a fire truck. Police had already taken a woman into custody. She was handcuffed and draped in a dark gray flannel blanket, which hid her face. An officer covered her head with his hand, pushed downward, and guided her into the car. She stared straight ahead without blinking an eye.

Once we entered the house, there were no signs of a break-in, no broken glass from a door or window, and nothing seemed to be moved or out of place. Coming from the bedroom we could hear another female crying hysterically. I didn't have the time to make any assumptions after I saw a gunshot victim lying partially unconscious in a puddle of blood in the middle of the bedroom floor. The fireman from their local station briefed me as we took over. We knew at this point, time and technique were critical to sustaining his life.

In the next room I could hear the officers discussing the report as the "girlfriend" gave it. It was safe to assume the woman in the police car was a wife who was caught off guard by a cheating husband in her own home. I counted two bullet holes in the headboard. I believed at least one if not both was intended for her.

Judging from the victim's blood loss we had no time to waste. In sync we prepared and passed supplies until the situation was under control. Carefully we moved him from the bed to the stretcher and got him into the ambulance. Even though he couldn't talk his eyes rolled in anguish as he begged us for relief. I drove while my partner stayed in the back of the ambulance to monitor his stats, assuring him we would do everything possible to ease his pain.

Lights, siren, and action. The large rotating tires squealed as we pulled into the street. The ambulance appeared, then disappeared as a blur of white with flashing red lights. On Interstate 10 traffic divided evenly on either side of us as drivers took heed to the urgency of our situation. As we passed, one by one they fell back into formation and reformed their perfect lines.

As soon as we got him in the doors of the ER, we received another call. This time a street brawl on Bourbon Street. On my way out, I stopped to grab a Snickers bar out of the vending machine. I shuffled through my pockets looking for that last dime I needed, looked up, and the reflection I saw looked like Maria. I spun around but only caught a glimpse of her going around the corner. This person had on scrubs. No way it could have been her.

MARIA

My junior year in nursing school had been successfully completed. For students who desired the experience or simply needed the extra money, our academic counselors regularly provided us with job postings available in and around

New Orleans. Ready to apply my skill in a setting somewhere other than the classroom and clinical rotations, I communicated my interests to the counselor and inquired about the application process. She provided me with the specifics and I followed through. Within two weeks I was offered a weekend student nursing position.

Proud of my new job, I held my picture identification in my hand and read it aloud to myself. Tulane University Hospital. Maria McCory. Student Nurse—Emergency Department. I wasn't oblivious of the fact that working on the weekends during my senior year would be difficult. Zeal for life had become a part of my repertoire; fear of life and its many deterrents had lost its place long ago.

New Year's Eve was my first scheduled workday on my new job. With all New Orleans had to offer I anticipated that the parties and drinking would start early in the afternoon. Whether you preferred a mild romantic evening or an experience that would have to stay hidden within and follow you straight to your grave, Bourbon Street had it. Natives and visitors alike would blend flawlessly as they partook in the undeniably uncensored activities. The partygoers, fueled by their own anticipation of a good time, would weave in and out of the bars and nightclubs. Bourbon Street never slept; open doors would be on a swivel all night long. We mentally prepared ourselves to deal with the minor head gashes, broken arms and legs, bruised ribs, and broken noses . . . all typical wounds sustained by the drunken partygoers.

Describing my day as fast paced would have been an understatement. I'd admit the most interesting case of the night was a gunshot victim. The details were stunning as the victim's girlfriend uncandidly told the nurse training me. Some things you hear are hard to believe. This was one of those unlikely situations.

"My boyfriend wanted us to celebrate at his house. He called me on my cell and told me he was on his way and to meet him there." Obviously, they decided to celebrate during their evening lunch breaks.

"I didn't think nothing of it. He said his wife, June, was in Baton Rouge for the whole freakin' weekend."

Neither of them considered the possibility of his wife coming home early from her trip.

"He said he knew her and I didn't have anything to worry about because she was like clockwork. If she said she wasn't coming home until Tuesday at noon she wouldn't arrive one second sooner, so he thought."

Only judging from his shot wound they were foolish enough to make it an official date.

"We couldn't wait to get inside and started to undress before he could unlock the side door. With our lips locked tight we barely made it inside the house. Caught up in the moment we left our clothes scattered on the kitchen floor and scurried into the bedroom. I saw the car lights in the driveway, but he didn't listen to me. He was moaning and groaning when I told him I heard something in the front room. Then I forgot about it and let myself get all caught up, you know?" Her hands shook as she reached into her purse and pulled out a crushed package of cigarettes.

"June opened the bedroom door, called his name, but before he jumped up to say, 'Baby, I am sorry,' she started to fire. One bullet hit him in the stomach, the other is lodged in the headboard."

Wow! My life had never been so exciting, I thought to myself as we completed his chart and explained to the girlfriend he'd be in surgery several hours, then rushed to close the door.

The nurses scurried around as they responded to last-minute admission orders. Their movements were brisk as they catered to the admitting physicians with solemn facial expressions ready to receive verbal requests in any attempts to deter life-altering situations. I weaved in and out of the human maze formed by impatiently waiting family members and staff. The hall was filled with patients, lending unrelinquished support to each other, as they lay in wait on a promising or not so promising diagnosis. The antsy father, praying for the birth of a healthy girl or boy with ten fingers and ten toes. The little boy, who didn't look both ways before he crossed the street. The husband, knowing benign indicates the strong possibility of survival. The elderly transport patient, pushed flush into the far back corner, refusing admission into a nursing home.

Patients were moved hurriedly in and out of rooms, up and down the halls, around the corner, and through the flexible doors all night long. The admitting physician depended on his dark black, no-sugar-or-cream fuel. I observed as he entered the rooms, asked the few necessary questions, then relied on his expertise or someone else's for the answer. Not much time to think, only time to respond. Just in case, I kept my right hand plastered to my small pocket notebook. The momentum of the night was like a loaded freight train whose wheels screeched as they met metal to steel, late for its next destination.

CHAPTER 22

Take no thought of what shape you'll be.
For the master jeweler has a plan, you'll see.

"Man, what's up?" Tony sounded alert for seven o'clock in the morning.

"Hey, big brother, how's life treating you?" I responded.

"Good. Check your e-mail. Found something you may be interested in."

"Really? I'll take a look at it." I unofficially put Tony in charge of my job search in Texas by convincing him that with enough help I'd consider the move. Willing to accept the task, he considered only a few simple Internet queries, his search started after Christmas. However, there was one stipulation along with his title. I made him swear not to tell Mom I was trying to move back to Dallas or anywhere within a one-hundred-mile radius of her home. I didn't want to get her hopes up, then disappoint her if things didn't work out the way I thought they should. If she knew, she'd rent a U-haul and move me herself, with or without my father's help.

"Yeah, I found a very detailed Web site for emergency health-care workers, so I forwarded you an advertisement for a position available in Dallas."

"Thanks for your help, I appreciate it."

"No problem, that's what big brothers are for, right?"

"All right, Tony, I'll keep you posted." I checked my e-mail, printed the information, and faxed a resume to the person listed as contact.

The response time was impressive. Someone from human resources called me within a week to schedule an interview. They understood my circumstances and reviewed the calendar with me over the telephone to assure we scheduled the next best available date. Ready to set the plan into motion, I arranged the interview during my next four off days.

My last scheduled day at work before my interview was stressful as I doubted my decision and wrestled with the idea of packing everything and moving back to Texas. When I finished my shift I stopped by the bar to have one beer. My intention wasn't to get intoxicated, only to calm down before going home and getting ready for my flight the next morning. I sat down and watched television until the bartender realized I was there. He turned around and I nodded for my usual, Heineken. He gave a thumbs-up, turned to fill a glass, then set my beer on the counter.

"Here it is, your usual. Anything else for ya tonight?"

"Man, I'm good. Keep the change." I paid him and told him that would do me for the evening.

I would have liked to talk, but who in the hell would believe me? Wrinkles formed in my forehead as I leaned back in my chair and allowed the beer to quench my thirst. As I glanced around the room the smiles and the laughter associated with those smiles told me they were having a good time. As I became more mellow the loud conversations and music became whispers to my ears. Two more sips and I was done.

While driving home I wasn't afraid to take it all in and reminisced over my past thirteen years in New Orleans. When I had moved at the age of twenty-one, everything was fresh, new, and exciting. Now I'd gotten older and my feelings toward my life had changed. I opened my apartment door with no regrets of having no one waiting for me on the other side. I closed it, kicked off my shoes, tossed my keys on the kitchen counter, and went into my bedroom to pack. I'd only be gone for two days, so I grabbed some jeans, a jogging suit, my black suit, white shirt, necktie, and black dress shoes. I inspected my suit before I put it into my garment bag, then hung it over my bedroom door. I folded my clothes, placed them into my suitcase, zipped it up, and set it down on the floor beside my dresser. Everything was packed and I was ready to go.

I slept well but woke up with second thoughts. Then I realized I was being stupid. If it was meant to be it would be. Nothing, good or bad, would happen to me before it was supposed to happen. Now if I could have this philosophy about the rest of my life I'd be okay. I grabbed my suitcase and garment bag, checked the apartment, set the alarm, then headed to the airport.

For a moment I felt guilty about going to Texas and not letting anyone in my family know about it, but the end results would make them happy. I fastened my seat belt and held on to the small armrests to stretch my legs. During the flight announcements I closed my eyes and nestled my head in the headrest. When I opened my eyes again the attendant was thanking us and giving exit instructions.

MARIA

Ten minutes prior to my clocking out, a sixteen-year-old in her seventh month with no previous prenatal care was transported to the emergency room. Her school called 911 after she passed out in gym class. When the ambulance arrived she was toxemic with an elevated blood pressure. No one, including her mother, knew she was pregnant. Explaining the circumstances forced me to sympathize with the heart-broken mother while we prepped her for an early delivery. Her stomach was no more than a little pouch; I could see how she hid it so well. Forty-five minutes later I gave my relief directives before rushing into the dressing room to change out of my scrubs into street clothes. I unzipped my garment bag to remove my double-breasted navy blue suit, got dressed, then sat down to slip on my pumps. *Good,* I thought to myself when I looked at my watch. My timing was perfect. I had one hour before the session started at the recreation center.

I opened the door and was relieved to see the chairs were still arranged in a circle from last week. Not having to re-arrange the room gave me time to prepare for today's meeting. Five minutes later the attendees started to enter the room. I counted each one as a blessing. It took a lot of courage to attend our meetings every week; I knew it. It wasn't very long ago that I had been the new victim in the session.

"Good evening, ladies. I'm so happy to see you here this evening. We're pleased to have a new member. We'll start the session with brief introductions using first names only for the purpose of confidentiality."

"My name is Shawn, my name is Joanna . . ."

I smiled in approval. An older member was happy to start us off. As the introductions rotated around the room our new member, Cassie, became distant. Joanna leaned forward to show emotional support.

"Healing is a process. Remember, with time all wounds will heal."

As Shawn reached out to hold her hand I was reminded of my first session when Juanita held mine. She was so supportive and became a very good friend. I missed her at our weekly meetings. After coming to the sessions week after week for a solid two years, she was confident that she'd received all the healing and nurturing she needed from the group. Rather than continuing to come to the sessions at the center she began volunteering the same few hours on the crisis hotline. Through strength and perseverance I'd become the group leader.

ROWAN

The first impression of my job interview in Dallas was a little intimidating. The receptionist led me to a small conference room where a rectangular conference table with eight chairs sat in the middle of the floor and no outside windows. Before leaving the room she offered me a seat, then said someone would be in momentarily. Ten minutes later, two gentlemen and a lady, all wearing dark suits, filed into the room. They each extended their hands and introduced themselves as they entered.

"Mr. Miller, how was your flight?" the gentleman on my left asked while the woman thumbed through my application and resume.

Not willing to become too relaxed during the interview, I answered his question professionally. "It was great. I didn't experience any delays or complications." I turned to acknowledge the interviewer as she asked the next question.

"Your resume states you have several years of experience as a paramedic in New Orleans. How do you anticipate dealing with the mental and physical demands of a larger city?"

"Being in a city like New Orleans gave me the opportunity to display my ability as a paramedic. Yes, the city may be smaller, but it caters to tourists throughout the year. So, as an emergency health-care worker my knowledge was constantly put to the test."

She smiled and made notes on my application as the other gentlemen each asked more questions. My interviewers were impressed and offered me a position.

"May I have three days to consider your offer?"

Without hesitation they granted me the three-day grace period. Mentally, I'd already accepted the offer but didn't want to come across too desperate as they concluded the interview with firm handshakes.

Glad the interview was over, I got inside the car, took off my jacket and necktie. Before leaving the parking lot I called Tony on my cell phone to tell him the good news.

When he answered the telephone I decided to withhold the information a few minutes.

"Hello."

"Tony, how's it going in Texas?"

"Things are going okay. See you got my message. I called you about ten minutes ago."

"Yeah, ahh, really?" I couldn't keep a straight face and chuckled behind my own response to him. "All right, man, I gotta tell you the truth. I'm in Dallas. The last e-mail you sent me was a dead ringer. I just finished my interview."

"You did what? Not that I'm not happy and all, but you didn't tell me. I feel so used."

I imagined the expression on his face as he laughed. "Yeah, I knew you would go straight to Mom and tell her everything."

"Naw, I wouldn't have told everything."

Some things would never change; I was certain he'd call them if he knew an interview had actually been scheduled.

"Well, cut to the chase. How did the interview go?"

"It went well. They offered me a position and the pay is far better than in New Orleans. I told them I needed three days to consider the offer. You know I've already made up my mind. I'll call them back tomorrow morning."

"That's my brother. So, when are you moving back to Texas?"

"I've decided to move in May."

"Why May? You could move next month if you wanted to."

He was right, at any time I could move. Other than my job and apartment, I had no obligations.

"I gotta have somewhere to stay, right?"

"You can crash with any of us, including me."

I'm sure he meant well. His hospitality was appreciated, but I wasn't trying to become anyone else's roommate.

"I know but May just sounds right to me. I want to take my time, turn in my resignation, and tie up my loose ends in New Orleans. I need to find a nice place, with your help, that is, in Dallas."

"Yeah, I guess you're right. It's only four months from now."

"I know and it will be here before you know it." His words echoed in my ear, *It's only four months from now.* In four months I would be leaving the past behind me, including the first time I saw Maria.

"Hey, now that you've made a decision are you gonna tell Mom?"

"Yes, I'm going to tell. It's still early, maybe she and Dad can meet me for dinner."

"Ro', congratulations. It'll be good having you close to us again. We've really missed you, man. Maybe now I can start a family with an uncle to babysit and all."

"Hell no, don't get too carried away. You know I don't babysit until they can use the restroom alone. You know the rule, no diaper changing. But all fun aside, thank you for your help. It really meant a lot to me." I drove into the parking lot, found a space, then turned off the ignition.

"You're my baby brother, man. No problem."

"Talk to you later."

"Peace."

I grabbed my suit coat and necktie, got out of the car, and walked toward the front entrance. Before getting on the elevator I decided there was no need to stop by the reception area to check for messages; no one knew I was there. I unlocked the door, tossed my suit coat and necktie on the chair, sat on the edge of my bed, and rested my face in my hands. Everything had been set into motion. In two months Dallas, Texas, would be my home. I picked up the telephone and dialed Mom's number.

"Hello."

Just hearing her voice confirmed moving back home was the right decision. "Mom, how are you doing?"

"Fine, baby, how are you?"

"I'm doing really well."

"Hmm . . . really well? Does this have anything to do with the conversation we had at home?"

Mom's optimism regarding my situation with Maria was unbelievable. She'd have no parts of the conversation if I told her I'd given up on ever seeing Maria again.

"No, it doesn't. I think you'll enjoy this much better."

"Okay?"

"Mom, I'm in Dallas right now." To refrain from any other thoughts of Maria, I stood up, walked to the window, and looked out across the parking lot.

"What! Dallas . . . as in Dallas, Texas?"

"Yes, as in Dallas, Texas. I wanted to know if you and Dad could meet me for dinner this evening."

"Why, sure we can. For you it's not a problem at all."

"Can you think of a good place for us to meet?"

"Hmmm . . . let me think. Hold on a minute and let me ask your dad." She yelled Dad's name. I could barely hear his voice in the background. "What hotel are you staying in?"

"I'm at the LaQuinta by the airport."

"Okay, your father knows where it is. If we leave now we'll be there in thirty or thirty-five minutes. We need to get out of the house anyway."

"Mom, I don't want to be an inconvenience if you have other plans."

"Would you hush. You're not an inconvenience. We'll call you when we've made it to the lobby. Deal?"

"Deal." I'd have a few minutes to freshen up before my parents arrived. I unbuttoned my shirt, took off my shoes, and found a change of clothes. Thirty-five minutes later my telephone was ringing. I knew it was Mom and Dad so I didn't answer it and hurried downstairs.

"Mom! Dad! Good to see the two of you. Wow, you look great." I gave them both a hug and kissed Mom on the cheek.

"Thank you, Son, this is a pleasant surprise. There's a new steak house with the most tender sirloin you've ever had near your hotel. We think you'll really enjoy it."

"Sounds good, let's go." The restaurant was only ten minutes away from the hotel. Judging from the wait alone they were right, so we sat outside on the patio until our table was ready.

"So, Son, are you going to tell us the reason for your visit?"

"Mom, Dad, when I came home for Christmas I thought about moving back home. I didn't tell either of you because I didn't want you to get excited before I really made a decision. So, I swore Tony to secrecy and made him promise not to tell either of you." Mom crossed her arms in front of her and rolled her eyes at me. "Every weekend he would fax job listings to me. Well, here I am."

Mom's face lit up as she playfully nudged me on my shoulder. "I can't believe you didn't tell me, but how did your interview go?"

"It went well and I've decided to take the position. I explained to them the details of my move. I told them I would call back within three days, but I'll call them tomorrow to accept."

"Rowan, I'm so happy for you. It will be great to have you so close to us now." Mom leaned over and hugged me.

"Yeah, I know, I've thought about that too."

"How difficult will it be for you to move?" Mom said, then folded her arms in front of her.

"I really don't foresee any major issues other than finding a place to stay."

"Do you need us to help you find a place to live? You know we could make it a lot easier for you if you need us to."

Dad's response was just as I expected. "I know you would help and I really appreciate the offer. I haven't decided what I'm going to do yet. I recently bought all new furniture before I moved into the apartment I'm living in now. I haven't determined if it will be easier to sell everything and start over or to hire a moving service. Since I'm single, either way would be okay. At this point in my life nothing holds any sentimental value."

Mom nodded her head, but I was sure she was ignoring me and organizing my move in her mind.

"Miller, party of three. Your table is ready. Miller, party of three. Your table is ready."

We spent the rest of the evening talking about the family and my decision to move. At this point there was no pressure, only planning.

Over the next month Mom called several times to offer her assistance. From the tone of her voice she sounded ready to catch the next flight to New Orleans. Each time, I assured her everything was okay and all of my plans to move were still in place. It was May and I felt it was an appropriate time to turn in my letter of resignation.

"Rowan, the coffee is good and hot this morning."

"Thanks, just how I like it. Lieutenant, when would be a good time to talk?"

He put cream in his coffee, then looked at his watch. "Now is good. What you got?"

I poured my cup of coffee and followed him into his office. He put his cup down on the desk when I handed him my written resignation; then he opened it and read it.

"Please shut the door and have a seat." There was a look of disappointment on his face as he pulled his chair out from his desk and sat down. "Rowan, you've been a valuable employee and I hate to see you leave."

"It was a hard decision but I'm ready to move back home. I've been away several years." I made it clear that it was time for my life in New Orleans to end.

"I'd like to take this time to personally thank you for the years of service you've given to the city of New Orleans." He stood and extended his right hand.

"Thank you."

Immediately following our meeting we made the announcement to the rest of my shift. I had gone through the entire process without telling anyone, and they understood it was a very hard decision to make.

"Look, guys, I've really enjoyed working with all of you. But most of you know I moved here from Texas to attend college. After graduation my plan was to move back, but I decided to stay awhile longer. Well, I think now is the perfect time for me to relocate back to Texas."

"Yeah, Rowan, we understand. I'm sure it gets hard living alone in a state without your family and all."

Suddenly, everybody got serious after Chef made his comment.

"Man, we wish you the best." Parker nodded his head, then put his hands in his pocket. We'd been partners almost four years. "Hey, look at the bright side. It gives us an excuse to get together and have a few drinks to see you off. Tell you what, Rowan, since it's your party we'll let you pick the place. When is your last day?"

"My last day here will be the fifth of May. I'll start my new job on the twentieth."

"Guys, check it out, maybe we can throw in a coupla strippers." Fakes would never change.

CHAPTER 23

The mystery of a woman will unfold,
when you go deep inside man and into the
depths of his soul.

This morning as I sat at my vanity looking at my reflection in the mirror, I saw an accomplished woman. The big day I had been waiting for, my graduation, had finally arrived. A few years ago I could barely visualize this day in my future, and after the rape, it seemed to fade even more so in the distance, but I had been bold enough to persevere. While sitting there I decided not to cover the three-inch scar on the left side of my face with foundation. It would be a proud reminder of everything I had gone through, overcome, and accomplished. He told me no one would want to look at this pretty face again. He was a liar. Yes, at first I was ashamed and wanted to hide my past in a box and store it in a dark place, a secret place. That was no longer the case; no longer was I ashamed. If anyone asked me, I would tell them the truth. They would have to be capable of dealing with my truth if they were curious enough to ask. My truth could be their resolution.

My relatives weren't able to attend my graduation and sent their regards and best wishes by cards and telephone calls. Juanita only had her daughter, and since we'd become close, we decided to make it a joint day of celebration, spending it together. I'd packed a small overnight bag with an appropriate dress for the commencement and a couple of clothing choices for tonight's festivities. I'd finally agreed to go with Juanita to her hot spot, Enchanted Notes, a jazz club downtown. She had been telling me about the club for months, and while I had never agreed to go before, today I was excited by all she said the place had to offer, in anticipation of having a great time. As I drove to Juanita's I envisioned the new me . . . mature, developed, whole, and complete . . . celebrating and dancing the night away. Pulling into Juanita's driveway, I could only smile at myself.

Before I could ring her doorbell the door was opening; there she stood with outstretched arms to give me a congratulatory hug. We locked our arms elbow in elbow as she led me into the extra bedroom, showed me where I could find everything, then put away my overnight bag. Now with only a few minutes to spare she took a look at her hair and makeup in the mirror and chattered nervously as she removed her cap and gown from the hallway closet and headed out the door. We paused to seize the moment, reflected briefly, took deep breaths, then got into the car. Excited as we were and not talking about one thing in particular very long, our conversation continued as I drove.

The adrenaline of the accomplished graduates filled the room. Starting out, we had all been slightly indecisive and questioned our ability to complete the program. But we all knew that we had what it took. As I found my place in line, I thought about Aunt Bethany. This was one time I wished she was here. In dual concession we marched down the aisle. One by one, in a single-file line, we veered off into our appointed seats—standing proud—until prompted to sit. Our program started with a prayer.

"Dear Heavenly Father, we want to thank you for this day. Thank you for allowing us to reach milestones in our educations and careers. Continue to bless the families represented today. Please, dear God, allow them to see and reap the benefits of the sacrifices they have made. Please bless the future endeavors of the graduating students. Continue to lead and guide them as they make many more life-altering decisions. Allow them to touch and leave lasting impressions on everyone they meet. Dear God, please hear and answer our prayers. Amen."

Amens rang across the auditorium as we lengthened our backs from pride. Next, we took pleasure in listening to melodic selections from the choir. Small, neatly folded sheets of Kleenex appeared, then quickly disappeared as many of us wiped tears of joy, anticipation, and appreciation from our faces. No one verbally shared their private thoughts, but instead held their heads up and smiled. The city's state representative delivered a speech. Among many things, she encouraged us to allow this day to serve as a stepping-stone marking a new beginning and not an end.

Now the time we all waited for; individually we were given our moment of recognition. With pride and distinction, I approached the stage as my name was called by the dean of nursing.

"Maria A'Twanette McCory." As I stepped forward, I suddenly realized that my feeling about Aunt Bethany's absence was inappropriate. She was there; she had been with me the entire time. I envisioned Aunt Bethany on the stage reaching toward me to hand me my degree. Her memory further encouraged me as I walked to the stage. I accepted my degree with a firm handshake and a proud smile. As I walked back toward my seat I silently thanked Aunt Bethany, honoring her for making this day possible. *Aunt Bethany, thank you for praying. Thank you for unconditional love. Thank you for believing in me when no one else did. Mom and Dad, thank you for teaching me to forgive. First, how to forgive myself, then how to forgive others.*

This degree—no one could steal, destroy, or violate. My knowledge, my passion could not be taken from me. I was no longer a person of unwavering firmness of character and indecisiveness, but rather a woman of strong will and determination. I uplifted my experiences and my degree in my heart. My future stood before me like a bright beacon of light. I was now equipped and my positive energy glowed around me. This energy would attract and embrace nothing but the best life had to offer me. My newfound confidence and love for myself brought a fresh wave of tears to my eyes.

Immediately following the ceremony, the graduation committee hosted a reception for the graduates, family, and guests. Someone from each department stood by the door to congratulate us as we entered the reception area. The room was beautifully decorated with flowers, balloons, and the like, and a serving station was set up in its center. An ice sculpture of the university's mascot, used as the focal point, invited all to mingle and partake in the assortment of meat and cheeses, fresh fruits and vegetables, quiche and pâté.

My eyes quickly darted around the room until I spotted Juanita. I rushed over to her and hugged her tightly as the day we met flashed in my mind. I almost didn't want to let her go.

"Congratulations, girl," she nearly whispered, sensing the emotion in my embrace.

"Congratulations to you and thank you for all of your encouragement. I wouldn't be here if it weren't partially for you. Girl, you're the best."

Juanita and I fixed our plates, then sat down to enjoy our

refreshments and say our last good-byes to classmates we knew we might never see again, promising to keep in touch. We only stayed about thirty-five minutes; we both wanted to be well rested for our evening out.

ROWAN

That was it; I finished off my last day at work. I had begun to separate myself emotionally from my job and coworkers the day I submitted my letter of resignation. From that point, the passion and desire I had was no longer for my career in New Orleans but for my new opportunities in Dallas, Texas. Everything at the apartment had been packed and was ready to go. A truck was scheduled to come and move me first thing Monday morning. That left me with three days to live out of boxes. Hell, that was easy; it had been worse. At least this time they were labeled and arranged in my apartment and not strewn all over the damn yard or sidewalk.

As I pulled out of the station's parking lot for the last time, I didn't have any feelings of regret or resentment about any of the decisions I'd made. Except where Maria was concerned. The way I just up and disappeared, questioning if I could truly love her the way she needed to be loved, wondering if she would even allow me to try . . . I sighed heavily to myself. I had always had a strong desire to know what true love felt like and knew I had experienced it with her. Even so, in my state of confusion, I had allowed it to slip through my fingers. Maria probably never wanted to see me again. What a fool I'd been. The next time love came, if and when it ever came again, I would recognize it, welcome it, cherish it, and never let it escape my grasp again. But until then, it was time to move on.

As a final farewell, the guys were meeting me at Enchanted Notes for a round or two of drinks. I dug through a box and pulled out my tan and white silk shirt and coordinating tan slacks, then made my way to the shower.

I tilted my head back, closed my eyes, and stood motionless, letting the hot water pelt into my face. I couldn't help but think of Maria once more. Living in New Orleans was my last and only connection to my memories of her. Remembering her face, her features, and the pure essence of her beauty, I longed for her presence. I imagined her being right there in the shower standing directly in front of me, watching the water transform her hair from thick straight strands to beautifully coiled tendrils framing her face. I visualized her leaning against the shower wall, letting me massage her body with my warm soapy hands; in my mind I turned her toward me, embracing her and kissing her neck and shoulders as she laid her head on my chest. Drops of water danced on her long eyelashes . . . I had a hell of an imagination, but it was just that, imagination. I knew I'd never see that woman again. I blocked the vivid images and with my eyes still shut I grabbed for my towel.

While I got dressed, I took a thoughtful look around my bedroom, then out toward the balcony. I had to laugh at myself; my hopes were high for this place. I sprayed on my favorite cologne, then took one final glance at myself in the mirror. I looked pretty damn good.

I grabbed my keys off the counter and headed toward the door. Before I could get the door shut, my telephone started to ring. After a few brief seconds of contemplation, I decided to answer it.

"Hello?" Other than someone nervously clearing their throat, there was no response. "Hello!" I said again, letting the caller know that I was clearly irritated.

"Rowan . . . hey . . . don't hang up . . . this is Josh."

Josh? I felt a huge wave of anger immediately rise up from the pit of my gut and into my head. It wasn't a collect call; what the hell was he doing out of jail?

"Why are you calling me?" My tone was cold and harsh.

"I only need one minute of your time. Please don't hang up the phone in my face. I only have a few seconds to talk."

"Ten freakin' seconds and I'm hanging up."

"Rowan, you owe me more than ten seconds—"

"Owe you? I don't owe you a damn thing but an ass whuppin'!" My blood was beginning to boil.

"Man, I know you hate me for everything I put you through, for kicking you out on your ass . . . and for . . . for . . ."

"You know what? You're wasting my damn time," I said through clenched teeth.

"Rowan . . . please listen . . . I'm sorry."

"Josh, you can go to hell!" Infuriated, I slammed the phone down and stared at it, not believing he had the freakin' balls to dial my number. I was mad enough to punch a hole in the wall. Instead, I stepped out on the balcony and took a few minutes to calm down. He'd already done enough damage and I refused to let him mess up my last night with the boys.

MARIA

As the evening approached, I became increasingly excited about going out tonight with Juanita, but I was also a little apprehensive. I hadn't covered my scar this morning, but I found myself contemplating whether or not I should apply makeup for the evening. Because it was such a deep scar, it drew a bit of attention to my otherwise very smooth skin. I looked into the mirror and traced its outline with my fingertips, remembering how it got there, then remembering how much I'd grown since then. How I overcame a situation intended to put me in my grave. Again, I smiled at my reflection; there was no need for me to cover it. I dismissed the thought completely and focused on other more important things . . . like whether I was going to style and profile in my silk and chiffon pantsuit or flaunt this dress!

Wrapped in a thick towel, I padded to the bathroom adjoined to Juanita's guest bedroom. On the way, I wiggled my toes in the carpet. Its plush fibers tickled my soles as I practiced a couple of dance moves. I laughed to myself, sensing a new appreciation for the little but delightful things in life. I adjusted the showerhead to produce a pulsating massage, then stepped into its stream, allowing the circulating beads of hot water to drench my hair and skin. I lathered my body with a mango-scented body wash, and inhaled deeply as the citrus-infused scent mixed with the steam and created a relaxing aura of aromatherapy. As I stood directly beneath the flow of the water, I sensed something else. I knew I was alone and didn't have to convince myself otherwise, but it was like the presence of someone in the shower with me. It felt like someone was embracing and adoring me in a way that I'd never known before. I closed my eyes and stood still, succumbing to the feeling, but opened them abruptly, shocked to hear my lips whisper Rowan's name. Immediately, I shook him from my thoughts, turned the water off, and patted myself dry.

I decided on the fuchsia Jones of New York halter dress with a fitted bodice and a hemline that flared around my calves. I accented the V-neckline with a choker and matching earrings and slid my feet into a pair of clear sandals, which showcased my beautiful, French-pedicured toes. I let my hair dry into soft natural curls, gathered it into an elegant up do, secured it with four bobby pins, then allowed a few tendrils to fall about my face and at the nape of my neck. My makeup was also simple, yet elegant, just touching my eyelids up with a little shadow and lining my lips in a soft hue of brown, coupled with a clear lip gloss. I looked into the mirror and blew myself a sweet kiss. I looked absolutely radiant as I grabbed my purse. Ready to leave, I caught a glimpse of my journal, which was sticking out of my luggage. Juanita told me that the club allowed poets to share their works with the audience. If the atmosphere was right, I might get the nerve to share one of my poetic journal entries. I pulled the small book out of my overnight bag and slipped it into my purse. I was ready.

"Good evening, ladies." The rich voice of the man working the door pleasantly greeted us while the smooth tones of reggae invited us into the club's walls. I immediately felt comfortable in the mellow atmosphere and absorbed my surroundings. My attention was drawn to the dance floor where there were both couples and individuals grooving to the beats while onlookers relaxed at their tables. Juanita had already warned me that if I couldn't hang on the dance floor, I might be spending the majority of my evening alone. I wasn't intimidated; I had full intentions of dancing the night away. She wasted no time in pulling me on the dance floor with her. We easily blended in with the others, keeping with the fluent syncopated rhythms, both fast and slow. I fully gave in to the vibrant musical textures and choreography, and laughed like I hadn't laughed in years, when the live band switched to a Latin American arrangement. Before I realized it, I'd become separated from Juanita, having danced my way to the opposite side of the room. When the song ended, I pardoned my way back to her to let her know I was going to find us a table. Finding one adjacent to the stage, I sat and ordered myself a glass of celebratory wine.

ROWAN

I told the guys to meet me at the bar. I spotted those characters as soon as I walked through the door. They shook their heads and laughed as I walked toward them. Each one greeted me with "dap," pulling me into his chest and thumping me on the back before I sat down and ordered my drink.

"We thought you weren't gonna show up for your own party, man! What took you so long?" Chef asked.

"Something came up, but I'm here now." I forced a smile on my face, although Josh's call sped through my mind for a split second. "So, guys, what do you think?"

"Man, it's great. The music is on point and the women are . . . fine. No, no, they foine!" Leave it to Fakes to be checking out the ladies. "You have already missed the grand entrance of most of the ladies."

"I'm moving first thing Monday morning. I'm not here to hook up with any females."

"Aww, come on, man, take you a little sumptin' home just for the night. You know, something to remember the city by." Fakes chuckled, patting my shoulder.

"And what are we gonna do, lie up on some boxes, or get rug burn? Man, please."

We all laughed, and then Parker started in with his attempt. "Just keep your mind open about the situation. I mean you still a man, right? Don't get all soft on us, man."

"Y'all fools crazy," I said, turning my glass upward.

"Seriously, though, I did see one woman that just might change your mind. She was on the dance floor doing the salsa, cha-cha, merengue, or something . . . whatever it was, she was doing it! I don't see her anymore, but you can't miss her. She has on a pink dress. Whew!"

"A pink dress, huh?"

"Yeah, man. I'm telling you, you gotta see it."

"Well, if the woman is all that, why you ain't tryna get her? What you passing her off to me for?" I eyed him suspiciously.

"Man, I tried to talk to her and she dismissed me so quick—I couldn't even finish getting my sentence out!"

I couldn't help but laugh at him. "So you wanna set me up for the kill too, huh? That's how you gonna let me go out? Defeated? Man, y'all ain't right." We high-fived each other and ordered another round.

MARIA

Tired from her energetic display on the dance floor, Juanita finally made her way to the table just before the MC announced the first poet.

"My goodness. Juanita, you are drenched!"

"Girl, I know, I haven't danced like that in a long time. So much for taking this dress back tomorrow!" She tossed her hair out of her face with a quick jerk of her head and laughed. "Pass me a couple of those napkins."

"I don't know whether to call you Paula Abdul or Janet Jackson for dancing like a madwoman, or Cita for tryna take that dress back!" I shook my head and laughed with her. By the way, I ordered you a drink," I said, pushing the small glass toward her.

"Thanks, girlfriend."

The lights dimmed and the music played softly in the background as the MC approached the stage. I was impressed by the encouragement the MC solicited from the audience before he introduced the poets.

"Good evening, people. Everyone looks well in the audience tonight. I want all of you to give yourselves a hand." The applause echoed around the room as the poets approached the stage. One by one they made their entrances and each of them left me with an impression of themselves or an experience they wanted to share.

As the next to the last poet read her poem I thought seriously about reading one of mine. I tapped Juanita on the shoulder and told her I was going to give it a shot. Her smile, as she turned to look me in the eyes, confirmed my decision.

"Ladies, did you feel her tonight? If you didn't get it, I did. I understand we have a newcomer tonight who wants to give you a taste of something new. I'll let her introduce herself. Please welcome her to the stage."

ROWAN

I leaned back in my chair and took another swig of my beer.

"Rowan, look up. The girl we saw is going to the stage."

I didn't bother; I told them I wasn't interested in hooking up with a strange female tonight.

"Man, you have got to look at this girl. She is beautiful."

I nearly fell out of my seat when I heard the next poet's name and spun around to look toward the stage. I could barely make out her facial features due to the dimly lit stage, and I wasn't going to accept what I had heard as truth until I saw this woman up close. Like a zombie, I stood up and moved toward the stage, but before I could get a clear view of her face, she began to speak further. My heart stopped in my chest. It was Maria.

MARIA

"Hello, everyone, my name is Maria A'Twanette. As the MC said, I'm definitely a newcomer to the mic. I want to share one of my poems with you." Overcome by nerves, I didn't look up to see the facial expressions of the audience. I took a deep breath as I found the page I wanted to read from my journal. I had written my poetry from my heart and that was the only way I knew how to read it . . . from the heart.

Sensational.
Motivational.
Extraordinary.
Out of the ordinary.
Woman, that's me.
Curvaceous.
Flirtatious.
Gorgeous.
Like a peach from Georgia.
Woman, 'hat's me.
The walk.
The talk.
The stance.
The glance.
Every man knows he does not have a chance.
Woman, that's me.
Ability.
Mobility.
Ah, the tranquility.
That mesmerizes the minds of all mankind.
Woman, that's me.
Sweet.
Tender.
Dare to remember.
Woman, that's me.

I looked up, then glanced over the audience and spoke a humble thank you. The audience responded with a standing ovation while the MC maintained his position at the rear of the stage, where he also applauded and whistled loudly. After several seconds, he stepped forward to receive the microphone.

"People, my girl was deep. Let's give it up for Maria A'Twanette."

The encore of resounding applause moved me to tears. An outlet for me proved to be a moving experience for the audience. The MC led them in a tribute to me with their cigarette lighters and simultaneously, their flames flickered across the room. I graciously thanked them with a slow nod of my head and a smile I could not contain. As I turned to exit the stage, a light tap on my shoulder from behind stopped me. I turned around to look directly into Rowan's eyes. My heart skipped beats. It had been months since I last saw him. Months since the unreturned telephone call. Months since he told me of his friendship with Josh.

"Maria . . ." He reached for my hand, excitement dancing in his eyes. "Maria, you are the—" The loud music masked the end of his greeting.

"Oh, my goodness . . . Rowan." Before I could say another word, he complemented his greeting with a warm embrace, and I genuinely returned his display of affection.

"He's proud of his woman, isn't he, y'all?" The MC spoke into the mic and the audience again cheered and clapped.

I blushed as Rowan loosened his embrace, took me by the hand, and escorted me to my table. His eyes were wide with both unbelief and elation. Before I could take my seat, with pleading eyes he leaned toward me and whispered in my ear.

"Can I please talk to you . . . outside?"

ROWAN

Once again, fate played an unfair game with my life. My arms were twisted and tied behind my back with a Boy

Scout knot. Just when I decided to throw in the towel and move back to Texas, my soul mate appeared to stop me. I waited nervously on the patio while Maria took a few minutes to go to the ladies' room with her friend. Before I could pull my thoughts together, she was walking toward me. I had no idea what I was about to say, but I wasn't going to let the opportunity pass.

As she approached, her warm smile slightly took away my nervous edge, though I struggled with my starting words. I looked straight into her eyes, wanting her to see my sincerity as I prepared to bear my very soul.

"This is so vague . . . but here it goes. The day of that horrible incident, I was one of the first paramedics to respond to your call. It was very hard for me to accept what I saw, and that was the amazing part. When I saw you, something happened to me that day . . . that very second. I've never been able to describe it but I could feel it. There was some sort of . . . connection. And I tried to shake it. I was in a relationship at the time, and didn't know exactly what I was feeling. Before I knew it, I had fallen in love with you. I held back from telling you because I wanted to respect the boundaries of our friendship, but I swear to you, from that day until this one, I haven't been able to let go of you mentally or physically." I wanted to pause, but I was too afraid to stop. Afraid that she would walk off the patio and out of my life, which was exactly what I deserved.

"The day that I found out it was Josh . . . Maria I was devastated, embarrassed, ashamed. I didn't know what to say or do, so I did the worst possible thing, I ran. I was confused. I didn't know how to embrace you. I didn't think you could ever love me knowing that I was connected to such a . . ." I searched out in the distance for a word or words to describe what I thought of Josh without being totally offensive. Her eyes were tender as she stood there and listened to me go on and on. "But because I did love you, I knew I owed you one more visit to tell you the truth about Josh being my friend. But after that . . ." I did pause this time, feeling as if I'd run out of words. "So many times I wanted to call you, but I knew I'd let too much time go by. I didn't think you would have me, and I . . . I've accepted a new job in Texas and . . ." My thought dissolved into thin air.

"Rowan, your concern and level of compassion meant so much to me. And yes, I did think about you and wondered what happened. I actually missed you. Our kiss . . ." I gently touched my finger to her lips. "Maria I'm so very sorry. I should have been there for you, I disappeared at a critical point and I don't even deserve to be in your presence tonight. I . . . I love you so very much. Please forgive me."

"Rowan, my feelings toward you never changed, even after you told me you were friends with Josh. I never held you accountable for his actions. That was something beyond your knowledge or control. It hurt me when you left like that."

I grabbed both her hands and focused intently again into her eyes. "I never meant to hurt you. Please believe me. I know it's impossible for us to relive the year. But if you would be generous and just give me tonight I'll remember it for the rest of my life."

After what seemed like an eternity, a slow smile spread across her face and she subtly nodded her head. I immediately pulled her into my arms, experiencing a little piece of heaven. While I held her, I looked toward the night sky and mouthed *Thank you* to God, Jesus, and the entire heavenly host of angels. Surely they all had a part in bringing my soul mate back to me.

MARIA

"Maria A'Twanette McCory, would you like to dance?" Rowan's voice was gentle, humble, loving.

"Yes, I would."

Together we found a spot in the middle of the dance floor. He held my hands as he stood back and looked at me. Now I thought I was beginning to accept our love for one another. No, I didn't understand the previous chain of events ... maybe it wasn't meant for me to understand. With our arms outstretched we started to sway to the music. He gently pulled me closer to his body, then closer than before. He wrapped one arm around my waist and took my hand into his while my other hand rested on his shoulder. He began to serenade me, accompanied by the band.

I looked into his eyes, and peered into his soul. Yes, I was there. Passionately we kissed, confirming that this wouldn't be our last night together despite his plans to move to Texas. Yes, fate had played another nasty trick, but destiny would prevail and allow our paths not just to cross again but to be ultimately joined together. In his arms I felt weightless as we seemingly levitated above the dance floor. I wasn't going to deny myself this moment. I rested my head on his shoulder as I succumbed to the beats of his heart.